Doc Martin:
Mistletoe and Whine

DOC MARTIN: Mistletoe and Whine

SAM NORTH

ISIS
LARGE PRINT
Oxford

Copyright © Buffalo Pictures, 2013

First published in Great Britain 2013
by
Ebury Press
an imprint of Ebury Publishing

Published in Large Print 2014 by ISIS Publishing Ltd.,
7 Centremead, Osney Mead, Oxford OX2 0ES
by arrangement with
Ebury Publishing
a Random House Group Company

CIP data is available for this title from the British Library

ISBN 978–0–7531–9280–1 (hb)
ISBN 978–0–7531–9281–8 (pb)

Printed and bound in Great Britain by
T. J. International Ltd., Padstow, Cornwall

CHAPTER
ONE

For Louisa Glasson, schoolteacher, happiness arrived with a swoop, like a windblown bird, across the cliff tops above Portwenn, because she was with Martin, and everything was settled, and good. She was sitting on the grass while Martin threw a stick over the edge of the cliff and then turned to the dog and commanded, with a stern voice and a pointing finger, "Fetch!"

And then, in the bright sunlight on top of the cliff, with a view of Cornwall's northern coastline on either side, Martin sat down next to her on the grass, of all the unlikely things. She looked down at the ground — and only a few inches separated her hand from his. And it was wonderful that she could, if she wished, simply reach across and pick up his hand, or cover it with her own; that was allowed, and after all it would be easy — just one movement. She counted all four of her fingers and a thumb, and the same for him. Her hand was feminine and slight; his was heavier and workmanlike. And the grass grew, and the sun shone, and inside she was smiling, and there was no danger. And she could only wonder at the number of sword-like stems of grass growing thickly over this patch of ground, so densely covering the earth that spun around and carried them —

Her train of thought was interrupted by Martin's voice — a note of alarm — and by a startling sight: the grass had moved, fractionally, as if the stems were lines of soldiers and, smartly, all at once, two lines had taken a step backwards from one another to open between them a sliver of dark, of nothing. Her eye was taken in both directions as the split lengthened and ran instantly to left and right like a crack in an eggshell.

And then there was a movement, yes, as if a monstrous creature stirred under the ground on which they sat, and she thought it could only be she who imagined such things, but one look shared with Martin told her he'd felt it too, and he too saw the fracture between them open wider by an inch with a sudden jag — it was an earthquake. The look between them changed from alarm to panic. Both were climbing to their feet just as the ground bucked violently; it had them trying to ride on the earth's back, keep their balance, stay on. Thunder filled their ears; it was as loud as a train, more than one, a herd of trains tearing through the ground. In the same moment, the gap tore wider still, opened like a pair of jaws, and Louisa, with the sudden acceleration of the ground under her feet, could only tip forwards onto her hands and knees, except the awful earth's mouth opened wider and there was nothing for her hands to lean on except thin, dark air and she turned at the same time as she fell. She scrabbled at

2

this cliff face that had opened under her feet and managed to hook both elbows over the top.

Through the wild sound of thunder she could hear Martin's voice calling, while the opening jaw of the earthquake split further sideways and, she realised, it was going to swallow not just her but the entire town of Portwenn: houses, boats and people were going to be tipped into it and become just like so much debris. With her elbows planted on that same grass that she'd first stared at so intently, she tried to haul herself up; her knees scraped against the cliff face and she tried to listen to Martin's voice at the same time as pull herself onto her stomach, climb out, but the further vigorous shaking of the ground lost her the progress she'd made and she felt the yawning gap beneath her feet. Now she'd sunk further: her fingertips clung to the cliff top and her scissoring legs felt nothing but thin air. She looked up to see Martin's face, blazing with fear and anger, and his hand reached out for her. But to loosen her grip just for the one second necessary to grab his hand meant she'd surely plunge into the earth's shaking jaw. An intense pain built in the muscles of both her arms as she strained to hold her own weight. She looked helplessly at Martin and saw in his eyes her helplessness. He leaned closer; he was going to pick up her hand, or her arm, and try to pull her out, but he wouldn't have the strength. She must, with that last inch of possible exertion, lift herself out of the chasm despite the trembling that had entered her every muscle.

He shouted at her, "I've got you." And then again, more savagely, "I've got you, you filthy stinking dog. Give it to me." At the same time she saw the strain on his face, and felt her arm being hauled up. She knew it wasn't going to work and her desire to fly upwards, to join him, mixed with the sensation of falling, a giddy acceleration downwards that opened up a hole in her belly. All her limbs were lost and became uncoordinated; there was nothing to keep her the right way up. She was swallowed by darkness, and gravity pulled her faster, so fast that when she hit it would mean without question instant death.

Strangely she could still hear his voice — it would be the last thing she'd ever hear if she didn't somehow rise to the surface. With the same force of acceleration as in her fall, she now was certain she was heading in the other direction, upwards, with heart-stopping speed. She felt a small "mew" of despair escape from her lips at the same instant that she opened her eyes — and she found her head already half lifted from the pillow. All her muscles were tense, but her bedroom calmly waited, her whole life waited, carelessly confident of her return. She had the sense she'd travelled a long way and come back from the dead.

The one constant thing that had run throughout her dream had been the sound of Martin's voice and it was still there. His words came through the tightly shut window and through the curtains: "Give it to me. Come on. Come on!"

The narrow cobbled street was just beneath her bedroom window, and he must, she thought, be standing right there. What was he saying? "Let go! Drop it, you filthy dog." There was the sound of growling. She swept back the bedcovers and it was only a couple of strides through the sudden cold to where the curtains were drawn across the window. She didn't want to be seen, so she tentatively drew the curtain aside and looked down. She saw Martin bending over the dog, both hands on its jaws, from which hung his stethoscope. "Drop," he said, "you wretched thing. It's not a stick." He prised open its jaws and the stethoscope dropped to the ground. He snatched it up, lifted it high, and the dog barked and leaped for it.

Now that he had his stethoscope back, and even as he was wiping it with a handkerchief, Martin's gaze swung upwards to Louisa's window and their eyes met. Instantly she dropped the curtain and stood, frozen, listening to the sound of the dog barking, and, after a second or two, Martin's footsteps. The sounds diminished. She teased the curtains open by an inch and watched his stiff back retreat down the slope.

She was cold, so she wrapped her arms around herself and hurried back to bed, grateful to find the warm spot and seal herself back under the duvet. "Brrr," she said to the empty room; and she was aware of the empty house, waiting for her to rise and occupy it.

What had that dream meant? An anxiety dream. What had happened? Falling, that sensation of the plummeting depth opening up beneath her. And there had been someone's voice. Who was it, who had rescued her? She couldn't remember. But the anxiety was fresh, it was still with her and she didn't want to leave the warm comfort of her bed.

The summer had begun to falter, and August's blue skies had turned to September's greyer ones. The young mothers of Portwenn prepared their children's uniforms and replaced the missing items from their pencil cases, so they'd be ready to attend the school where Louisa Glasson, at the moment, was making an application for the post of headmistress. The population of the village began to dwindle as tourists packed up and went home, and there was the sense of a new season beginning; the village, as it were, with its roofs mended and its boats repaired, headed into the wildness of a winter on the Atlantic shore. The sea began to flex its muscles, ready for the yearly onslaught it would make on Portwenn's sea walls, washing the stonework so vigorously and so continually as to wear it away, a fraction at a time.

For Doctor Martin Ellingham, autumn was his favourite time of year. It had never lost that feeling of being the true start of a new year — perhaps because, in childhood, that was when new achievements had made themselves felt: the move upwards through the school, a new class, a size bigger uniform. He liked the sense of the world throwing itself anew into the world of work — because after all that was the world he lived in all the time; he wasn't one for holidays.

And yet, this year, it seemed that autumn had no sooner started than it was over. Three months of calm, orderly work as Portwenn's doctor went past in a flash.

The days shortened in quick succession, the sun rising later and disappearing earlier behind the cliffs at the back of his house. Suddenly autumn was gone, and the village of Portwenn descended into the oddity that was the most mystifying holiday period of all, the holiday that was in some ways a charade, that had the most illogical conventions and the most bizarre traditions and the most incomprehensible events — Christmas. During autumn, Martin had put his head down and worked, fending off the idea of Christmas for as long as he could; but it was like being on a conveyor belt moving into the jaws of a machine.

And, sure enough, here it came: the first of December.

In the Lexus, Martin followed Joan's Land Rover — there was a fragment of orange string tied to the tow hitch at the back, which was distracting. It was a battered, ancient vehicle and swayed from side to side like an old boat in the narrow lane. His aunt, he could see, was cheerfully upright, a silhouette behind the steering wheel. Her engine sounded louder than his own. The lane was white with cold, and the hedgerows were shorn, and still, and lifeless.

He slowed down, following the Land Rover as it swung into Muriel's driveway. The suspension bounced harshly: the mud and stones were as hard as the tarmac. His own breath puffed from his mouth as he exited the car and the chill immediately found the gaps in his coat and suit.

"I should be in the surgery," he called out as he slammed the car door.

"Won't take long!" answered his Aunt Joan, and she gave a skip to hurry to the front door. She pressed down on the latch and let them in.

Martin ducked his head to fit under the lintel. "Well, let's hope her condition is grave."

"Oh come along Marty, buck up."

The warmth of Muriel's house breathed in their faces. The kitchen was crowded: an oak table and four chairs were the centrepiece, there was a dresser stuffed with crockery and papers, and also a comfortable chair hard up against the stove, with a dent in the seat from the hours of Muriel's sitting there, presumably. Martin heard himself say the same old thing, "House calls are not an efficient use of my time."

"If we were all efficient with our time," said Joan as she weaved between the furniture, "we'd all be Swiss, wouldn't we? Come on."

He followed her into the hallway, with the walls at each elbow and the ceiling beams low enough to knock his head.

A voice floated across from the living room. "And you shouldn't be on the airwaves if you can't speak properly."

As they went in, Muriel was saying into the telephone, "No, I don't take calls in the afternoon," and then the receiver was sent tumbling back into its bracket. Muriel continued seamlessly to Joan, as if the latter had been in the room all along, "Call Nick Wright? Call Nick Wrong if you ask me." She was a

8

strong-boned woman with a fierce eye, sitting in the best chair, covered in two thick blankets. "But I've complained to the Culture Secretary and there's little else I can do." She stared at Martin. "Who's this?"

"Mu, do you remember, my nephew, Martin? Doctor Ellingham? He's come about your ankle."

"Oh now he comes."

Without thinking, Martin judged Muriel's general health: the strength of her voice and movements, how her eye moved from object to object, the strength and colour of hair, her posture, the condition of her teeth . . .

"Where were you yesterday," went on Muriel, fixing a sharp eye on him, "when it was up like a balloon?"

"Yesterday? I thought this was an emergency?" He turned to Joan.

"I was worried," said Joan firmly.

"Well, quick about you," said Muriel, "I'm busy."

Martin felt a sudden leap of astonishment and irritation. "Mrs Steel, I've driven out here to see you —"

"What d'you want, a medal?" interrupted Muriel, flipping back the blankets and lifting a leg out for him to examine.

"— when I should be in my surgery," finished Martin.

"It's my fault," chipped in Joan helpfully. "I left some letters on the stairs and she stood on them and slipped. Silly of me."

Martin pressed the ankle gently. "Any sensitivity here?"

"No."

"Here?" He moved the pressure to the top of the foot.

"No."

"What about here?" Martin sounded impatient. There would be some pain; it was swollen. She was acting up, the tough old boot. Pretending that nothing hurt. But it was not an emergency, and certainly it didn't warrant a house call.

"Um . . . I'll . . . go and put the kettle on," said Joan and she was quick to leave the room.

Muriel fixed Martin with a beady stare. "I suppose it's the way of things," she said solemnly. "You get on in years, you're not sure of yourself. Maybe you slip up here and there. And you start to lose your nerve."

"How long have you been slipping up?" Martin's professional instinct sharpened.

"No, not me. You," said Muriel impatiently That same beady eye blinked, twice. "I was told how you couldn't keep up with the big boys in London. Came running back to little old Portwenn."

"You've a mild sprain," said Martin. "I will prescribe some painkillers and anti-inflammatories."

"No thanks." She turned to Joan who'd walked back into the room. "Oops. Look at his face. Reminds me of when I used to spit on my hankie and wipe the choc-ice from round his mouth."

"Keep the weight off it for a few days," said Martin. He seemed to be involved with the leaves of a pot plant, and the ceiling had come down to attack him also. He was having trouble finding a spot to lean on to write the prescription. He signed it and held it out to Joan. "Any problems, come and see me in the surgery." He really had to get out of here.

"Sure you won't stay for tea?"

"Goodbye, Mrs Steel."

"Doctor."

Martin snapped his bag shut and walked from the room.

Joan followed him out. "So how is she?" she asked in a low voice, as Martin fought his way around the kitchen furniture to find the door.

"She's rude." Martin pulled on his gloves and shrugged into his overcoat.

But Joan was on a different track. "No, but do you think she's muddled in any way?"

"Muddled? No. Why d'you ask?" Martin stopped.

"It's just that Danny, her son, thinks she's losing her marbles. But I think she's fine. What do you think?"

"Oh she's functioning all right, wouldn't you say?" asked Martin with a degree of sarcasm.

"Yes, I think so. So . . . do you think you could tell Danny that you've examined her?"

"Aunt Joan, if you . . ."

"Martin, she's a dear, dear friend."

". . . if you want me to assess your friend's mental state, then please arrange an appointment in my surgery."

"She is just in there, and you're right here."

Martin, with his stern face, looked into the anxious face of his aunt, and realised he would have to agree. In a few strides, during which he had his usual feeling of being too big for a Cornish cottage, too tall and broad for its doorways, he was back with Mrs Steel. He stood squarely in front of the mantelpiece and turned to her and asked, "Mrs Steel, have you any idea what time it is?"

"Hmm?" Muriel's eyebrows went up. Then she thought for a second and asked a dry question. "How can I tell the time accurately if you're standing in front of the clock, which I suppose was deliberate, wasn't it? But I can make a guess, can't I, since I am actually *compos mentis*, and I'd say it was about half past eight."

"D'you know when the Second World War started?" Martin didn't even realise how impatient he sounded; his only concern was to get this done, and be out of here. But her answer startled him.

"Nineteen nineteen," she replied promptly.

Martin shared a brief look with his Aunt Joan. Maybe there was something wrong with her . . .

"At the Treaty of Versailles," explained Muriel shrewdly. "The Germans were humiliated. It was a sham. In the aftermath of World War One were planted the seeds of World War Two."

"Thank you, Mrs Steel," said Martin politely, and for the second time he carried the medical bag from the room.

He was rather impressed with this friend of his aunt's. She was a formidable and admirable woman — someone worth looking after. Mrs Steel — yes, steel indeed.

"So she's all right?" asked Aunt Joan, shepherding him back to his car.

"She is more than fine," said Martin. "She is impressive."

ALWAYS AVAILABLE FOR ADVICE said the sign on the pharmacy door, which curdled Martin's blood slightly, and his disapproval was exacerbated by the trail of fairy lights which ran along the shelves, and the festive Santa whose arm moved up and down woodenly. It was only 1st December — but he supposed that the commercial interests of Christmas were always bound to make themselves felt as early as possible. And yet, there was something unutterably sad about Christmas decorations in a shop devoted to ill health, to the eradication of spots and boils and facial hair, and to the cleaning and maintenance of one's fingernails, thought Martin. He took two steps into the shop, but then saw that Louisa Glasson was being served at the counter — that swatch of long, dark hair tied in a ponytail, the sheepskin coat pinched at the waist and warm boots. He turned straight back around to leave again.

His exit was blocked by Portwenn's plumber, Bert Large, of Large and Son. There was no way round Bert.

The plumber's wistful face, under its usual bobble hat, but currently pulled right down over his ears, took in the doctor and he said, "Ah, morning, Doc. All right?"

Martin gave the shortest possible answer, "Yes," but he felt his voice fill the small shop; it would undoubtedly reach the ears of Louisa Glasson.

"Er, has Paul arrived?" asked Bert. His cheeks puffed out and he moved his hat back and forth on his head.

"Paul?"

"Yeah, Paul . . ."

By now Louisa had turned round and their eyes met. "Hello, Martin," she said in a meaningful tone.

Martin felt all the confusion that surrounded ordinary human intercourse return to him and befuddle his reactions. "Hello," he said.

Bert rocked on his feet. "Sorry, Doc, you're on your way in, or out, or . . ."

"Um . . . yes," said Martin. He stepped towards Louisa. "Um, I'm glad I've bumped into you. I've been meaning to —"

"Yes, well," interrupted Louisa, "considering we live in the same village, it's actually quite impressive that you haven't managed to 'bump into me' for the last three months, Martin."

A wall of difficulty faced Martin, which he simply had no idea how to climb over, or why he needed to climb over it. And Louisa seemed determined to make it more difficult. "Right. I wanted to say —"

Mrs Tishell, the pharmacist, popped up from behind the counter. "Sorry, I am sorry," she said.

Was Mrs Tishell joining their conversation, Martin wondered, or was hers a different one?

14

"I know they're here somewhere," said Mrs Tishell. She was looking for something on the shelves, so Martin felt the pressure land on him again to carry on.

"You were so rude," said Louisa, shaking her head. She had taken a few steps, so they had a modicum of privacy between the shelves.

"I'm a doctor," explained Martin. "I can't help it." Surely she could see, that because he was a doctor then —

"I cannot believe," said Louisa, interrupting his train of thought, "that you could think it was acceptable to . . . kiss me." She glared at him. "And then imply that I had a problem."

"I know they're here somewhere," came Mrs Tishell's voice. Louisa's chin was set firm. "We'd both been up all night. Drinking hospital coffee for God's sake. I can tell you what *your* breath was like, if that's useful."

"Here they are," said Mrs Tishell. She was clutching to her breast three bottles of something and sidestepping to the till.

Louisa wasn't finished. "I was having kittens over Peter's accident. And all you can bang on about is dental hygiene. You kissed me, Martin," she hissed, "and then you told me I had bad breath! That's not on, is it? It's just not on." She swung back to Mrs Tishell, who was waiting patiently, putting all three bottles down carefully on the counter. "Thank you, Mrs Tishell. How much do I owe you?"

"It's three for the price of two on this particular brand," said Mrs Tishell. "So that will be three ninety-eight, please."

Louisa dug in her purse and handed over the money, sweeping up the three bottles but not having any bag to carry them in.

One of the bottles slipped out of her hand, and landed at Martin's feet. He picked it up, just to be helpful.

It was Listerine. His eye was caught by the slogan, "Kills The Germs That Cause Bad Breath".

Woodenly, he handed it back to Louisa, who snatched it. "Thanks," she said abruptly, in an injured tone.

"D'you want a bag?" asked Mrs Tishell.

"Yes, please."

Martin stood and watched while Louisa tumbled the clumsy bottles into a plastic bag. He couldn't think what to say.

"And that was your apology was it?" said Louisa in a low voice, " 'I'm a doctor'? Well, frankly, that's a pretty rubbish apology."

"Louisa, your change," said Mrs Tishell.

Louisa took her change and, with her face burning, walked out. Martin and Mrs Tishell were left uncomfortably in the shop.

"Oh dear, I only wanted to save her some money. It's three for two on the . . . um. Was she upset — d'you think I upset her, Doc?"

"Yes, Mrs Tishell, said Martin. "I think without question that you did."

It was one of those mornings when the village of Portwenn seemed to set out deliberately to confuse and

16

irritate Doctor Martin Ellingham. As if all the cottages in the narrow streets swapped positions as soon as his back was turned. As if people were in front of him at one moment, but when he turned round they were suddenly behind him. As if the cliffs, the sea, the boats, the cottages and the people were all made of plasticine and papier mâché, and he was in the middle of a child's game. Sometimes he thought the entity who was in charge of Portwenn, who controlled them all, was this flea-bitten, mangy, matted-haired dog that insisted on hanging around . . . he passed the dog and went into his surgery, where he was faced with a complete stranger sitting behind Elaine's desk — just sitting there as if she owned the place. "Who are you?" he asked.

"Morning, Doc," she said breezily. "Three appointments for this afternoon, the lab called about something, lots of Latin words, couldn't catch them all, number by your phone, and a cup of coffee on your desk."

"Do I know you?" asked Martin.

She was dressed in the most extraordinary clothes: there seemed to be a lot of ruffs, and frills, and different colours, and things stuck in her hair. She looked like something you might win at a fairground.

"Paul," said the girl.

"Paul," said Martin. It was clear to him that she was a girl. It would appear to be deliberately obstructive to give yourself a boy's name. Why would anyone do such a thing?

"As in Paul-ine?" suggested the girl. "Elaine's cousin," she explained.

"Where's Elaine?" This was like chewing on a piece of spaghetti and never finding the end.

"Pompee," said Pauline.

"Pompeii? Italy?"

"Nuh-uh. Pompee. Where Greg's got his Road Studies, or whatever. Her boyfriend? So I'm here."

"What d'you mean, 'So I'm here'?"

"Eh? What?"

"Well, it's not for Elaine to decide who should replace her while she's away."

"Elaine's a bit busy. *Cognito urgo sun*, isn't it? I am therefore I think." She shrugged. "So here I am. Covering for her. Both of us are totally relaxed about it. And it's not forever."

"Would you get me Elaine on the telephone, please?"

Pauline was about to answer that she really, really didn't need this when she was only doing a friend a favour, but instead she was taken with the sight of Eddie Rix bursting in, blood running from his temple. "Goddd," she said, and covered her mouth with her hand.

"Think I've messed up my ribs."

"Oh my God who've you been fighting?"

"No one," replied Eddie in a low voice. He had a solid, bricklayer type of build, was middle aged and sorry for himself, clutching his back.

Martin felt his own pulse rate lift, suddenly, at the sight of raw, open blood on Eddie's temple. Each time he felt this panic it was as if he visited again all the other times, one after another, that he'd panicked at the sight of blood — making the incision in Peter Cronk's chest in the back of the ambulance, seeing what he thought had been the blood-soaked shirt of Bert Large in the bar of the Crab and Lobster — until he arrived back at the very first time that the sight of blood, and the smell of cauterised flesh, had caused him to panic: when he'd been a successful surgeon, and for the first time he'd realised that what he was cutting into was not just human flesh, but an alive human person, very alive, and the panic had meant that he'd never been able to operate, since that moment. He'd had to walk away from his career as a surgeon. On this occasion, the blood wasn't flowing, he was quick to notice. Nonetheless he had to fight a strong compulsion to turn on his heel and leave the room. "Name?" he asked.

Both Pauline and Eddie answered at the same time, and the clash of their voices gave Eddie a kind of fame. "Eddie Rix."

"Wallop yourself, then, did you?" called Pauline sarcastically, grabbing a packet of wipes and following Eddie as he went through to the surgery.

"You stay here," said Martin.

"I thought I'd —"

"Stay," repeated Martin. He almost added, "Sit", but thought better of it.

The door closed between them.

In the consulting room, Martin was pleased to examine the bruising on Eddie's back, where the blood was out of sight. He moved his stethoscope across from the left-hand side of the spine to the right. Although bruises, of course, were made of blood. But it wasn't blood let out, blood escaping . . .

19

"Won't stop me going out on the boat, will it?"

"Yes, it will. For a couple of days."

The surgery door opened and Pauline stepped carefully in, balancing a cup of tea. "I thought he'd need this," said Pauline, "for the shock." She put the tea down next to Eddie. "There you are, Eddie."

"He's not in shock," said Martin, squeezing a dollop of antiseptic cream on his fingers. "I suspect you've broken a rib," he said to Eddie. "So we'll have to send you to A and E I'm afraid."

"Whoever did that wants locking away," said Pauline.

"No one did it," said Eddie sharply.

"Ribs don't break themselves," said Martin, irritated at the man's pride, unable to accept he'd been hurt.

"I mean . . . I mean, I didn't see who did it. Some guy jumped me and ran off."

"You were mugged?" Pauline seemed to be chewing the same bit of gum as her predecessor, Elaine. Perhaps they shared it back and forth. "Actually mugged? No way. In Portwenn? Cool."

Pauline left the room, and Eddie eased his shirt back into position tentatively.

"I'll give you something for the pain," said Martin. "The A and E doctor will give you a report, which you need to bring back to me."

Eddie winced. "It will heal by itself, won't it?"

"Let's see what the X-rays tell us, shall we?"

By the time Martin and Eddie had finished and stepped out of the consulting room, Police Constable Mark Mylow was leaning on the reception desk, talking to Pauline. The benign expression of Portwenn's very own policeman took in all human suffering, from whatever quarter, and remained always conciliatory, always understanding. "Ah," he said, "Eddie. Heard about your misfortune." For some reason, he seemed pleased with himself. "Very sorry," he added.

Eddie was thrown at the sight of the gregarious policeman. "What . . . how did you . . .?"

"Paul here phoned me." Mark nodded at Pauline. "Nasty bruising, I gather. A mugging, no less."

"It's nothing," said Eddie, who was barely able to take a breath, he was in such pain. "Just one of those things. You know."

"You say that," said Mark, kindly, "but d'you know how many muggings I've had in Portwenn? Go on, have a guess. Doc?"

"No."

"Guess, go on."

"I don't want to."

"None. Not one." Mark sounded proud, either because there had been no muggings up until now in Portwenn due to the deterrent effect of his uniformed figure walking up and down the village, or because there was, now, like a prize awarded to a village policeman for long service, a mugging for him to deal with. "This," he said solemnly, "is a bleak day for Portwenn."

The morning's list of patients continued: there was a flu going around, which was dangerous for the elderly, heading into the coldest and wildest months of the year, when the village became bleak and almost empty.

There was the odd injury caused by motor accidents or mishaps on board the fishing vessels; sometimes the less sure-footed would fall on the rain-sluiced cobbles. During the summer months, the sun and the leisure business would throw up their own seasonal variety of accidents: a burn from a camping stove, a bruise from a surfboard, a child who'd made himself sick by eating too much chocolate, a bald man with sunburn on the top of his head. Now the numbers had reduced, and it was mostly the elderly needing repeat prescriptions for chronic conditions. Martin was conscientious; he looked around the edges of his patients to be sure that one condition did not mask another: sometimes a complaint would be a symptom of a different illness. High blood sugar could cause infections, for instance, with the sugar like an accelerant, a food for the bacteria, and it would be important to treat the high blood sugar, as well as the infection.

And as the morning list of appointments was drawing to a close, a man appeared in Martin's surgery uninvited. There was nothing wrong with him. In fact Martin could see, as he looked up sharply from writing notes, that this man looked in perfect health: his stride was buoyant, his black hair glossy and the look in his eye determined. He could be considered handsome, with a face poetic in its sensitivity, and yet strongly masculine, the jaw set determinedly. He was confident, if not mildly aggressive. After all, he'd walked in uninvited.

22

"D'you mind?" Martin frowned. It was incredible what people did, how they behaved, sometimes. "This is my consulting room."

"I'm sorry, I've come down from London," said the stranger, as if the fact that he came from the capital city excused him from ordinary good manners. Martin could say the same himself, that he'd come from London — it was just that he'd been here for a bit longer.

"Have you any idea," continued the stranger, "what it takes to get someone into a decent care home?"

"I beg your pardon?"

"My mother. Finally, after months of waiting, and paperwork, and expense, it's sorted. And I get in the car and I drive down here, when I'm actually supposed to be in London, and I arrive — only to find the local GP has scuppered the whole thing."

Martin knew who this man must be, but he chose instead to say, "I'm sorry, but I have no idea what you're talking about."

"Muriel Steel. You saw her earlier this morning. And gave her the all clear. You and your auntie Joan, who, quite frankly, would do well to mind her own business. Muriel knew she had to go. She accepted it. Now she's refusing."

Martin felt intense irritation that his helpfulness — his going, frankly, beyond the call of duty — was now being thrown back in his face so impolitely, and his professional reputation questioned. "On good grounds," he pointed out. "Care homes are for elderly individuals in need, not for the convenience of offspring who've chosen to live three hundred miles from their elderly parent." Martin observed his answer have its effect: the other man's eyes shone with frustration, but a slight stutter had arrived now that he realised Martin wasn't afraid of a fight.

"Convenience?" said the other man. "D . . . Doctor, with respect, she's dementing."

"I asked your mother two standard questions used in the testing of cognitive impairment and she not only passed, she put the questions to the sword more effectively than most people half her age."

"Two questions?" The man's eyes glittered unpleasantly. "You are joking? I speak to her every single night. Most of the time she doesn't know whether it's Tuesday or Selfridges. Now whose fault is it going to be, when she gets hit by a car on the road, or uses a hairdryer in the bath?" Suddenly the anger went out of him as if on an outward breath, and he slowly sat down in the chair opposite Martin. "Look. Doctor. I understand you probably meant well, and I can forgive you that, I really can, but please trust me when I tell you that you've made a mistake. And I think we'd sort this whole thing out a lot more quickly if you'd just admit it."

As far as Martin was concerned there was no mistake. The rationale was straightforward, and this arrogant man, frustrated by the call on his time made by an elderly mother, needed to know that he, Martin, wasn't going to lie, or bend the truth, just so an ungrateful son could drive more quickly back to London. "I attended your mother for a medical complaint," said Martin calmly. "I informally assessed her cognitive functioning and was satisfied that no further examination was necessary. Now you can forgive me or not, but that is my professional opinion and this is my surgery." Martin felt a justified righteousness in his breast. "So I'd be very grateful if you'd bugger off."

Martin's irritation with every single human being stayed with him as he walked under a grey, lowering sky down the sloping cliff road to the village. Presumably a few simple groceries would not be impossible to procure, even in the depths of winter when every shop in Portwenn either shrank its stock by half, or opened for only two days, or closed completely. The Spar supermarket, though, on the first of December, had become a beacon of optimism, with a plastic Christmas tree in the window and a banner strung along its front reading, "Goodwill To All Men". The number of charity collection jars next to the tills had been increased to three, and each one had different-coloured tinsel wrapped around it.

Leaning casually against the wall alongside the Spar supermarket was PC Mark Mylow, who said something utterly irrational as Martin prepared to nod a greeting.

"Just walk on by, Doc," muttered the policeman under his breath.

Martin stopped. "What?" He frowned. "I was walking on by."

"No, I meant keep going. Plain clothes."

"How d'you mean?"

"Our friend —" Mark nodded to his right "— five eleven, Caucasian, dark hoody, has Eddie Rix's wallet." And then he asked meaningfully, "What's he gonna do with the credit card?" He wisely answered his own question. "He's going to use it before it gets cancelled. And, if he does show his hand, I'm here."

"Right." Martin frowned. "I'm not gifted with any particular insight into the criminal mind," he said, "but is it likely the thief would use the card of a local man in Portwenn? He'd go somewhere else, surely."

"I think what you're missing here, Doc," said Mark with kindly forbearance, "is that it's a visible policing thing. In times of uncertainty, people want to see their police force on the ground. They want to feel safe in their beds. You know?"

"But you're trying not to be seen," said Martin, grimly trying to hold on to the logic. "You're in plain clothes. You're meant to be invisible."

"That's right, I am. Which is why I'd rather not be seen chewing the fat with you. Everyone knows we're friends. If that's all right with you."

"That's fine."

Martin pressed on, trying to put the confusion behind him, write it off. In the Spar shop he saw Bert Large's bobble hat moving along just above the shelf, and, once Martin had fetched the spices and other ingredients he needed, he strode ahead to beat the plumber to the checkout.

"You'm light on your feet, Doc," said Bert.

"Yes," said Martin, handing over his items.

"What about that Paul, sweet Pauline, she settling in OK with you?"

"No."

"She's a lovely girl. Dawn — that's her mum — Dawn and I were in the water polo team. That's to say, some years back now." Bert looked regretfully at his stomach and patted it.

"Five sixty-two, please, Doc," said the cashier.

"I'd better have some cashback," said Martin. "Thirty pounds, please."

"Oh, I'm sorry, Doc, but I'm afraid we're not accepting cards today."

The nonsensical behaviour of Portwenn's policeman outside the shop, now added to the stupidity of the woman inside the shop, and Martin felt his disbelief turn into irritation. "Right," he said. "It was Eddie Rix who was mugged," he pointed out.

"Dawn is what you might call very motivated," interjected Bert.

"Yeah, horrible business," said the cashier to Martin. "Mugged. Never been lucky, Eddie hasn't. One injury after another."

"And I wasn't mugged," said Martin. "And you know who I am." He waved his card up and down.

"I should point out," said Bert carefully to Martin, "that Dawn is very ambitious for her daughter."

"Please don't point anything out, Bert," said Martin sharply. He could only deal with one nincompoop at a time. He turned to the shopkeeper. "This is completely illogical."

"It's not actually," said the cashier bluntly.

Bert was thick-skinned; it was easy for him to keep banging on about Dawn. "Once, when Paul was a one-year-old, she threw her in the pool, you know, trying to get her to swim early. Which is important round here, of course."

"Would you explain to me," Martin asked the cashier, "why I can't use my card, when it's someone else altogether who's been mugged?" He leaned forward to emphasise the question. "Can you explain that to me?'

"Surely I can," answered Bert, blithely. "She sank straight to the bottom, didn't she?"

"Not you." Martin glared at Bert. "Her." He glared at the cashier. "Apart from anything else, what criminal with half, or even a quarter, of a brain would try to use that credit card anywhere in Portwenn?"

"Dunno," said the cashier. "But I can tell you he won't have any joy in my shop in any event."

"I can't imagine anybody finding much joy in your shop."

"Not if they wanna use a card, Doc, no. 'Cos our card machine is broken." She indicated a sign leaning against the till — CARD MACHINE OUT OF ORDER. "So that's why I can't take your card, I'm afraid," she finished.

Martin felt as if he'd trudged over a thirsty, barren desert only to find out he had travelled for no reason, and was in the wrong place, and now had to trudge all the way back again. "Right," he said, and he believed utterly at that moment that for the human species ever

28

to communicate effectively was a forlorn hope. "Well. I shall just have to pay you tomorrow."

The cashier pointed at another sign. It read: MR AND MRS CREDIT HAVE PASSED AWAY. PLEASE DON'T MENTION THEIR NAMES — IT REALLY HURTS.

Portwenn harbour grew larger and then shrank twice daily with the tide. There was no quay built; since time immemorial fishermen had left their boats to lie on their sides on the beach at low tide, as if the boats needed to rest their weary frames and sleep, for a half dozen hours, before the water ran in again and sat them upright, ready for work. The two big sea walls, built from either side of the bay like the paddles on a pinball machine, protected the harbour and meant that surfers would never have any joy here, but other, less adventurous holidaymakers, come summer, would crowd onto the beach, and parents appreciated the calmness of the water for their small children. All of these latter groups had long since gone; instead it was only fishermen that could be seen here now, working with frozen fingers, and perhaps one or two well wrapped-up individuals giving their dogs the briefest of walks across the sand at low tide.

Yet, this afternoon, with the beach deserted and inhospitable and cold, there was the unlikely sight of an elderly woman walking towards the sea — unlikely not because she was dressed in a thick tweed skirt and sensible shoes, but because of her direction, and her gait: she appeared to have in mind a destination that could only be reached by walking on the surface of the water, because she seemed not to take account of the first teasing of the ocean around her feet. Perhaps, in her mind, she was somewhere else, as in a dream, and the sea was to her a favourite path, or the streets of her home town, or a metaphorical place: a long and dusty road with her journey's end beyond the horizon.

She walked in up to her knees. Her tweed skirt began to swirl around her and grow heavy.

Two witnesses noticed — their curiosity had turned to disbelief and quickly, now, to alarm. She would drown; she must be saved. They started towards her, and shouted for help.

It was Police Constable Mark Mylow who was the first to reach her. Alerted by the shouts, and his eye guided by several others moving towards the woman, Mark ran down the beach at full speed, calling out, "Just a minute . . ."

The woman dreamily walked onwards; she was up to her waist just as Mark skipped through the shallows, the cold water as sharp as knives in his shoes and round his ankles. In several bounds he'd reached her side and he could see who it was. He took her arm and gently stopped her.

"I need to buy a battery," said the old lady.

"Batteries are this way, up in the village, see? I think . . . there we go, that's it." He began to turn her round, and his peaceable and benevolent tone of voice, which naturally came out during any crisis or alarm, encouraged her to obey. "That's it, I think this is the way, we're better off heading in this direction."

"Mr Monkford will have a battery for me."

"He's in the post office at the moment, I'd reckon. He's not out on the water."

"A PP3."

"Yup, that's the one. A PP3. No problem. We're all set, one foot after another is the trick . . . post office dead ahead, in the town there, Mr Monkford waiting for you . . . with your battery all ready." He noticed she'd begun to shake with cold. "That's the way, you're doing just fine, Mrs Steel."

The doctor had been called for, and Martin rushed down the few hundred yards to the beach. It soon became clear, as he walked fast towards the gaggle of people, that the person they were gathered around, lifting the blanket across her shoulders, was the woman to whom he'd given the all-clear — Muriel Steel.

PC Mylow caught his eye; also among the group was her son — what had been his name, Daniel?

Martin was astonished. Was this the same woman who'd tricked him earlier by attributing the start of the Second World War to the Treaty of Versailles? It was unbelievable. "Good God," said Martin.

Danny, his arm around his mother's shoulders, said quickly and automatically, "Please don't take the Lord's name in vain."

The comment registered with Martin, but he was only concerned with his patient. "Mrs Steel?" he asked, making sure he was in her line of sight. "Muriel?"

"You're not Mr Monkford."

"No, it's Martin Ellingham. The doctor." Her shaking jaw told him she was losing body temperature, and she was confused, anxious. "Let's get her inside. Up to the pub, I think."

"I need to buy a battery for my smoke alarm."

PC Mark Mylow stood on a great big empty patch of beach and said needlessly, "Can we clear some space, please?"

Daniel leaned in close to his mother as they made their way up to the pub. "Everything's going to be taken care of," he said.

"We'll soon have you in the warm," said Martin.

Muriel looked him in the eye and said, "Tosser."

These were all the classic signs of dementia. Yet earlier she'd shown no signs of cognitive impairment — rather the opposite. Martin was immediately one hundred per cent professionally engaged in the conundrum.

By the time they were inside the Crab and Lobster, others had joined them: Louisa was there; and someone had phoned Muriel's best friend, Martin's Aunt Joan.

Louisa brought a cup of tea from the kitchen. "To warm you up on the inside," she said, taking a seat beside Muriel.

"Don't need warming up," said Muriel.

"Mu, what were you doing?" asked Joan impatiently. She knew the implications — this behaviour would have her friend locked up in a home.

"Oh what's it got to do with you?" said Muriel. Her head poked out like a turtle's from underneath the blanket.

32

"Mu?" Joan was shocked.

"She's dementing," explained Martin.

"Nonsense," said Joan. "She's just old. We all have our idiosyncrasies, Martin, you of all people should know that."

"Auntie Joan, there are idiosyncrasies and there's wading into the sea to get to the post office."

Mark tried to walk the situation forwards. "Danny's phoning up — to see if the home will still have her."

"No," said Joan sharply. "That will kill her. Martin, can't you do something?"

Martin drew breath, about to make his excuses and leave — he'd done all he could, after all. But his eye was caught by the son, Danny, walking back into the pub, pocketing his mobile phone.

"It's all arranged," said Danny. "High Trees will take her."

"That is her worst nightmare," announced Joan.

Danny's springy, youthful stride carried him across to the group surrounding his mother and he sank to his knees and took her hands in his. "We are all talking about her as if she isn't here," he said, looking at her carefully. "Aren't we, Mum?"

Muriel frowned, as if trying to understand a foreign language.

"I have prayed long and hard for her to get better," said Danny. "But she hasn't. And I can't look after her — I'm in London."

"Well, I can look after her," said Joan, "and I'm here."

"You can't look after her, I'm afraid," said Martin. "She needs around-the-clock care."

"I'm glad you see that now," put in Danny. His thumbs massaged the backs of his mother's hands.

"I promised her she wouldn't have to go into a home," said Joan.

"It's not a decision I've taken lightly," said Danny, pressing his mother's hands together as if encouraging her to pray.

The High Trees Care Home was a graceful former country house with a sweeping stretch of lawn; and the mature trees gave the grounds an air of permanence that suited the heavy stone walls and gabled roofs. The stone was honey-coloured rather than Cornwall's usual granite, which warmed the face of the property even now, in December, and made it less of an institution. It might have been true that Muriel Steel wanted at all costs to avoid going into a home, but from the outside, at least, it was a place where anyone would be proud to live.

When Martin stepped inside, he was impressed at how spacious it was. There was no Christmas tree or decorations, yet, which was a relief. Yes, it was the shopkeepers, he thought, the ones who had to retail goods to the public, who went for Christmas just as soon as November turned to December.

Martin was taken up the stairs, along the corridor, and once in Muriel's room he found his Aunt Joan already there. In here it was equally spacious — plainly furnished but clean and well kept. A large window looked onto the windswept front lawns.

The greetings between the three of them were quick, anxious. Martin settled immediately into an examination of Muriel's ankle. It was strange how her fierce look told a different story from before — her belligerence had turned from brightness and light, to dark. She had gone from being an independent, strong-minded old lady to being a vulnerable patient, clinging on to her sanity.

"I'm not happy with this," said Martin. The ankle was more swollen. He asked her, "Have you been taking the medication I gave you?"

"It's my ankle," said Muriel, as if she were answering the question.

"She's due another dose," said Joan hopefully.

"I'll give her something stronger." Martin reached for his medical bag. He turned to the care worker who'd led him here. "Can you supervise the medication?"

"I'll do my best," she said. "I'll get a glass of water."

Martin and Joan stood together a short distance away from Muriel, who looked peacefully out of the window.

"I thought she was all right on her own." Joan sounded anguished. "I mean, I've popped in almost every morning for years."

Martin kept his voice low, to match hers. "It's sometimes hard to spot a gradual deterioration."

"Yes, or maybe it was there all the time, and it was just . . . that I didn't *want* to see it."

A figure appeared in the doorway — it was Danny, Muriel's son, and he didn't spare a moment to greet anyone. "Look at the state of her." He was looking at his mother's ankle.

"Inflammation in the elderly can sometimes look alarming, but it's not as bad as it seems."

"Yes, but none of this would have happened if she'd been here in the first place, would it?"

Martin felt his usual irritation with this young man. "If you're so concerned, why weren't you watching her when she walked into the sea?"

Joan's voice was quiet and calm. "Maybe this isn't the place . . ."

In his anxiety Danny went to kneel in front of his mother — just as he'd done at the Crab and Lobster — and Martin, seeing him kneel, thought, yes, that's his thing, to kneel, and he remembered that phrase, about prayer, and about not taking the Lord's name in vain: this was a deeply religious young man. "Hello, Mum," he said. "You all right?"

Muriel looked at Daniel carefully, and then she peered at him even more closely, and asked everyone, "Who's he?"

Christmas is a time for parables, a time for human generosity and kindness, and in Portwenn a stranger appeared who seemed to embody these qualities. He wore a uniform that made him look like a policeman, or a fireman, or an ambulance man, or a parking warden, but he was in fact none of those things. He was of late middle age, around sixty, with a greying beard and a genial, calm expression. With an umbrella that seemed too small, like a child's, he went from shop to shop in the village, carefully lowering the umbrella once he'd gained shelter from the rain, disappearing inside for a few minutes, and then appearing again without any purchases, to lift the umbrella and walk steadily, under its cover, to the next doorway. The only contribution he made to the village's economy was to Mrs Hall's bed and breakfast up on the main road, the cheapest in the whole area, which got an unlikely visitor for nine days and nights in the middle of December. This figure, who persisted like a good fisherman — and perhaps that could be the name of this parable, "The Good Fisherman" — performed the same task in every shop, at every front door, and with most people that he might pass in the street. Any observer could see how it went — always the same way: he said a few words of introduction, he reached into his satchel for a set of photographs, and then came some kind of explanation, which took no more than a minute to deliver. And then from his listener would come a shake of the head, a regretful no, and the Good Fisherman would replace the photographs in his wallet and move on.

It was a mystery.

The next conversation that Martin had about old age was a more unlikely one. He was driving to the hospital in Truro and in the passenger seat was PC Mark Mylow, who had sprained a wrist. Portwenn's diligent policeman had seen a man in a hoody trotting past his house, and had asked the running figure politely to stop, since there was a mugger in Portwenn and a mugger would obviously be wearing a hoody. The fact that the man hadn't stopped or even paused was enough to have Mark Mylow running after him, and putting a hand on his shoulder to stop him, whereupon the "man" had turned out to be Al Large, the plumber's son, out for a morning run and wearing headphones. The hand on his shoulder had startled him, made him think he was about to be mugged, no less, and the unfortunate upshot was that Al — who was pretty quick on his feet — had upended PC Mark Mylow. Hence Mark's injured wrist.

Martin found the village policeman willing to wait for a couple of hours so he could share a car journey with Martin to the hospital.

"Having no girlfriend or family," said Mark, carrying his wrist in his other hand, "if I should need looking after when I'm older, who's going to run me to the hospital and whatnot? That's why we have to cherish our friends. Like your Aunt Joan and old Mrs S. And you and me. I can see us in old age, can't you? Looking in on each other? Obviously, if you should get a girlfriend, that'd be fine as well."

Martin solidly drove: clutch, gearshift, accelerator. Mirror.

"Although I have to say," went on Mark Mylow cheerfully, "that I admire you on that score, Doc. You're not needy. You don't pine for the opposite sex."

Martin could practically hear the gears crunching in Mark Mylow's brain.

"Or," said the policeman in an apologetic tone of voice, "are you . . . umm?"

"No," said Martin.

"Just a bit?" Mark sounded hopeful.

"No."

"No problem if you were, of course," said Mark. "Still be friends. That's possible."

"Mark, shut up," said Martin. If you were to cut open the policeman's head, he thought, a whole load of magazine articles would spill out.

"Though actually, as it happens, I have to warn you," said Mark.

"What about?"

"I have seen someone I like."

"Well, that's a start," said Martin helpfully.

"And I think I've got a new secret weapon —" Mark imitated casting a line, hauling back on the rod, winding the fishing reel "— to help land her in the net."

At the hospital, Martin was first to the reception desk because Mark appeared to know so many of the staff and lagged behind. "Dr Martin Ellingham," said Martin. "I've brought in a patient from Portwenn with a sprained wrist. Needs an X-ray. I'd appreciate it if you could see him as soon as possible."

"You'll have to wait for triage," said the receptionist.

"No I won't. I've already diagnosed him."

"That's triage."

"Yes. And that's what I've done," said Martin testily. Was no one allowed to break through the bureaucratic nightmare of hospital red tape?

"That's not how it works," said the receptionist. But then her bureaucratic face broke and her smile showed. "Oh, hiya, Mark," she said. Portwenn's policeman had carried his own wrist as far as the reception desk, now.

"Hiya," said Mark.

"In the wars?"

"It's a jungle out there." Mark winked at her.

"Go on through. You know the way."

Martin had to step beyond his own irritation — that was what it was like, so often — but at the same time a trolley was wheeled past; a smear of blood on the gurney caught his eye and made him giddy.

He could only escape from his own reaction by closing his eyes and walking for a step or two and opening them again to see only the hospital corridor, the floor, the ceiling, and people walking past who were complete, all their blood inside their skins, safely contained. He headed for A and E, and stopped the first doctor he met. "Dr Ellingham," he introduced himself. "Mr Rix is a patient of mine. Suspected broken ribs. I wanted to know if the X-ray showed anything?"

"Rix? You mean the burns injury."

"No, suspected broken ribs."

"That must be a separate trauma. We had a Mr Eddie Rix for a burns injury. Not serious, though." The A and E doctor peered into Martin's face and placed a hand on his arm. "You all right?" he asked.

"Yes, yes," said Martin, distracted. He barely noticed the A and E doctor go on his way. Instead he went quickly back to the car, not thinking to wait for Mark Mylow, and drove swiftly back to Portwenn. The car slid to a halt outside the surgery and automatically, without thinking, Martin found himself seated behind his desk in the consulting room, computer mouse falling under his hand. He searched the patient records for "Rix" but found nothing. "Pauline?" he called. He wouldn't ever be able to call her "Paul".

"What?"

He could just about see her through the open door of the consulting room. "I can't find a patient's records."

"They'll be there. What's his name?"

"Rix."

"Eddie."

"Yeah."

She came and looked over his shoulder. "OK, you're looking under 'R', yeah?" She pecked at the keyboard. "Shall we start again at the beginning? Eddie Rix, so we look under 'E' . . ." She pecked twice more. "There. See?"

"Pauline, I can't have patients' records filed under their first names."

"It was good enough in Newlyn."

"Well, what sort of surgery was it, a vet's?"

"You say that, but it was, actually. Still a surgery, though, isn't it. Learnt a lot there. Minor ops. Splints. Stuff like that. Could have sorted that sprained wrist for you. Saved Mark the journey." She started to head back to her desk, but he stopped her.

"By the way, did Mr Rix bring a letter from the hospital regarding his ribs?"

"Not that I know of." She continued on her way.

Martin said loudly, "Perhaps it's filed under 'L' for letter, or 'P' for piece of paper." He didn't hear Pauline's sarcastic reply; he was frowning at the list of Eddie Rix's past injuries: a dozen or more, all in the last few years. Bruised neck. Elbow joint. Whiplash . . . What was going on? A solidly built, middle-aged fisherman: was someone beating him up?

Martin's professional curiosity was aroused; and it was an enquiry that would lead him, oddly enough, to the sight of Louisa's name written alongside the name of Danny Steel.

The names were written, among others, on the "Get Well" card given by the community to PC Mark Mylow. Mark was proud to show it off. In the fishmonger's, where he happened to bump into Martin, he clumsily unfolded the giant card. Martin had the impression that Portwenn's policeman might have been carrying the card around for a number of days showing it to anyone who cared to look. "There you go," said Mark. "See? Everyone's been making a bit of a fuss of me, which is unnecessary, of course. Because it was all in the line of duty."

In the middle of the card the words "OUR HERO" were written in giant letters in marker pen. Around this exclamation were written the various signatures.

"But you didn't actually confront a mugger, did you?" commented Martin.

"Technically, no, that's right."

"Well, not technically. Actually." It seemed to Martin that one of the qualities necessary in a policeman was truthfulness. "Actually, what happened was that you jumped on Al's back by mistake and he threw you to the ground."

"You say that, Doc, but that's only one way of looking at it. Another way of looking at it is, I didn't know Al wasn't the mugger, did I? So I did confront him, didn't I? Anyway," he went on in a pained voice, "the public likes to know the police are making progress on these sensitive issues. Makes them feel safe."

"That's better than knowing the truth then, is it?"

"Well, it is the truth. Progress was made. I found out Al wasn't the mugger, even though he runs around the streets wearing a hoody. Process of elimination, see. Detective work, in effect, that is."

"The truth is," said Martin, "there is no mugger."

"You can't know that."

"Well, I do know that. I can't tell you how I know, but I know for certain there is no mugger in Portwenn."

"Well, let me tell you something," said Mark, "the illegal use of a credit card in Portwenn was only to purchase cigarettes. So we're looking for a mugger who smokes."

"That is as maybe. There might be a smoker who is illegally using a credit card. But there is no mugger."

"So you're telling me I sprained my wrist for nothing?" He held up his bandaged club of a hand.

"Yes."

"But everybody's signed my card," said Mark, as if this were proof there had to be a mugger in Portwenn. He opened the card again and pointed at the names. "Lucy Holmes. Rick. Bert. There's Al himself. Lovely apology from him. And Lou and Dan — that's a blast from the past, to see those two names together. Young Peter Cronk signed it . . ." The slight tone of complaint in his voice made it sound as if he was implying that not all these people could be wrong. "It's embarrassing, now," he finished.

"Lou and Dan? Is that . . .?"

"Yeah, Louisa and Danny. God, in the old days, Danny used to bring out the green-eyed monster in me, I can tell you. When I thought Louisa was The One, you know."

"Right." Martin felt an unaccountable tightening in his chest, a feeling similar to the panic he felt at the sight of blood. Yet there was no blood. The feeling persisted, and was joined by intense irritation at the picture in his mind's eye of Mrs Steel's son, Danny, standing next to Louisa Glasson: both dark haired, both a similar height and build, both with similar glowing, well-favoured looks. Even as he imagined them standing there, he could see that Danny's hand reached for Louisa's, and there they were, hand-in-hand, standing next to each other like paper dolls. Lou and Dan. Why should their being together be of any concern to him? Was it a medical matter? No. But Louisa was his patient; he could advise her — strongly — against forming a liaison with a man who believed in a religion that she didn't share. But this was the province of the mind, and he wasn't qualified to judge. A personal matter, for her alone to . . . Nonetheless, he strongly . . .

Confusion reigned for a while, and he shook his head to clear away any unhelpful thoughts and see his way.

"And," said Mark Mylow, "look at this." He pointed to an extravagant signature bang in the middle of the card. "What about them apples, then?"

Martin leaned closer. The strongly female handwriting was writ large. It read, "With love and admiration, Julie."

"Who's Julie?" asked Martin.

Mark Mylow tapped the side of his nose and pointed at Martin as if holding a firearm. "Coming this way soon." His smile was huge.

The next time Martin saw Danny, the intense dislike came back — because of the latter's religious views, obviously — and Martin knew enough not to venture near the subject, to prevent himself from becoming even more irritated at spurious belief systems that sponsored ridiculous festivals such as Christmas, and had nothing to do with reality — and that stepped over, or around, proven scientific facts as if they didn't exist. He disliked the man's unbearably springy hair and his animal litheness and his glittering eyes. Danny was a handsome example of the human male, Martin could see that — but luckily there was an immediate preoccupation to divert his attention, because there was Mrs Steel, in her comfy chair in the window of her room at the High Trees Care Home. Her leg was up on a stool, and the ankle — again — was more swollen than before, not less.

The care-worker, a girl called Eileen, stood nearby anxiously. The son, Danny, stood behind his mother's chair, his face set determinedly — ready to blame, to criticise.

"And you've been giving her the Diclofenac?" asked Martin.

"Yes." Eileen nodded. "Twice a day."

Martin spoke to himself. "I don't understand why the inflammation hasn't gone down." He turned to look at Muriel, who kept a hawk-like eye trained on her bad ankle. "Have the tablets I gave you had any effect on the pain, Mrs Steel?"

"What?" Mrs Steel swung her gaze to him.

Martin took in the anxious demeanour of the care-worker, Eileen. He asked her, "You have been supervising her? She's definitely taking them?"

"I bring her the glass of water," said Eileen.

"Well, that's not enough, is it? That's not what I asked."

"Can't *make* me drink," announced Muriel.

With that emphasis on the "make", Martin didn't need to ask any more questions and there were several logical connections that were instantly made in his head. He stepped smartly to the little bedside cabinet, opened the drawer and then checked in the cupboard underneath. He lifted the pillows and felt underneath the mattress. He dug his fingers into the soft earth in the plant pot, and felt the hard capsules — three, four . . . He fetched them out in the palm of his hand and silently showed them to Eileen.

"She's supposed to *take* them," said Eileen.

"Don't want to," said Muriel.

"Mrs Steel," said Martin, but with such patience and kindness that it surprised the onlookers, "these tablets will help you with the pain and reduce the inflammation in your ankle. But, you do have to take them." He went to Eileen and dropped the tablets in her hand. "If these tablets were more critical, your negligence could have been lethal," he stated baldly.

A groan of complaint came from Mrs Steel. "I don't want to go to High Trees."

Outside the window, unmoving, stood the upper branches of one of the high trees after which the rest home was named.

There was silence for a while. Except there almost could be heard the snap as the connection strengthened in Martin's head. He thought he knew what was going on now. It was almost like a hunter, thrilling to the chase.

Danny broke the silence. "Mum, we're all doing the best we can to look after you in the best possible way."

His mother had already moved on. "I don't drink at night. Otherwise you wet the bed and they send you to High Trees and I haven't . . ." A crack opened up in her voice. "I haven't . . ."

Danny knelt at the arm of her chair and picked up her hand. "Shhh, Mum, it's OK," he began.

"I have not wet the bed," insisted his mother.

"Of course you haven't," said Danny. "Shush now, it's all right."

Martin turned to the care-worker. "Have you at any time seen her drink?"

Eileen could not meet his eye.

"Have you seen her drink anything at all?" asked Martin.

Eileen frowned. "Not as such."

Muriel interrupted their conversation. "I drink in the mornings, as I always do."

Martin asked Eileen, "Do you have any rehydration salts in your medical cabinet?"

"I don't know."

"A diarrhoea preparation will do." He turned to Danny. "I think your mother may not have been drinking properly for a long time."

"She must have been drinking," said Danny. "Otherwise she would have become ill."

"Joan always brought her a cup of tea in the morning, which would have helped, would have raised her fluids temporarily, and allowed her to become lucid for an hour or two."

Eileen returned with a sachet and Martin tore it, poured the contents into the glass that stood on the bedside table. He picked it up and carried it to Muriel's chair. "I need you to drink this," he said.

"No."

"Please drink it," said Martin.

"Come on, Mum," said Danny. "It'll help you."

"No."

"All right," said Martin. "We need to get a drip into her." He peered closely at Muriel. "Don't worry, Mrs Steel, I think you're going to feel very much better, very soon."

"Do you mean to say —" Danny was incredulous "— she might not be demented at all?"

Martin nodded. "Well, let's see. But I think not. Similar symptoms are caused by dehydration."

"Praise the Lord," said Danny.

"No," said Martin.

When Martin returned to the surgery it was to find a small plastic Christmas tree sitting on Pauline's desk, its red and white lights winking away, and then running around the tree in an orderly line, and then winking one by one, and then flashing on and off together.

Pauline herself was dementing over the wretched dog. She ahhed and cooed over it, stroking her hand along its back and all the way up its tail.

"Did I imagine it, or did I say no Christmas tree?" he asked.

"That?" said Pauline. "It's not a tree, is it? Made of plastic. That's a Christmas decoration." Under her hand, the dog smiled and wagged its whole rear end with pleasure. "Luverrrly dog," she crooned.

"No Christmas decorations, please," said Martin.

"Well, I've gone and bought it now, haven't I," said Pauline.

"When you say *you* bought it . . ."

"Well, petty cash. Important for our patients to be cheered up when they come in."

"Take it back," said Martin bluntly, "to whichever godforsaken motorway service station you got it from."

She shrugged. "All right."

"And don't do that," said Martin abruptly.

"What?"

"That. With that animal. This is a doctor's surgery."

"You're not an animal, are you, lovey?" She puckered her lips for the dog to lick. Again her hand ran down its back and along its tail. "What's your name?" She turned to Martin. "What's its name?"

"Dog."

"Hello, Dog," sang Pauline. "Have you wormed him?"

"No. Because it's not my dog."

"What about flea and tick? I can do that for you."

"No."

"Takes two minutes."

"Get out," said Martin — and he wasn't sure if he was talking to the dog, or to Pauline, or to the infernally winking Christmas tree, or all of them together. "Out!" He found he was pointing at Eddie Rix and his wife, who stood at the entrance to the waiting room. "Not you," he added.

The dog slinked past Eddie, making its way out.

"Come through," said Martin.

In the consulting room, both Eddie and his wife, Gloria, nervously took their seats on the other side of Martin's desk.

Martin had Eddie's notes open on his desk. "Eddie," he said, "you've suffered a significant number of contusions and fractures over the last few years."

"Well, not that many." Eddie stirred uncomfortably in his chair.

"Seventeen," said Martin. "The last one just yesterday when you fell out of the back of your pickup, luckily when it was stationary, and lost consciousness."

"Ah. Well —"

His wife interrupted, "That was because of his rib, see. He carried on working, and he was unloading a crate of fish, and he leaned over and —"

"Or was it because of the burns, which you went straight to hospital for, and didn't tell me about?"

"That? Oh, that was out of surgery hours, so . . ." Eddie ground to a halt.

"Do you have a problem with balance, vision? Hearing?" asked Martin.

Gloria rolled her eyes and tutted. "Don't hear me, does he, when I ask 'un to take out the bins."

"Are you on any medication at the moment?" asked Martin. "Anything you've not told me about?"

"Nope."

"Do you use recreational drugs?"

"No!"

"So what about those burns? What caused those?"

Eddie and his wife answered at the same time, but he said, "Bonfire" and she said, "Cooking." He added, "Trying to cook . . . on the bonfire, like." They looked at each other. "Cooking on a bonfire?" asked Martin.

"Barbecue," said Eddie.

Martin frowned. "Have you always been accident prone?"

"No," said Eddie at the same time as his wife said, "Yeah."

Martin leaned forwards. "Mr Rix, there's a strong possibility that you have developed one of a number of serious conditions which would explain why you keep injuring yourself. I've spoken to a colleague at the

51

hospital in Truro and arranged for you to jump several queues. You're going to have an ultrasound of your carotid arteries to determine whether you've suffered any transient ischemic attacks, which would cause temporary blackouts. You're going to have an ECG to record your brainwave activity, which would rule out epilepsy. Or not, as the case may be. But most importantly, you're going to have an MRI scan which will show us whether you have a primary or secondary brain tumour."

Eddie nodded humbly. "Maybe it's for the best."

His wife looked frozen, and glum. "Don't be stupid," she said quietly.

Eddie looked at her, and leaned towards her when she signalled that she wanted to whisper in his ear. He listened for quite a long time and they both looked at Martin.

"Right," said Eddie, and they both stood up. "No need to go to all that trouble," he added.

"Mr Rix," said Martin. "You don't seem to understand. If you have a brain tumour and you do nothing, you may well die."

"Doc," said Gloria in a tolerant tone of voice. "You've been very kind. It's very nice of you to go to all this trouble." She pushed her hand into her bag. "Look, have some of my smoked mackerel pâté." She gave a broad smile. "We smoke the mackerel ourselves." She put the jar down on the desk.

"Honest, Doc, we . . . we understand." They started to edge towards the door.

"Thanks for everything," said Gloria.

52

"We'll think about it," said Eddie, "and let you know."

"Yes, we'll be in touch."

The surgery door closed behind them.

Martin had seen Danny and Louisa's names written together — "Lou and Danny" — inside Mark Mylow's get well card, but even worse was to see them together outside the Crab and Lobster, together with his Auntie Joan.

"Oh, Marty," she called out in her commanding voice. "Just the person."

Martin stopped. Louisa and Dan, he thought. Danny and Lou. Louisa and Danny. They stood side by side. A mating pair. He frowned. Their relationship didn't concern him, but he was puzzled as to why Danny's religious views continued to irritate him so much. Normally, he could force himself to be perfectly calm when faced with whatever nonsense people were prepared to believe in. After all, he had long ago ceased to be surprised at the illogical nonsense a human brain could seize on and make its own. So why, with Danny . . .? Of course, it was none of his business, but he considered that for Danny to inflict his religious beliefs on Louisa was like crushing in your hand a spring bloom.

Joan wobbled a little in her tough old-lady way. "Muriel is back to her old self!" she exclaimed.

"You mean, annoying, then," replied Martin.

"Vile to everyone!" said Joan.

"Good. I'm pleased."

"She's fighting fit. So I'm very proud of you. And thankful. I've got my old friend back."

"Yes, well, I'll drop in to see her tomorrow," said Martin.

"No." Joan indicated the three of them. "Don't do that. We're going to fetch her. At three o'clock. She's coming home."

Danny was youthful and easy in his assured charm. "Yeah, I can't remember the last time I had a conversation with her like today. It's . . . it's like she's back from the beyond."

Danny's eyes were glittery, thought Martin. Like a snake's? No, they were like Christmas decorations. Like the lights in that plastic Christmas tree on Pauline's desk, winking one by one and then flashing all at once.

"So we'd like to thank you," said Danny glancing at Louisa next to him. "Er . . . do you know Louisa, Louisa Glasson?"

"Yes," said Martin, at the same time as Louisa said it.

"Of course," said Danny. "You forget, everyone knows everyone else. We're going for a drink." He nodded at the doors of the Crab and Lobster. "To celebrate?"

If that was an invitation, Martin didn't want anything to do with it. "Well," he said abruptly, "enjoy your evening." He took a step to indicate he would be on his way.

As they passed each other, Danny smiled and gave Martin's arm a definite squeeze, as if testing a vegetable

54

he might wish to purchase, and said, while calmly and steadily looking at him, "Bless you."

"I didn't sneeze," Martin pointed out.

The smile stuck to Danny's face, but rather woodenly now, as Martin walked away.

The next morning, as Martin carried a cup of coffee from his living quarters into the surgery, it was almost as if he were listening to a voice inside his head, a voice describing him, when he overheard Pauline saying, "He's too shy, he's always waiting for the girl to make the move." The coffee splashed a little from the cup into the saucer as his footstep faltered. He heard Pauline say, "It's like he's always waiting for permission. And, when you give him permission, he messes up." Was this him that she was talking about? He heard Al — he guessed it was Al — tut-tutting.

Pauline went on, "And of course *she* thinks that's just pathetic."

Was that "she" referring to Louisa? Martin wondered.

"I s'pose I can see why she went back to her old boyfriend," said Al.

It was Louisa — Louisa and Danny — they were talking about. Louisa had gone back to her old boyfriend. Was that true? In any case, he couldn't just stand here and look down on a cup of coffee that tilted dangerously in his hand. He straightened it, and carried on, walked in. He was pleased to see that the plastic Christmas tree was nowhere in sight. "Morning, morning everyone," he said.

"Morning," chimed Al and Pauline.

Martin went through to his consulting room and shut the door behind him. But instead of going to his desk he paused for a while and listened. The muffled voices of Al and Pauline came through.

"And what did she say yesterday?" came Al's voice.

"Oh I don't know. Nothing much." There was a pause and then Pauline's voice came again. "She said you had a nice bum."

"Oh. Well. Thanks for telling me that, Pauline."

"Al?"

"What?"

"She was right."

"Oh. Thanks . . ."

Martin quietly moved away from the door. They had been talking about Elaine, not about Louisa.

He heard the phone make its call, and then Pauline's voice. "Portwenn surgery?" And then came Pauline's voice again. "Doc? Putting through a call for you."

Martin had to ask her something. He ducked back in. "Pauline?"

She looked up. "Hmm?"

Martin said, "Do I gather Elaine is not coming back?"

"Um, no. Maybe not."

"Right, well, I wanted to make it clear that I'm going to advertise her job."

Pauline leapt ahead of him, "Yeah, good, 'cos I was going to say, you know, I can't cover forever."

"Oh. OK."

"The phone call's urgent." She pointed at him. "Mrs Rix."

Fifteen minutes later, Martin pulled up outside the Rixs' hillside bungalow.

Mrs Rix was hurrying to meet him, her gait uncertain. "Thanks for coming, Doctor. We are so, so sorry to have troubled you."

"I hope that you now see the need for a proper investigation," Martin said, pompously. Sometimes he couldn't believe how people had the truth described to them and yet they blindly refused to see it. As if they were on some other planet, where the rules of cause and effect were arranged in an entirely different manner. Why on earth couldn't they see that he, Dr Martin Ellingham, a man who had been trained in one of the most advanced medical communities in the world, who had years of experience as a surgeon, up to his elbows in the mechanics of the human body — every day for hours at a time seeing underneath the human skin, grasping arteries, livers, kidneys, intestines with his bare hands — was the one person they could trust to look after their best interests, to keep the air going in and out of their lungs, the food in and out of their stomachs, the blood rushing from the heart and rushing back to the heart, the muscles tightening and loosening, in short, to keep them not only alive, but as healthy as it was humanly possible to be? Could they not see that? "Another accident." He shook his head.

"He's upstairs," said Gloria.

Martin followed her silently through the carpeted corridor. He imagined what it might be: DIY, falling off a stepladder, probably, or something to do with a power tool. Why hadn't she said?

"He's in here." Gloria opened a door to what Martin supposed would be a bedroom, but it was dark inside.

"Can we switch on a light or open a curtain?" asked Martin. He had the sense of some kind of contraption . . . When the curtain went back, daylight brightened the room and showed Mr Rix in a harness made of black leather and plastic that held him like a torture victim, suspended with his arms out and his head bowed over. It looked excruciatingly uncomfortable.

Gloria said in a friendly tone of voice, "We'd appreciate your discretion, Doctor."

"What have you done to him?" asked Martin. There wasn't any kind of censure in his tone of voice, but instead professional curiosity; he was concerned with the task at hand: the diagnosis-prognosis-prescription paradigm.

"Well," said Gloria, "I was hoisting him up, and something gave."

"Don't say anything, Doc," pleaded Eddie. "The boys down at the harbour, I . . . I'd never live it down."

"Is this consenting?" asked Martin. He thought he'd better check.

"Eh?"

"Consenting?" asked Gloria. "Blimey. He loves it."

"My shoulder . . . shoulder . . ." Eddie's face was suddenly a mask of pain.

58

"Oh yes, sorry." Martin stepped towards the spreadeagled fisherman. "Which one?"

"Right." Eddie's head nodded to that side.

"OK. Can you move it?" Martin leaned down to look at it more closely, to see the shapes made by the bones and the musculature. He could imagine exactly how every bone and sinew and muscle and artery was arranged under the skin. "This hurt?" He adjusted Eddie's arm sideways a fraction.

"Agggh."

"Trapezius muscle," confirmed Martin. "I'll give you an injection of diazepam." And then he asked, "Were all the injuries caused like this?"

"Yes." Gloria nodded.

"The burns as well?"

"Uh-huh. Except for down on the harbour, when he fell out of the pickup. That was just an ordinary fall. Obviously."

"Why didn't you tell me?" asked Martin.

"Sorry, Doc." Eddie sounded like a remorseful schoolboy.

"Well, you've got to be more careful," said Martin. He drew his bag towards him and pulled it open.

"I know, I know," said Gloria humbly. "It's just that sometimes, you know, in the heat of battle, Eddie forgets his safe word."

"Don't tell him that," said Eddie. "He doesn't want to hear about that."

"Oh it's all right, sausage, he's a doctor." Gloria was getting into her stride. "You see, Doc, what happened was that —"

"It's OK," interrupted Martin. "You don't have to tell me." He withdrew the syringe from its wrapping.

"We'd been married a long time," continued Gloria, "and when the boys left home, we needed a bit of a spark, you know. Something . . . well, I don't know."

Martin wiped Eddie's shoulder with an antiseptic wipe. "This may hurt a little," he said. But then, as he was about to give the injection, he paused. "Injections . . . the needle . . . doesn't . . . arouse you, does it?"

"Oh no, Doc," said Eddie. "No, no, you're good to go ahead. No worries."

"OK." Martin slid the needle into Eddie's trapezium muscle.

"Ow," said Eddie and gritted his teeth.

"And then by chance," said Gloria, who was pleased to be able, at last, to talk about it to someone, "we found this." She waved at the contraption. "Opened up a whole new world." She smiled easily. "Now there's a spark, all right."

The eighth of December: by now, in the High Trees Care Home, the central heating had been switched from "all day" to "constant", the lawns were ignored, the leaves had been swept up and burned, and the high trees that gave the place its name clung on to their needles if they were evergreens, or stood as bare silhouettes if they were deciduous.

As Martin eased the car down the drive, he remembered coming here before, during the summer. He'd seen a group of elderly people playing a game of croquet, and it had seemed like a reasonable place in which to grow old in a civilised fashion.

It was too cold for that now — the croquet set had long since been packed away.

Martin parked his car and walked into the building. He asked for Muriel, and was directed to the billiard room, further along the ground floor. He saw the group he was looking for: there was Danny, Muriel's son, and Muriel herself and his Aunt Joan. They were among other residents watching a slow but steady game of billiards being played by two male residents, who had decided to dress in white shirts and black waistcoats and trousers — plainly it was a serious match. There was the satisfying "click" of ball touching ball, and the "thunk" as a colour dropped into the pocket. The two players, stooped and elderly but resplendent in their black waistcoats, took up new positions around the table, its baize surface bright green under the flood of light.

Martin joined the picturesque group observing the game. "You're much better," he said to Muriel.

She looked a bit peevish. "I suppose you think you're the bee's knees."

"No I don't," said Martin calmly. "Mind if I have a look at your ankle?" He crouched at her feet, and could see immediately. "Oh it's gone down considerably."

Muriel peered at him, her brow lowered. "Prescribe a glass of water and suddenly you're the cat's whiskers."

Martin didn't smile or even answer; instead he looked rather critical. "Can I ask you some questions?"

"What on earth for?" And then she warned him, "I'm not taking part in any kind of survey."

"No. It's just routine. If I had a hundred pounds and I spent seven, how much would I have left?"

"Wednesday," said Muriel.

They all waited to see if Martin had a sense of humour.

Muriel went on, "It's three-fifteen in the afternoon and Labour is in its third term of office and still hasn't done anything for the elderly. We are about to escape from High Trees, home for old codgers, near Portwenn, in the county of Cornwall. And you would have ninety-three pounds left, which, these days, little Marty, buys you very little."

"Correct," said Martin.

"Right," said Danny, standing up. "All fit and ready to go, then. I'll put your suitcase in the car."

Joan stood up also.

Muriel leaned forwards. "Yes . . ." she said, uncertainly. "But perhaps we ought to finish watching the match." She waved at the billiard table. "Rude just to leave."

Martin had been about to help her up from her chair, but she looked fixedly at the game. "And perhaps," she said thoughtfully. "I ought . . ."

"What?" Danny waited patiently.

"Could you possibly," said Muriel after a while, and she leaned back in her chair again and looked up at her son, "see about me staying on?"

62

"Stay on here, at High Trees?"

"Yes, I know — I was terrified of coming here, but, well, I mean, look at it. I can't think what I was scared of. And, er, more to the point, I didn't know what I was missing."

Joan, Danny and Martin were standing there, observers of this rather grand old woman, Muriel, at a crossroads in her life.

"I could ask," said Danny.

"Then ask," confirmed Muriel.

"You're sure?" Joan's face was a picture of kindness.

Muriel waited for a while, thinking about it. "No, I'm not sure," she said eventually. "There's a lot of flatulence in the ranks." Then she added, "But, if that gets too bad, I can change my mind, can't I? So yes, I think I have decided. Yes. If poss."

Danny leaned down and kissed her cheek. "I'll go and ask," he said, and walked off in the direction of the admin office.

"Well," said Joan to her old friend. "What am I going to do at half past eight every morning?"

"You've got a farm to run," answered Muriel.

They were interrupted by a call from the billiard table. "Shot, Jamesie." Then there was a drumming of the cue's end on the wooden floor to show appreciation for a difficult, final black.

"Muriel?" came a man's voice and one of the players turned towards her, his highly polished shoes turning easily, his white shirt immaculate. "Your turn." He lifted the fat end of his cue towards her.

63

Muriel pushed herself to her feet and strolled over. It could easily be observed that when Muriel took the cue from him, their fingers hooked together, just briefly, as he let go. The other man was already racking up the reds and positioning the colours, ready for a new game.

"Good God," said Joan.

"That would be to take his name in vain," said Martin, since Danny wasn't there.

"I didn't know she could play snooker, or billiards or whatever it is. How about that?" Joan stared. "I think we need to check that young man out," she said, staring hard, as the now-retiring player wobbled to a chair close by to observe.

A moment later Joan said, "You know, I think I know why she was so terrified of coming here."

"Why?"

"Because I was so ridiculously frightened for her."

"Is that because you're getting old, too?"

"I wouldn't have put it so bluntly," said Joan.

"Oh. Really."

They watched the game for a while. The soft clicking of the balls was soothing and the very fact of the game's existence added more beauty to the room, to the place itself and the people who played it. "D'you need a lift back?" asked Martin.

"No, no, I'm fine. Got the Land Rover," said Joan.

"All right then."

As Martin left, turning his car on the gravel at the front of the house, he wondered if he'd ever have to see Joan herself into a place like this, perhaps this very place, if she ever became incapable of running the farm. He believed not; he sincerely could not imagine his Aunt Joan leaving Haven Farm, except — unthinkably — in a coffin.

CHAPTER
TWO

The Good Fisherman had knocked on doors in the area of Portwenn closest to the harbour, and he'd done most of the shops, except for the ones that had half-day closing on Wednesdays, and those he'd pick up later. The residential estate at the top of the hill had been done, one of the neighbouring villages further along the coast, and, inland, most of Delabole. He wasn't having much luck. And he hadn't yet managed to talk to Portwenn's doctor, a certain Doctor Ellingham.

It was a shame that his instructions on this case didn't allow him to talk to the village's policeman, PC Mark Mylow, but the person he was looking for was known to have an unhappy relationship with the authorities.

He took advantage of a windy and rainy morning to stay in his room at the B & B for a while, and think again. He cleared the surface of the bed and laid out the evidence. First of all, at the top, he positioned the three photographs, and took a moment to consider the differences between them. There was one of the girl at eighteen, and she was thinner, with her hair parted at the side and hanging limply. It was a police mug shot, taken during a first warning for cannabis use, so the picture lacked vivacity and charm. Her face scowled; the dark eyes were hostile and resentful. Her complexion was pale, ill-looking. Probably, thought the Good Fisherman, it was how everyone would look if they were having their photograph taken in a police station. The second photograph was much larger — A4 — with a glossy finish, although dimmed with age. It had obviously been kicking around in a drawer for a few years. It was in the style of a model shot. The girl in the picture was sideways on, but as if glancing — and smiling — at someone who just happened to be passing by. The pose meant her dark hair, glossy and artfully arranged, in contrast to the mug shot, dangled like a curtain down her back. But, unusually for such a photograph perhaps, she was wearing no make-up so the same mole was evident — just a dot, really, like a full stop — halfway between her cheekbone and her ear. It was difficult to tell her age, but he would guess she was maybe in her mid-twenties. Instead of the hostility evident in the police photograph, this picture tempted the viewer to come closer. And it was a knowing look; this was a person who was aware of how to entertain, how to please, and what rewards that might bring her. The third photograph was a set of four from a photo booth, from which one had been cut. Each square was the same but with a fractional variation in the angle of the chin or the direction of the gaze. Her features — the same features that expressed such self-aware attractiveness in the model shot — were plain and inert, like a zombie's. The flesh was slightly heavier.

Every day he looked at these photographs, to make sure that if he and this girl chanced to be in the same place at the same time, he'd recognise her, and follow her to see where she lived. He had no doubt that if you were to draw with a red pen on a map of Portwenn all the paths she'd taken, walking here and there over the last few days, and if you were to draw on the same map with a green pen where he himself had been, the red line and the green line would have crossed.

The Good Fisherman began, in his mind, to list the features that someone couldn't possibly change about themselves. Height — except insofar as she could wear high heels, which were easily visible. The arrangement of her features.

But almost everything else someone could change: hair colour, length of hair and style. Weight — she might have deliberately put on weight or lost it. She could change her eye colour, although that was more difficult. Make-up — it was significant, he thought, that in none of the photographs did she wear make-up. She could wear glasses, and she could use hats and scarves as a disguise. For the umpteenth time he looked carefully at the photographs and in his mind's eye he changed her hair to blonde, he had her wearing glasses, she was thinner or fatter, long hair or short hair.

And of course one of the easiest things to change was her name. Her real name was Emma Lewis, but she'd called herself Jane Carpenter, Louise Wood, Miriam Rawlins, Julie Mitchell. Most often it was down to the credit card she'd got hold of.

★   ★   ★

It was like a fairy story: Police Constable Mark Mylow had opened the packet, taken two tablets and Julie Mitchell had run into his arms.

He'd spotted her first of all in the Crab and Lobster, with her lovely oval face and her bell-shaped blonde hair and her smile, that tentative, alluring smile she gave people. Although he'd stared hard at her she hadn't taken any notice. He'd wandered over to talk to Al Large, who stood at the bar, using him as an excuse to get closer. And he was such a good mate, Mark could be quite open about it. He'd leant his elbow on a soggy beer mat and said, "Don't mind me, I'm using you to clock the one at two o'clock."

Al had turned to him. "You what?"

"Top totty at two o'clock," muttered Mark. "Don't look now, though."

But it was too late — Al had already turned his head. "Oh, her," he said.

"Lovely isn't she?" said Mark. "Hold on, let me stand the other side of you." He'd stepped around Al, and unzipped his jacket. He needed to allow his bodily scent to escape. Now the girl was in his eye line, and it was easy to gaze at her every now and again, and wait to catch her eye. It would take a while, though, thought Mark, for the pheromones to carry on the air and reach her.

And then the fairy tale had begun: their eyes met. So strange it was — he'd think when he'd come look back on it — how it had seemed like they'd already known each other for a long time. It was definitely the pheromone tablets. He was sure that he even saw her nose twitching. And she held his gaze for maybe up to two seconds longer than was necessary before she broke off.

"Mark . . . Mark?"

He'd become aware that Al was talking to him.

"What?"

"Don't go mad on me. I was talking to you and hey, it was like I wasn't even here."

"Sorry mate . . ." But Mark couldn't continue. He'd been expecting things to take their usual course of action: normally, he'd look at a girl across the room, then he'd really stare at her, and she'd meet his eyes a few times. He'd stare even harder to try to get her to look at him again, and then he'd saunter over, only to find she was putting on her coat and picking up her bag.

Even now, with the pheromones working for him, he was expecting to have to do quite a bit of staring and then a good bit of talking, maybe a week or two of jokes and comments and following her around — but now this girl he'd never met before was stepping around a table, with her empty glass tilting in her hand as if it wasn't really for drinking at all, and she was looking at him steadily and walking towards him. He'd felt a rising sense of panic. Was she smiling at someone standing behind him? He dared not turn around and check; she was too close.

"Hiya," she'd said cheerfully. "I saw you were looking at me, so I thought I'd come over and introduce myself." She looked at Mark for most of the time, with the odd glance at Al. "Julie," she said.

70

"Hi, Julie," said Mark.

"Hi there," said Al. "Pleased to meet you."

"Me too," said Julie, but she was staring at Mark. "Can I buy you guys a drink?" she asked.

"God no!" Mark practically shouted. "Let me buy you one."

"Oh. OK then. Thanks. I'll get the next one. I'll have an orange juice, please."

That's it, thought Mark. The pheromones. It was just like the advert said. She'd caught wind of the pheromones, and she'd been dragged helplessly in his direction. Now all he needed to do was not muck it up.

Martin saw Louisa, or rather, he bumped into her coming backwards out of a shop. Some of her shopping, as she gave a startled "Oh", loosened from her arms and fell. Martin was quick to help her pick it up, while she tried to let him off.

"It's all right," she said.

Martin placed an orange and a loaf of bread on top of the items she already carried in her arms.

"Thank you," she said.

He caught sight of the bottle in her hand — it was champagne.

Louisa saw him look at the bottle and, guiltily, she felt she had to explain. "I fancied something different. An old friend . . . no, I didn't fancy an old friend, I mean, I'm having an old friend over for dinner tonight, so, I fancied, you know, something different."

"Louisa." Martin wanted to tell her how stupid it was that . . . but he stopped because Danny appeared from the same shop, and stood next to Louisa.

With an easy, forgiving manner, Danny greeted him. "Doc. How's things down at the surgery?"

"Danny." Martin felt as clumsy as a gatepost, standing there. He was so busy fending off the younger man's ghastly condescension that he forgot to answer the question.

"Come on you," said Danny to Louisa, "I could eat a horse."

"OK." Louisa frowned at Martin.

"Night, then," said Martin abruptly.

"Goodnight," said Louisa. It sounded — in her own ears — like a cry for help.

Martin didn't hear it.

It wasn't too much longer before Martin next had occasion to look down on Danny's Christian soul. From the window of his bedroom, one morning, as he knotted his tie, his glance landed on the springy stride and the optimistic cheer of Louisa's old boyfriend, or maybe her current boyfriend, as he walked past the surgery and, of course, with his infinite patience and kindness Danny had the time and the inclination to stop and stroke the wretched dog that Martin would just as soon have kicked.

There he was — and, thankfully, not coming to see him, after all.

The sight of Danny with his wiry, corkscrew hair, his actor-ish good looks, his deconstructed clothing, his open collar, his pointy shoes . . . all this had sent Martin further, irretrievably, into his bad mood.

When he walked downstairs to the surgery it was to find Pauline talking to a patient, and the patient at the same time talking to Pauline; altogether there was too much noise and confusion. "Shut up," he said — to everyone. To anyone.

Both Pauline and the patient looked startled.

"Shut up," repeated Martin. He recognised the patient — Mrs Richards. She had brought in her son earlier in the week. Now there was more confusion: the dog had been let in by Mrs Richards's son. "Get out!" said Martin.

The boy turned around to leave the surgery.

"Not you," said Martin. "The dog. You. In there." He pointed into the surgery. "Has he got something else stuck up his nostril?" he asked the mother. "Come on, in you go, in. In." He was aware, just as he closed the door, of Pauline's smile, which annoyed him.

In the consulting room he sat the boy on the sofa and without preamble moved his head to face the light. "It's a skin infection," he said. "Impetigo. Highly contagious. I will prescribe you some antibiotic cream." He pulled off his gloves. "You will have to wash his face four times a day and apply the cream to the blisters. He will have to remain at home for at least two days."

Having hardly caught her breath, Mrs Richards exclaimed, "Two days?"

"That's what I said. No contact with others. No sharing of toys or clothing or towels." He turned to the afflicted boy. "And don't scratch at all." He turned back to the mother. "Cut off his fingernails."

"I can't keep him home," said Mrs Richards, nudging her son as if prompting him to agree with her. "I work all God's hours."

"Well get your husband to help," said Martin.

"Oh yes, OK," said Mrs Richards in a sing-song voice, "I'll mention the impetigo and he'll ditch his girlfriend straightaway, drive overnight from Glasgow and give our marriage one last try."

"Good," said Martin, "that's all right then." He gave them both a little sort of push to get them out of the room. "Give that to Mrs Tishell. She will give you the tablets. One in the morning before food, one before going to bed." He handed them the prescription as they left. The waiting room, he noticed, was blighted by the presence of the dog, which wandered along the line of patients gathering strokes. "Get that dog out of here," he demanded. "Who's next?"

Pauline shouted, "Cameron PARIS."

Martin winced. "It's all right, he's not deaf."

"He is, actually," said Pauline calmly.

"Oh. OK. Cameron?"

In the consulting room, Martin looked through the otoscope into the sci-fi world of the human ear. The mother explained, "He woke up this morning and was stone deaf."

"It's bad news." Martin's gloves snapped as he pulled them off. "A dangerous build-up of fluid in the auditory canal."

"Good God," said Mrs Paris. Her hand flew to her mouth.

Martin sat back in his chair. "I'm sorry to have to tell you," he said, "but it's only a matter of time before his head explodes."

"What?" Cameron was frightened. Both their faces were frozen.

"Back to school, I think," said Martin with a steely tone. This was what was needed for a bad mood: swift forward progression through the diagnosis-prescription-prognosis paradigm.

Mrs Paris's face hardened and she turned to glare at her son. Her arm flew out quick as a donkey's kick and slapped him on the back of the head. "Cameron, you are in big trouble," she said very quickly, and turned to Martin. "Doc, I am sorry for wasting your time. He's always trying to bunk off. You don't need to tell the teacher about this, do you? I mean, I know you probably have to and all, seeing what's your position . . ." She rocked back and forth in her chair.

"My position being?" asked Martin.

"Well, one of the school governors, and everything."

"I'm not a school governor."

When he'd escorted the Paris family from the consulting room, he checked with Pauline. "Am I a school governor?"

"Yes, you are," said Pauline. "At least, there's a meeting in your diary. Look. Friday, twelve-thirty, school governors."

★　★　★

Unknown, microscopic in size and thus unseen by anyone, what was thought to be impetigo passed from hand to hand, from door handle and towel to light switch to school desk to dinner tray and window catch. The school became the centre of the outbreak of what would initially be diagnosed as impetigo, just as Louisa was about to try for the job of headmistress.

The school was working hard to keep its pupils warm, the old boiler roaring away and pumping the warm water around the radiators, and the children were all beginning to reach that optimistic time when Christmas was in sight, and their timetable included nerve-wracking, exciting things like the nativity play.

"You going to be our new headmistress?" asked Peter Cronk. He ran his hand along the wall as he went along.

"It's not for me to say," said Louisa. "But I'm going to try."

"Will you do something about the IT department?" Peter sounded old enough to be the school bursar.

"What IT department?" asked Louisa.

"Exactly," said Peter. He pushed against the swing door and stepped ahead of her into the classroom.

Louisa had the feeling that Peter ought to be headmaster.

During playtime, Michael Sands came and stood with her. The children buzzed like heavily wrapped-up insects or stood in corners with chattering teeth, gossiping. One girl made the mistake of trying the first rung of the climbing frame: it was so cold it burned and she immediately let go. The pair of teachers stood together, arms folded, in a different world from their charges. "Any news?" asked Louisa. She felt a little vulnerable, like it was wrong to ask him.

"As of 6p.m.," he answered, "which was the cut-off point for applications, it's between you and two external candidates."

"So d'you think I'm in with a chance?" She realised she was fishing for compliments, but also she was suddenly aware that for her to succeed, others must fail. She didn't like being in this cruel position. "It wouldn't be a bad Christmas present to go home with."

"Well, the odds are three to one," explained Michael Sands reasonably. He blew his whistle. "Oi! Matthew. I'm watching you." He took a few steps, made a small circle, and folded his arms against the cold. "Have we got a problem?" he asked and nodded in the direction of the school gate.

Louisa saw Martin walking towards them — a stiff, formal figure, his gait as always purposeful, direct, almost like a march. She wondered what he wanted. She felt like running away, but she told her feet to stay planted where they were, not to move a muscle. Her arms tightened around her body. I never kissed him, she thought. Surely, I never did. But she had.

The two teachers were ready to give the usual social greetings, but Martin wasn't concerned about such niceties. "Mr Sands," he said in the worst kind of patronising voice, "can you give me one good reason why anybody would think I was a governor of this school?"

"Well, Doctor Sim was a community governor before you. Doctor Blake before that."

"And does that mean I am automatically a school governor, without anyone taking the trouble to ask me?"

"On the contrary, you were asked, and you did say you'd be happy to be a school governor."

"When did I say this?"

"In the letter you sent. Some few months ago, but I can show it to you, if you like. We'll have it on file still."

"Did I sign this letter?"

"Yes. At least, it was signed on your behalf."

"By my receptionist?"

"Elaine, yes."

"Elaine, who was an utter imbecile. Which suggests, I hope, that your letter is null and void. I have no wish to be a school governor."

As they spoke, a child came out of nowhere and hurtled, like a thrown object, against Martin's legs.

Louisa sprang forwards. "Oh . . . Oh . . . are you all right?

The boy bounced off Martin, feet tangling comically, but with one stumble and hardly a backwards look he was away again, still in his game.

Louisa turned to Martin. "Are you all right, Martin?"

"Fine," said Martin shortly. "Fine. Never better. Thank you."

"Well," said Michael sensibly, "if you really can't make the meeting on Friday, we'll have to reschedule the interviews."

"What?" Louisa was dismayed.

"If Martin doesn't want to be a governor—" Michael held out upturned palms "—what can we do?"

"But I'm all geared up for Friday." She only had to think about it for a second to realise there would be quite a delay, which would mean they might have to re-advertise and other candidates would come out of the woodwork.

"I don't understand." Martin frowned.

Michael explained, "Louisa's one of the candidates for the headship. We were hoping the board could appoint someone this week."

"We need to get on with this," said Louisa. "Please Martin?" Inside, she begged him to forget about the kiss she'd landed on him, to forget about her kicking him out of the taxi and leaving him to walk home, to forget about her not wanting him to get *his* job. "Please?" And yet she could see from his face that he was going to say no. She knew that stern frown well enough, now.

"All right. I'll be there," Martin said abruptly and nodded.

Louisa felt the tide of relief. "Thank you," she said, and meant it.

"But don't expect any favours." Martin turned on his heel and marched off, at the same time as Louisa replied, "Of course not."

She watched him go and, with Michael's trotting over to see to a child who'd fallen, for a moment she found herself alone, in the middle of a playground cut into the side of a Cornish cliff, surrounded by children, but standing alone, and it might be the case that this school, these children would be, in a way, her own — if she were to win the job of headmistress — and she felt a deep sense of awe, and love, at the thought of this responsibility being divested on her.

She had a lot to do; there wasn't time to dawdle, or indulge in reverie. "Tom," she called out, "Connor! Amelia. Chess club?"

Martin happened to be walking past the school the next morning when, surprisingly, he saw Mrs Richards at the school gates. He called out, "Mrs Richards?"

"Yes, Doc?"

"Did you bring your son to school?"

"Yes, I did."

"Did his highly contagious impetigo clear up overnight?"

"Miss Glasson said I should bring him in as normal."

"Oh, well, if Miss Glasson said so, then it's all right. By all means feel free to infect the entire school. Well done." Martin walked off quickly, and Mrs Richards's wails of complaint fell on deaf ears. He swung into the school.

Louisa was separating Cameron and Bobby Richards from fighting. They were actually on the ground by now, with Cameron hauling on the straps of Bobby's rucksack. "Oi," she said mildly, "Cameron, off. Get off him. Both of you, inside now." She turned to Bobby. "What d'you think you're doing, Bobby? It's not playtime."

"He called me spotty," said Bobby.

80

Which was the truth, as it happened, thought Louisa.

"I did not," said Cameron in an aggrieved tone, and then he turned to Bobby and said accusingly, "Spotty, spotty."

"Just stop it," said Louisa. Out of the corner of her eye she noticed Martin coming towards her with a purposeful tread. "Go on, in you go," she said to the two boys. She was ready to face Martin. And with Martin, she always felt she had to be ready: shoes polished, hair brushed, everything proper.

"Louisa, could I have a word?" asked Martin.

"Could I ask you to call me Miss Glasson in front of the children?" asked Louisa.

Martin rolled onwards, unstoppable. "I gave clear instructions that the impetigo case should stay at home."

"Bobby Richards, the impetigo case, well, his mother works. Now it might have escaped your attention, but for a lot of people in Portwenn, work is an economic necessity."

"Well, this is a medical necessity. Unless you want all the working mothers of this school to have to stay at home, instead of just one? Because if the case is not isolated, the disease spreads. Is that clear?"

"Yes, Doctor."

"So you will send the boy home?"

"I will deal with the situation straightaway."

But it was only the next day when Cameron's mum, Mrs Paris, was on the path leading up to the surgery and thrust her son's hand towards the doctor. "Ah, glad just to catch you. Could you look at the boy's hand?" she asked.

"Congratulations. Impetigo," said Martin. "Follow me, and I'll write you a prescription." He turned and went back into the surgery, followed by Mrs Paris, still holding on to her son's arm as if it were a garden implement she was required to carry.

But despite Martin's diagnosis of impetigo, and prescribing the correct antibiotic cream, Mrs Paris was back in the surgery only one day later. Cameron's rash was worse, not better. She took hold of both of her son's hands and thrust them towards Martin. "I know it hasn't been long, but they're worse, aren't they?" she said. "I did everything you told me to, Doc."

"Have you been applying the cream four times a day?"

"Twice yesterday, myself, and Miss Glasson took care of it during school this morning."

"What? He's still going to school?"

"Yes, Miss Glasson said."

"Miss Glasson said, did she?" He put a gloved hand under Cameron's chin and lifted. "Look up."

And the same day, with a different pair of gloves, with a different child, he was doing the same thing. "Look up, Lucy." He turned to Lucy's mother. "Yes. Impetigo. Has she been in touch with Bobby Richards or Cameron Paris? Of course she has, because Portwenn has one doctor and nine hundred and sixty-six people who know better."

The following lunchtime he kept an eye out across the bay and waited for the children to appear like dots

82

moving against the chill grey of the tarmac playground: they'd come out for their lunch break and there was a good chance he'd catch Louisa. He didn't want to phone; this was a message he wanted to deliver face to face. And then he thought, of course, they wouldn't come outside in this rain.

He shrugged on a raincoat, and walked hurriedly over to the school.

It was such foul weather that by the time he reached the school rain rattled the roofs and you could think the tiles were in danger of being broken. Safely inside, the damp leaking under his collar, he walked the corridors looking for Louisa. He recognised, first, her gait, the sway of her figure as it walked away from him, and the ponytail between her shoulder blades. "Louisa?"

She turned to meet him. "Martin."

"You allowed infected children into the school. As a consequence, three more of your pupils have impetigo. Did you think you could ignore my advice?"

"Martin, please, I —"

"What would happen," Martin interrupted, "if everyone in Portwenn ignored medical advice? Disease would rampage through the village. Bodies would pile up in the streets awaiting burial. Rats would scrabble among the wasteland that the village would become."

Louisa took in his sarcastic tone; and she understood his point, but she had an opinion, too. "Martin, I think you should just listen to me for one moment."

"In years to come," Martin went on, "when archaeologists unearth the ruins of Portwenn, someone will ask the question, 'How did this unspeakable contagion occur?'" For a while he just held his breath and glared at her. "And the answer would turn out to have been, 'Because Miss Glasson said so,'" he finished.

Louisa tried to remain professional. She answered firmly, "I arranged for the sick kids to be taught in separate classrooms. Well away from everyone else. No one has swapped books, shared towels, or done anything they're not supposed to do."

"Well, it's not working, because there are three more cases of impetigo."

"And that's not my fault, or the fault of this school." She wasn't sure she was right; in fact she began to understand that all her precautions couldn't have been enough, but she spoke with conviction. She watched Martin's upright, forceful figure as he turned and walked down the corridor. He was carried along, she thought, by self-confidence, you could practically see the bow wave of it coming off him as he strode along. Sometimes, she wished for that amount of self-confidence for herself, but at the same time she knew that part of her humanity, her empathy and kindness, came from the lack of it.

Martin returned to his surgery to find it was Bobby Richards's turn to come back and tell him the cream wasn't working.

"He's no better," said Mrs Richards and, underneath the part of the unsightly rash that spread across his face, Bobby looked startled that she might be talking about him. "If anything, he's worse."

Martin pulled on his gloves and went to his store. He took out a swab and broke open the packet. "The cream hasn't worked at all," he said.

"Is it the wrong cream?" she asked.

"More likely to be the wrong infection." Martin drew the swab back and forth across the rash on the back of Bobby's hand.

"What, you made a mistake?"

"No, it was a perfectly reasonable hypothesis."

"So if it's not impetigo, what is it?"

"The swab will tell us," said Martin. He bagged it and carried it through to Pauline. "Get this to the path lab for analysis, asap."

"Is it bad news?" asked Pauline.

"There's a vague chance it's not impetigo," said Martin. "Nothing to worry about."

That evening, Martin carefully diced the beef into the same size squares ready for his stew. At precisely different times he would put in the different vegetables and, in an hour, add the last touches of seasoning. With mashed sweet potatoes heated with a touch of paprika, it would make for a good wintery meal and last for another two days. He sliced the broccoli florets quite small, ready to blanch them in boiling water for only a few minutes, to keep them crisp, but hot. As he did all this, he was very conscious of his hands, of everything that he touched — knife, chopping board, tap, colander — because each of these objects would carry a microscopic trace, a fragment that was capable of carrying a charge of infection . . .

At the solid "clunk" of the knife connecting with the chopping board, the doorbell called its summons.

He walked through and found on his doorstep Louisa Glasson. "Louisa," he said.

"Martin, can I come in for a moment?"

"It's not the best time," said Martin. "I'm in the middle of cooking."

"It won't be for long," said Louisa, "and I won't disturb you."

"Well, all right then," said Martin.

Louisa sat at the kitchen table, and wasn't surprised that she wasn't offered a glass of water, even, let alone a cup of tea or a glass of wine. She was becoming used to the idea that Martin travelled only along the one track in his mind, and it was pointing only in one direction; anything else, the niceties of life, didn't register. It was exciting when she was on the same track as he was, but it was a bewildering and cold place to be when she wasn't. "I came to apologise," she began tentatively, "for not taking full account of your medical advice. I was trying to think of families as a whole. It's a very serious thing to send a child home, with, you know, fairly disastrous economic ramifications for parents, but I should have consulted with you and worked out a way that it would actually work. I do listen to what you say, and there's nothing more important to me than the kids' welfare, and there's no way I'd do anything to put their health at risk." She watched him slicing his potatoes, and waited for a response. It really was true — he was in the middle of cooking, and he'd taken her at her word that she wouldn't interrupt him. She felt like seizing the knife from his hands and hurling it across the room.

"Why are you being like this?" asked Martin.

"What?"

"Like this. It's nothing to do with Friday, is it?"

"Friday?" Louisa felt the cold drench of embarrassment sluice through her.

"Your interview. You will, Louisa, have my full support, but only if you're the best candidate for the job."

Louisa stood up. "Why do you always do this?"

"Do what?"

But Louisa was already leaving.

It was a mystery to Martin why people behaved in such illogical ways. What had he done? he wondered. He had given her an expression of his wholehearted support, insofar as he was capable of giving it before having sight of the other candidates, whereupon she had made some kind of complaint about his behaviour and stormed off.

Louisa, as she walked down the slope to the harbour, felt in her throat the ache of repressed tears. Once again she found herself wounded from an encounter with Doctor Martin Ellingham. It had taken a lot of courage to go there and admit she'd been wrong, and yet all he'd done was to accuse her, in effect, of having an ulterior motive: sucking up to him because he was on the panel that would, on Friday, decide on her application for the post of head teacher at Portwenn primary school. She walked fast up the other side of the valley, squirrelling through the alleyways to find, with relief, her own front door.

Inside her own home, even, there was no comfort, as it seemed to her that from across the bay, from that small house set into the cliff, came Martin's signature disapproval. It was infuriating.

Fourteenth of December: from time to time Louisa stood in front of the mirror and practised what she would say to the interview panel. She made up a list of questions she herself would ask if she were on such an interview panel, and recorded herself giving the answers. She played them back through headphones, leaning forwards earnestly over her kitchen table to listen to her voice, ". . . a very good question. Enjoyment. Enjoyment is the birthright of every child. And teaching should give children the chances that they deserve. Setting standards. Aiming high. This kind of thing—" She pressed the pause button and made a note never to say "this kind of thing". It was vague. It sounded as if she didn't know what she was talking about, or — worse — that she didn't care. She might as well say, "Blah, blah, blah."

The results of the swab that Martin took from Cameron's hand came back via a telephone call from Brian Deal at the path lab. Martin paused in the bagging up of his medical waste, and pressed the speakerphone button.

"I've got the results from the swab you sent me. Very interesting."

"Why very interesting?" Martin's professional curiosity sharpened.

"It's not impetigo."

"Not?"

"No. You're dealing with a highly resistant stapherysipelothrix."

"That's a zoonosis, isn't it?"

"Yes indeed. A rare creature, very rare. It can't be passed through humans, only through animals."

An image came to Martin's head: the dog wandering along a line of patients in his surgery waiting room, gathering strokes from each person. Pale hands reaching out to stroke along its back.

When he'd finished talking to Brian, with five strides Martin went immediately through to Pauline and asked her to call PC Mark Mylow. "Tell him there is a dangerous dog here at the surgery. I want it caught and I want it put down."

"Put down?" There was disbelief and cold disapproval in Pauline's voice.

"Destroyed, Pauline. Killed. Sent to that big dog basket in the sky."

When Mark Mylow came, he gratefully accepted a cup of tea from Pauline; and with his usual mild manner he delivered what he thought would be good news both for Martin and for the dog, which stood there, idly drifting through life, giving a vague pant and a solemn wag of its tail, looking from person to person with the mournful enquiring eyes hidden in the depths of its long hair. "I've spoken to the vet," he said proudly, "and the dog can be treated."

"I want it put down," said Martin.

"The vet —"

"I don't care what the vet says. I want the dog killed."

Dog looked at Martin, trying to guess what might happen next.

"Guess who won't let me have any Christmas decorations in here, neither," said Pauline. "Does the name Scrooge ring a bell?"

"Well, I've checked, you see." PC Mylow stood there with his cup and saucer like he was at a village fete. "And there's a list of notifiable diseases, and this staphy-whatever-you-call-it isn't on it. We don't have the power to have him destroyed."

Martin pointed. "It's a dangerous dog."

"But has he actually hurt anyone?"

"Yes."

"Not by attacking them. He didn't actually bite the children, did he? So we can't go by the Dangerous Dog Act of nineteen ninety-one." He sounded pleased to be able to give the name of the act and the date. "He doesn't deserve the death sentence, even if you were able to give him one, which you're not."

"These children have an unpleasant skin condition."

"Not as bad as having your throat torn open. Or your ear chewed off. That would be unpleasant. That would be nasty. We'd be looking at the death sentence for that." With his spare hand he picked up an ophthalmoscope and squinted through it.

"Put that down," said Martin.

"Guess why I'm in such a good mood?" said Mark.

"No."

"Go on, guess."

"You've passed your eleven-plus."

"Ha ha. No. I've well and truly found myself a girlfriend." He beamed. "Christmas gift number one. She's got the most gorgeous little mole—" he tapped his cheekbone "—right here. And she's got—"

"That's enough, Mark," interrupted Martin.

Of course it was Peter Cronk who leafed through the pages of a medical dictionary until he found the word "stapherysipelothrix". He took his newfound knowledge through the school gates and into the classroom. Once he'd told everyone what it was, he could run at them with his arms outspread, and, gratifyingly, they'd run away shrieking.

Louisa Glasson went to take the rehearsal for the nativity play only to find the shepherds, the wise men, all the sheep and the cows plus Joseph and Mary cowering against the walls in the gymnasium, while Peter, dressed in ordinary school uniform, ran at them like a zombie, herding them from one end of the room to the other. "Peter Cronk!" she called out. "What are you doing here? You said you didn't want to be in the nativity play. You're supposed to be in room three."

"I've got a flesh-eating bug," said Peter.

"No, you haven't."

"Yes, I have. It's got a name like a dinosaur's. It's called stapherysipelothrix. Doc Martin said." He ran, arms outstretched. The shepherd dropped her lamb.

The wise man tripped over the hem of his robe and his hat fell off.

"Right, all of you calm down," called out Louisa, as fresh screams erupted from the cast of the nativity play. "Peter. Out. Out."

On this, the day of the interviews for the headship, the school assumed a solemn air, despite the Christmas decorations which festooned the entrance hall, and the Christmas tree which stood, a signifier of goodwill, alongside the hatch which served as the portal to the school office. The white-painted, converted chapel, secure on its bluff overlooking the harbour, had seen head teachers come and go, and would continue to host the young of Portwenn, and try to press on them, from within stone walls that still retained their religious grace, the fruits of human knowledge and experience. But for all the enviable continuity of the school, which the young passed through like so many wild bullocks through a cattle crush, the character of the head teacher — and the initiatives that he or she would undertake — would formulate its new spirit. The school would be as stern or as kind, as adventurous or as staid, as energetic or as slow, as the person who would, this very afternoon, take the helm of the little human vessel, Portwenn School, carrying at the present count 108 souls.

Doctor Martin Ellingham, the new governor whether he liked it or not, dressed in his usual dark blue suit and a shirt as white as the golf ball that somehow came to be thrown by the wintery ocean against the sea walls guarding Portwenn harbour, was introduced to the other members of the panel by Michael Sands. "Mel Collins, our LEA governor. Stu Mackenzie. And Tim Barton, our other community governor."

When it came to shaking Tim Barton's hand, the other man said, "It was just a mole."

"I beg your pardon?" Martin was wrong-footed.

"That *spot* I was worried about. You said I was being stupid."

"Oh. I was right then."

Michael Sands wanted to move them on from the reception area, into the head teacher's study. They began to walk in a group down the echoing school corridor. Each was aware of the portentousness of the occasion.

Martin found himself alongside Stuart Mackenzie. "So what's going on with this impetigo business?" asked the other man.

"It's not impetigo," said Martin. "It's a zoonosis."

"Sounds nasty."

"I'm giving the affected children a dose of penicillin while I'm here."

"Surely they're off school?"

"Miss Glasson felt . . . or rather it was felt that the children would be better off attending school."

"That doesn't sound very wise."

As if to punctuate his announcement, there came from some invisible place further down the echoing corridor a child's scream. And as the group rounded the corner it was to see Louisa Glasson holding on to a handful of the sweatshirt that stretched between Peter Cronk's shoulder blades.

"One more time, Peter Cronk," said Louisa, and she yanked his sweatshirt higher and pulled him from left to right and left again, "and I am going to throttle you and feed your body to the gulls. Stay out of my classroom and stop frightening my students!" She dropped him and watched with satisfaction as he loped away down the corridor. And then, strangely, the hairs rose on the back of her neck, as if ghosts assembled behind her, and the next moment she heard a breath, a footfall, and realised they weren't ghosts. She was already turning around and the shock coloured her face and neck when she saw the group — Martin, a man she didn't know, Mel Collins, Tim Barton, Michael.

The entire interview panel had seen her verbally and physically abuse one of her charges.

"Miss Glasson," said Michael affectionately. "One of our candidates."

"Hello." Louisa summoned a smile — or the semblance of one — and shook each of their hands.

After an embarrassing silence, they moved on. Surely they'd see, they'd understand . . . wouldn't they? She cursed her bad luck and told herself to put her head down and carry on with the lesson, attend the interview and do her level best when the time finally came to face them.

The interviews were conducted in the school gymnasium, and, for Martin, brought back to mind the occasion when he himself had faced a panel of

Portwenn's finest, most interested residents. Louisa had been sitting where he was now, and she'd had acute glaucoma.

As he observed the current interviewee take yet another sip of water from the glass in front of her, he had the doleful wish that Louisa would have succeeded; he'd be somewhere else, and at least he wouldn't be having to sit on a hard chair in the middle of a freezing cold gymnasium listening to . . .

A new question was proposed by Mel Collins, the LEA governor. "If you were going to improve the school's equal opportunities policy, where would you start?"

The candidate again picked up her glass of water. Martin concluded it was a delaying tactic: it gave her time to think.

Martin frowned. "And more to the point," he added, "how long would it take you to start?" He watched the candidate blink, and an expression of fear crossed her face. He might have been rude just then.

The candidates swapped from one to the next — a male one, with a beard and glasses and therefore seasonally in tune, because he looked like Jesus Christ. He was a much quicker talker. "It goes without saying—" he was confident of his opinion "—that we have a duty to provide for all children regardless of race, gender, religion, colour, creed, sexual orientation or disability of mind or body."

"If it goes without saying, why are you saying it?" Martin was fed up with this kind of glib patter.

Last of all came Louisa and, when she walked carefully across the gymnasium floor and took her seat facing them, Martin felt an unaccountable fear, or at least he could identify a release of adrenalin into his system which might signify hunger or low blood sugar, yet he had eaten sufficiently at lunch time.

Louisa knew that the career ladder was in front of her, and every answer she gave would work either for or against her, and with her natural grace she instinctively knew that all she could do — should do — was be true to herself and to say what she thought in the simplest terms. "So, um, we need to understand how progress in . . . in one subject can feed through to progress in others. And we need to look for ways to make good teaching . . . and good learning . . . cross over from one part of the curriculum to . . . other parts of the curriculum. If you see what you mean. I mean, I mean." This kind of stumbling wasn't going to get her anywhere.

And yet she knew that if all the residents of the village of Portwenn were gathered on the other side of that table, they would rush to give her the job.

It was Mel Collins who asked the next question. "What would you say were your strengths in terms of this position?"

This was the worst part — being asked to talk about herself, which she generally never did. But she'd known this question would come, and had prepared an answer. She reached into her memory to retrieve it, but found it wasn't there. She had stood in front of the mirror and actually rehearsed the answer . . . No. It wasn't there.

She reminded herself to be herself, to tell the truth in the simplest possible terms. "Well," she began, "I did prepare an answer to that question. I had a long list of my good qualities, ready and waiting, but in the heat of the moment —"

"What about an answer you haven't prepared?"

She could have kissed Martin Ellingham all over again, she really could have, for just that nudge forwards. It allowed her to hear the question properly, and think properly, and therefore answer meaningfully. "I think I'm good at listening," she said.

"Is that something a head teacher should be able to do?" This came from Stuart Mackenzie.

"Absolutely, yes," answered Louisa. "Because I think it means you're still prepared to learn. And how can you encourage others to learn if you refuse to learn yourself?"

Stuart Mackenzie said, "So, if a doctor, say, gave you some medical advice, you would listen to him, presumably?"

At a stroke, Louisa found herself in a trap. She looked at Martin's expressionless face. A trap laid by Martin.

Stuart Mackenzie went on, "And yet I gather from Doctor Ellingham that he advised you that certain infected children shouldn't come to school, to prevent the spread of this impetigo or whatever it is —"

"It's a form of zoonosis," interrupted Martin, as if everyone knew what that was. "But as I said, now that I know what it is, I can treat it with the penicillin that I've brought with me."

Louisa recognised that this was Martin backtracking — he had laid the trap and was trying to appear not to be to blame for it. She watched as Stuart Mackenzie leaned forwards and said, "Your decision to allow the children to come to school could have put dozens of children at risk. How can you justify your refusal to take his advice?"

Louisa had no trouble answering this question. She found herself already on the front foot, because she believed she had right on her side. "Most parents have to work. They can't keep their kids at home without paying someone to look after them. And they can't pay anyone anything because they've got barely enough for themselves. Unlike some people, I understand the reality of life in this village. I know which parents need help, I know what sort of help they need, and how to give it. And of course I would never put any child at risk of infection."

"With respect, you did exactly that. You encouraged kids to come to school. You brought them together."

"No. We took special precautions. We hired an extra classroom assistant. Every infected child was segregated. They were taught away from the others. Given separate play times. And, as I told Doctor Ellingham, there was no sharing of any books, pens, papers or anything of that kind. We provided a service to the kids, to the parents, to the community. And we followed medical advice to the letter."

The interview panel — all darn men! thought Louisa — sat like a row of magistrates, and, as the interview meandered to a close, she had to remind herself not to be wildly defiant in her manner, but just evidently, squarely, firmly in the right.

The other interviewees had gone home, to be informed of the result later by telephone, but Louisa knew the decision was to be made this afternoon, immediately following the interviews, and she'd asked to be told in person. She chose to wait, sitting on the same chair in the corridor outside the gymnasium from which she'd walked into the interview such a short time ago, with a misplaced sense of optimism, as it now turned out. She couldn't have imagined, then, that such a blow was about to be dealt to her.

Around her, the school quietened; pupils were leaving for home. But then she heard a familiar cough and a familiar footfall: it was Peter Cronk, who had been looking for her.

Like wind through a cornfield, the rumour had gone around the school that Miss Glasson's chances of getting the job had been ruined because she'd been caught red-handed by the interview panel throttling Peter Cronk and throwing him out of a classroom by the scruff of the neck and calling him a seagull. "Come to say sorry," said Peter Cronk.

"It's not your fault," said Louisa. "It wasn't the reason they won't give me the job anyway."

"Why won't they give you the job?"

"Because I subjected pupils to the risk of an infectious skin condition," she said calmly. She was perfectly happy in her current job. There would be other headships. She was young.

Peter Cronk leaned forwards and whispered something in her ear.

Louisa absorbed the information. "Thanks, Peter," she said. "That's good to know."

Eventually, Stuart Mackenzie appeared and, as if from far away, asked her to come in. As she stood up, Martin appeared, and nodded to her blankly, before starting off down the corridor. She was close enough to say what she wanted to. "Whether or not I've got this job, Martin Ellingham, I will never forgive you for stitching me up like that."

"I didn't stitch you up." Martin frowned. Why was Louisa using the language of gangsters suddenly?

"Then who told them I'd ignored your advice, if it wasn't you?"

"I'd have been perfectly entitled to have told them that, if I indeed had told them that, because I'm telling you—"

"Because you never listen," interrupted Louisa. "Why don't you listen? And now Peter tells me, in case it has escaped your attention, that the skin infection came from your measly old dog." She couldn't waste any more time on this conversation.

"It's not my dog," said Martin to Louisa's back, as it turned on him and disappeared into the gymnasium. He heard Stuart Mackenzie's voice, "Ah Louisa—" before the door shut.

He made his way to the medical room, where the group of infected children waited for him. Among them was Peter Cronk who asked, "Can't I have a flesh-eating bug for one more day?"

100

"No," said Martin. "Bend over." He swabbed the pale flesh of Peter Cronk's buttock. "There," he said, "feel that?"

"No," said Peter, impressed. "I didn't feel a thing."

"That's because I haven't done anything yet." Martin pressed the syringe home.

"Oww!" shouted Peter Cronk.

"There you go."

It was one syringe-full after another — four in total.

By the time he'd finished, Louisa Glasson was standing in the doorway. He packed away the syringes and balled up the swabs and chucked them in the bin. "Congratulations," he said.

Louisa felt this huge smile, a thrill of triumph, bursting to get out. "Thank you," she said. "I thought I was the last person you'd want to see running the school."

Martin clipped his bag shut. "You were the most suitable candidate by far," he said stiffly.

"Thank you." She wanted to hug him; she wanted to dance.

"You're welcome."

"I'm sorry . . . if I misunderstood."

"Easily done," said Martin, stepping towards her. She was in his way.

"Don't you think we should sit down, with a drink, in the pub, and stop having these mini-rows, and sort out what we really think of each other?"

It was as if the words leapt from his mouth without his doing anything about it. "Yes, all right. Let's go now."

"Well, not tonight, because tonight we're—"

Martin found himself interrupting, "You've got a prayer meeting at the chapel, have you?"

"I'm not seeing . . . he isn't . . . no. It's just there's a whole group of us, tonight, meeting to celebrate the job. And you'd be very welcome to come to that, as well, if you fancy it. You can either join us or not join us; it's up to you."

"Thank you. I'll be there."

"Definitely?"

"Definitely, at eight o'clock."

"Right. Great." Louisa felt like they ought to shake hands or something.

That evening, the lights of the Crab and Lobster slowly brightened as darkness fell, and points of colour — red, silver, gold — threaded through the Christmas decorations strung along the front of the pub. The neon Santa Claus had finally achieved its usual position on the wall of the pub that faced out to sea, and the pub's illuminated face thus wore an expression of good cheer. People arrived warmly dressed in scarves and gloves and hats to celebrate with Louisa her elevation to the headship. The Crab and Lobster offered warmth; and the determination of the people entering it or leaving it to keep warm under their insulating layers of wool and fleece was in opposition to the deadly and massive cold of the ocean, which breathed its in-and-out on the shore, not a hundred yards away, sending a shiver through the heart of anyone if they imagined they might be caught in its chilling embrace.

Leaving the pub, after the quickest of congratulations to Louisa, were PC Mark Mylow, with an arm around Julie's shoulders. The arm moved to her waist, then rested on her hip, and then they stopped so they could — yet again — embrace; and Mark Mylow was swept away by the full torrent of love that had suddenly broken over him in the most unexpected way during the past week. The workings of his heart and mind had been accelerated to a dizzying speed and he felt invincible and yet more vulnerable than ever. A new kind of truthful light bathed him in its glow and he felt that he not only understood the words of pop songs but that they'd been written especially for him. He felt ruthless and alert, and yet at the same time kind and utterly forgiving, and, all in all, as if he were in a dream. For the first time, a woman had straightaway offered him the whole of herself, from the tips of her toes to . . . well, to that favourite tiny mole, like a full stop, positioned just between her right cheekbone and her ear.

Two minutes after Mark and Julie had walked out of the Crab and Lobster, the Good Fisherman walked in, making one of his regular visits to see who else he might show his photographs to.

Inside the pub, Louisa was drawn by her friends to a position right next to the fire, in the most favoured seat, and everyone's eyes were gladdened by her smile, by her happiness and pride at her new job. She took off her fur hat and her sheepskin coat and sat down. Arms went around her, and someone started a round of applause for others to join in. A glass of red wine warmed through by a dash of boiled water was her Christmas drink, and it stood in front of her, courtesy of the landlord. Around her were the smiling faces of people she'd known and loved for a long time now. Yet still she looked at the door, waiting for Martin's appearance, and at the clock face, handsomely mounted in an old ship's brass barometer; and she watched as the minute hand moved from ten to eight, to eight o'clock, to one minute past . . .

On the bluff of cliff that rose from the westerly side of the village, Martin could look down at the Crab and Lobster. The dark patch of its roof was strung about with coloured lights, and that ridiculous neon Santa that, with the variation in the different neon tubes that remained lit or unlit, lifted its arm and flicked the whip to keep the team of electric blue and pink reindeer at the same endless gallop. The pub's closed windows issued a light that was softened by a veil of condensation made by human breath, the warmth of human bodies, touching the glass that kept outside the cold wintery air. He could imagine the human voices from within, and knew in advance that when he entered he would stick out like a sore thumb; he was forever incapable of joining in with any small talk. Nonetheless, he felt compelled to go by forces that he could only frown at, and try to ignore.

From this front window, he could hear the rush back and forth of the ocean rubbing at the sea walls and at the cliffs below his home and for a while he stood there and wondered why he was going, what for.

To make his peace with Louisa — that was all.

When he had showered, shaved and changed clothes, he went downstairs. The chill darkness of the house enclosed him as he switched off the lights. He would leave the outside light on, to guide his steps up the path from the road on his return. Even as the switch went downwards under his finger, there came a knock at the door, right there, which gave him a jump. It would be Louisa — something told him it would be Louisa. Sharply he moved to the door, pulled it open, and someone else, not Louisa — birdlike, covered in a sensible beige Mac — hopped over the threshold as if concerned not to touch the ground, not to fall down the gap between outside and inside. She took three or four more steps until she was further in, and, when she looked at her watch twice in quick succession, he recognised who it was. But he didn't have time to draw breath because she said, as if continuing a conversation they'd started some weeks ago, "All right, if you say you can help me, I'll listen. I'm ready."

It was Tricia Hawkins. She'd first come to him with sore hands; and he'd been impatient with her, and recommended she use P45 emollient cream, and wear gloves while washing up.

Martin said, "Well, as it happens, this isn't a good time. I have to be somewhere."

"You can't leave me." She checked her watch. It was one minute past eight.

"Well, I can."

She shook her head vigorously. "I can't go out there again until eleven o clock. I can't go in or out of anyone else's house until the hour hits a prime number. I know it sounds mad."

"Yes, it does," replied Martin. "You are." He stared at this lonely woman, rocking from one foot to another, dressed in her shapeless Mac. He'd cottoned on to what was really wrong with her when he'd happened, one day, to walk past a little alleyway, and he'd glanced sideways to see Tricia standing outside her own front door and making this same rocking motion, from one foot to another, while compulsively checking her watch. He'd stopped and asked, "Have you locked yourself out?"

"No."

He'd walked down the alleyway towards her. The front door was tiny, like that of a doll's house. "You keep looking at your watch."

"No I don't." Her hands had writhed in a washing motion.

"I know what's stopping you from going inside," Martin had said.

"You don't." She'd stretched out a tentative finger, touched her door handle, and then snatched it back again.

"Obsessive Compulsive Disorder," said Martin.

"What?"

"You've never wondered what's wrong with you? All your excessive hand-washing? You've never looked up your symptoms or read about OCD?"

"There's nothing wrong with me," Tricia had said, and she'd checked her watch one last time and then

106

unlocked her door and skipped over her threshold as quick as a mouse into its hole.

And now she was here, and she was admitting that she knew what was wrong, and that she needed help. Martin's interest sharpened, and all other thoughts — of Louisa, of the Crab and Lobster, of the impossibility of small talk and not drinking alcohol — fled from his mind. He observed the woman in front of him: pale hair colour, thin frame, anxiety drawn on her face, lack of eye contact, nervous agitation. "Let me see your hands," he said. She held them out, and he turned them over — the backs of the hands, the knuckles, were raw and the blistering covered the whole surface. "This is just from scrubbing them?" he asked.

"Sometimes only at home. When it gets bad, they notice at work. So how can you help me?"

Martin noticed she still couldn't meet his eye. "Come through," he said.

They went into the consulting room. Martin took the chair on his side of the desk, and Tricia perched on the chair on the other side, and words spilled out, dozens, in quick succession, from a woman who hardly said an unnecessary word, and rarely talked about herself, and who had never uttered a syllable about her suffering. ". . . just an hour or so in the morning, then I started to find I couldn't actually get out of the bathroom, because if I touched the door handle I'd have to wash my hands again, so I was trapped . . ."

One minute ticked into the next; Martin listened. He didn't check his watch or even think about the Crab and Lobster.

It was for Louisa to check the time obsessively as the minute hand crawled around to half past eight.

Martin wasn't coming.

Even after this realisation, she shared her glances, still, between the clock and the animated faces of the friends surrounding her and the door to the pub which might open to admit Martin. For two seconds she held her breath because the door did open, but only to admit Danny, who thus gratifyingly found her gaze on him as soon as he entered. He waved; she waved back. He came over and commented on the firelight that was reflected in her expression, and he congratulated her on the hew job. He indicated the spare seat next to her on the bench — which she'd been saving for Martin — and he asked, "Anyone sitting there?"

She smiled and patted it. "You are!"

CHAPTER
THREE

In winter time, the houses that clung to Portwenn's cliffs no longer enjoyed the brilliant sunlight that reflected off the many white-painted walls; and the village, the hills that surrounded it, the sea that lashed at its shore, became more grey. The windows that stood open in summertime were shut fast against the cold and against the storms that blew in from the south-west. Closer to the harbour, within sight and sound of the more tumultuous sea that poured against the sea walls, over and over, the more picturesque cottages, the ones with the crooked roofs and walls, which had worked so hard as holiday lets and second homes during the summer, stood dark and empty. The gift shops and the cafés either closed up completely or shortened their hours. And yet, within sight of the Christmas holidays, the village's Christmas spirit fought off this impression of gloom that was carried over the village by the towering clouds, the stinging rain and wind, because strings of coloured Christmas lights looped from house to house, then borrowed the telegraph pole to cross the street and decorate the pub; and in people's front rooms stood Christmas trees, fairy lights moving in pre-set patterns; and, here and there, in the modern fashion, was a house ablaze with illuminated ornament, standing out like a cross between a spaceship and a toyshop: Santa still galloped his reindeer across the pub, but there were other Santas as well, and neon Christmas trees, while waterfalls of silvery lights imitated snowfall flowing from the gutters to the ground. But still, any front door that opened did so quickly, to let out an inhabitant muffled in coat, scarf, gloves and boots, before it shut again to keep in the expensive heat.

Vernon Cooke had the good grace to come early, before the surgery opened. Pauline had had to give up the little novelty plastic Christmas tree on her desk and was reduced to one strand of tinsel, which Martin hadn't noticed yet, Sellotaped around the outer edge of her computer screen. She had just printed off Martin's appointment list when she caught the unmistakable smell and turned to see Vernon, with his wispy hair standing on his crown any old how, his friendly little round eyes and his baggy jacket and worn corduroy trousers, the satchel slung across his chest. It was all Pauline could do not to be sick; and she noticed Martin lift the back of his hand to his nose as the deathly odour filled the waiting room.

"Came early, see?" said Vernon. "Hope you don't mind."

"God," Pauline couldn't help saying. The full strength of it hit her, what with Vernon advancing towards her desk. She covered her nose and mouth with her hand.

"Sorry, love," said Vernon. "I know I smell, people keep on saying, and sometimes I get a whiff of it myself . . ."

Martin waved at him as if directing traffic around an accident, and tried to speak and hold his breath at the same time. "Go on through!"

Vernon and his satchel humbly trod over the remaining distance to the consulting room and sat gingerly, as if not allowed, on the chair.

Martin had to keep a handkerchief in front of his mouth while he opened the window. Cold wintery air rushed into warm surgery. "Right," he said.

"I am sorry, Doc, it's why I came early."

"No, that's . . . er . . . fine." He took a lungful of clean air, held it in for as long as possible and went to examine Vernon. For that rotten smell to be gusting from him like an ill wind, the inside of the mouth was the likely answer. "Open wide." The circle of light from the torch played over Vernon's teeth and gums to the back of his throat.

And then Martin had to go and take another draught of air from the window.

Vernon sat there, his satchel on his lap, his round eyes regarding Martin steadily.

"Aside from the odour, there's no indication of ill health, Mr Cooke."

"Well, that's a start," said Vernon.

"There's no infection of the tonsils, no gum disease, no atrophic rhinitis. But I'd like to take a swab to send away for testing. It's quite a powerful smell."

"Is it, yes, they tell me so, like I say, from time to time I catch a whiff of it myself, so I know there's a problem." Vernon's humility and goodwill couldn't help but shine through his shabby exterior.

"In the meantime," said Martin, "I'd like to go back to basics."

"How do you mean?"

"Well, let me make some calls. I'd like you to come back and see me this afternoon, and we'll try to sort you out with something then." The smell, Martin thought, was strong enough to lift off the roof. It was the smell of death, he realised. The smell of gangrene. "There are no wounds or sores on your body?"

"No, none."

"What about your feet, are they in good order?"

"One in front of the other." Vernon's eyebrows lifted. "Same as always. Tickety boo, walking along nicely."

"Nothing else wrong . . . anywhere else? Anything at all?"

"No, the only thing to say is that I've been a bit unhappy perhaps. A bit low."

"And why's that?" Martin broke open a packet of swabs.

"Well, since I've been on my own," said Vernon.

"Oh, you mean your wife's died recently?"

"Wife? No, I mean since Freddie left."

"Who's Freddie? Could you open your mouth." Martin had to hold his breath again to lean closer and wipe the swab around the inside of Vernon's cheek.

"Ahhhh . . . My greenfinch. He flew away, weeks back. I loved that bird. He could sing that song . . . how does it go . . . pomp-a-pomp pom pom pom . . ."

"Sorry, can't place it."

"Pomp-a-pom, pom pom pom . . ."

Martin shook his head. "No idea. Never mind." It really was beyond him how people formed such illogical attachments to any variety of moth-eaten animal that was put in front of them.

"Freddie knew it perfect," said Vernon. "Twiddle his little wings, he would, and his beak would snap open and from the back of his throat would come that tune. Not bad for a greenfinch. Not a parrot mind, or a mynah bird, a greenfinch."

"Very good," said Martin.

"And this was his time of year, see. He loved to perch on the Christmas tree. Like a little decoration, he was, among the branches. So bright and colourful. And loud, singing his heart out."

The next day, when Vernon came in again, Martin had done some homework, but the idea was hurtful to Vernon. "Social Services?" he said. "What do I want them for?" He was wearing the same clothes and carrying the same satchel, and his breath sounded in his throat in the same way as before.

"They'll give you a bath," said Martin.

"I can bath myself. I can jump in and out of a bath with my hands tied behind my back. I can touch my toes, you know."

"But they'll give you a bath and they'll launder your clothes," insisted Martin impatiently, "and your sheets and towels, and they'll give your house a good clean."

"I'm not having charity," said Vernon grimly. "No."

"It's not charity."

It was only two strides to the window and Martin took them, and found two lungfuls of cold clean air. "Mr Cooke, as I explained, I can find nothing obviously wrong with you for the moment. So it makes sense to see if this will improve things before we try anything more invasive. As your doctor —"

"Doctor?" Vernon's normally humble expression hardened uncomfortably, as if he was disappointed, himself, to be angry, and ashamed. "What do you know? You're frightened at the sight of blood."

"I know you stink to high heaven," said Martin shortly.

"Ahhhh . . ." Now it was the shame that eclipsed the sudden, brief appearance of his anger. "Is it really that bad?"

As if to answer the question, Pauline came in with a handkerchief over her nose and mouth. "Social Services are here." Her voice was muffled and there were tears in her eyes. She turned sharply on her heel and left the room.

Martin and Vernon looked at each other.

Vernon was crestfallen. To see a young girl behave like that, he thought, and it was his fault . . . maybe it was time to do whatever was necessary. It wasn't that bad, as far as he was concerned — just the odd whiff —

114

but it did seem that everyone else thought he was pretty foul, and he should own up to it, and accept any help that he was offered. Social Services. To clean him up. Like he was one of those people stuck indoors who never threw out their rubbish. He got to his feet. "I suppose . . ." he began. "Well, I suppose . . ." He didn't say any more until he reached the door on his way out. "I ought to thank you," he said, without looking at Martin, and then he left the room.

As Martin went about his business that week, he wondered whereabouts Vernon Cooke lived, and he pictured one of these little cottages — probably not very close to the harbour, which were mostly holiday lets and second homes, but further up the hill — with Vernon sitting there, filling it with fumes, and the smell would leak out, and fill this Cornish bay. Sometimes the scent came back to him, he could swear, when he was walking down by the harbour and the dense, cold air sank down and weighed heavily on the half-empty village.

The next time Vernon had an appointment, a week later, Pauline made sure to have a dish of aromatherapy oil burning on her desk, and when the familiar old figure came in, dressed in different clothes and his silvery hair waving in all directions because it was so clean, she poured fresh drops into the burner and said in as lovely a voice as she could manage, "Hello, Mr Cooke!"

He smiled shyly. "Good morning to you." Clutching his satchel on his lap, he sat on the third chair along. Pauline made sure to notice so she could rush over with

115

the spray disinfectant and a cloth as soon as he left, because the smell was still there — it rushed into the room, an invisible enemy, and remained behind.

When Martin appeared in the waiting room Vernon said mournfully, "Told you I was clean."

Martin swallowed. "Right, come through, would you?" Martin made sure to take up his usual position by the window.

Vernon, with his different clothes and his skin scrubbed clean, occupied the familiar chair. He couldn't help himself, but it was humiliating nonetheless to force everyone to the windows and the doors the minute he came into any room. It was like he was a walking disease, himself. "I'm sorry, Doc," he said mournfully.

"No, Mr Cooke, it's not your fault." Martin cleared his throat.

"Those two old ducks were good as gold," he said. "The Social people I mean. Clipped my toes and fingers, scrubbed me from top to bottom. They had me gargling every day. Wouldn't leave before they'd seen me gargle. Timotei shampoo, the expensive kind, in a bottle that stood upside down, mighty handy. They said they were going to burn my socks, if only they could catch them first. So they had a wonderful sense of humour about the whole enterprise. Which I couldn't share, of course. The pair of them, you know, smelled wonderful. Like . . . I don't know. Like I imagine one of these department stores in London. Giddy-making, it was."

116

"I'm going to send you to the hospital in Truro," said Martin bluntly.

"Oh."

"They're going to want to keep you in for a while. Just to monitor what's going on."

"Oh dear. You sure? Not something you can sort out here? Not like I could put myself through the car wash every morning, though, is it? You sure it's hospital for me?"

"Yes. We'll get Pauline to book you in."

Martin walked swiftly to the door and held it open for the poor old man to walk through.

"Penalty of age, I suppose," said Vernon.

They stood by Pauline's desk. She was busy clicking the lighter to try — again — to set the oil burner to work.

"Pauline, call Truro Hospital and find a bed for Mr Cooke, and book in those tests."

The flint spun in Pauline's hand, quicker and quicker. A spark jumped, but there was no flame.

"Goodbye, Mr Cooke," said Martin. He was already safely back in the consulting room.

Mr Cooke was disconcerted to see the young lady receptionist so anxious to light the oil burner.

"God, stupid thing," said Pauline. The lighter rasped in her fingers repeatedly.

"I've got some matches somewhere," said Vernon helpfully. He tugged his satchel round to the front and opened the flap.

The intensity of the bad smell instantly tripled. Pauline's eyes watered. She swallowed, flung a hand in front of her mouth and ran for the consulting room. "Doc!" she called.

Martin strode back with Pauline. Vernon looked at them with his mouth open, uncomprehending. "What's up?" he asked.

Martin held a folded handkerchief in front of his nose and mouth. "Mr Cooke," he said, "give me that bag."

Vernon looked mystified, but he unhooked his canvas satchel from around his neck and handed it over.

Martin took the bag gingerly using only one hand in order to keep the handkerchief in front of his nose and mouth. He lowered it onto Pauline's desk and flipped it open. Then he gently shook out the contents. There on the desk was a packet of rolling tobacco, an old paperback, a wallet, some crushed letters and utility bills, a men's grooming kit, a pen, an address book — and a dead bird. A greenfinch. Beneath the dull, lifeless feathers its skin seethed with maggots.

Vernon stared, aghast. "Freddie," he said.

The local community radio station, from its tiny insulated Portakabin next to the hotel, bathed the village in the warmth of the human voice. "Welcome to Radio Portwenn, with me, Caroline Bosman, bringing you the latest local news, as well as interviews and, of course, music." Caroline's voice was cheerful and it had a sing-song quality.

It was Portwenn's senior residents, mostly, who listened, but Martin had tuned in for a different reason.

He leaned on his kitchen table and cocked an ear towards the instrument.

"Today, and every day for the next week, right up to Christmas Eve, we welcome to the studio local boy made good, successful London architect Danny Steel, no less." She sounded very proud. "Thanks for coming in, Danny."

"It's a pleasure."

Martin frowned. He didn't want Danny's voice. It was Caroline he was listening out for.

"Can I just say it's been super having you back in Portwenn."

"Well, it's lovely to be back."

"Any chance we can persuade you to stay for good?" Caroline's voice dripped with honey.

"Well, if anyone could, Caroline, it's you."

Martin muttered an obscenity at the radio.

"And we're welcoming you every morning this week, because it's Christmas time, isn't it, coming up soon, anyway, and the clue is in the title, isn't it?"

"That's right, it is. Christmas — Christ."

"Exactly. And let me explain to listeners how this came about, because we were in the pub, weren't we, me, you and Louisa Glasson."

"That's right, we were."

"And the conversation turned to all things Christmas, and we were all saying, it's almost forgotten, isn't it, the jolly old business of Christ, Jesus Christ?"

"Yes, it's his birthday. Christmas is a birthday party."

"So, ladies and gentlemen of Portwenn, Danny and me, there in the pub, Danny and I, that is, if we're going to be correct, we dreamed up the idea there and then to have a half-hour every day talking about the Christian side of Christmas. And we came up with a good name for it, didn't we?"

"Yes, we're calling it 'Contact with Christmas'."

"Well, let's kick off with the basics then. Who the heck was he, this Christ bloke?"

"Well. Shall we start with his parents? Mary and Joseph?"

Martin dabbed the button on the radio, switched Danny right off. He went smartly through to the surgery. "It's bad," he said to Pauline, who was unwrapping her scarf and taking off her coat, ready to start work.

"Yeah, tis, isn't it. Poor bloke, having to put up with that old trout flirting with him on live radio. She must be forty if she's a day."

"Not the flirting. The slurring of her words."

"Exactly, both!" cried Pauline. "Awful, innit. She's going to trip over herself one of these days, but he'll step out the way, won't he; he won't catch her. No one will."

Martin had already gone through to his consulting room. For some inexplicable reason he had the image in his head — a memory — of Danny's hand rubbing Louisa's back, the flat palm of it, up and down a few times, a gesture not just of affection but of consolation, sympathy. The memory disturbed him and he quickly dispensed with it.

Martin had taken the trouble of listening to Caroline on Radio Portwenn because he had been told she would be coming in later, and he wanted to stop an example of bad practice brought to his attention by Mrs Tishell, the pharmacist.

"Caroline," he said when Pauline alerted him she was there. It was 5p.m. and black as night outside, and yet another storm tested the windows of the doctor's surgery. Sometimes it seemed like the storms queued up like airliners ready to land on Portwenn. "Come in."

Caroline was wrapped in her coat and shook the rain off her hat. She could barely look him in the eye. "Oh, Doc, sorry, no time to chat. I'm not properly parked. Blocking the lane, got to dash. Just a recurrent condition, I usually get the stuff over the counter, but Mrs Tishell —"

Martin interrupted, "Mrs Tishell quite rightly thought that a recurrent condition should be investigated by your physician. What's the medication?"

"Oh. Was it . . . is it . . . Fluconazole?"

"So the condition you suffer from is thrush," said Martin.

"I mean, it's only the third time, the fourth at the most. I mean . . ." Caroline glared crossly. "She's such a busybody."

"Go and park your car," began Martin. An extra blast of wind against the badly fitted windows almost made their ears pop with the sudden difference in air pressure.

"Haven't got time today," interrupted Caroline. Again came that bright-eyed glare, that look of panic. "I mean, can't you just fix me the bloody prescription?"

Martin was determined. "Firstly, I'm not in the habit of 'fixing' prescriptions, bloody or otherwise. And secondly, I'd like to see you. Now, if you really can't make it this afternoon then make it tomorrow." He returned to his consulting room, so as not to give her the opportunity to answer back.

Caroline was flustered; she turned on her heel and walked to Pauline's desk. "It seems like I'm to have an appointment tomorrow," she complained.

Pauline responded insolently to Caroline's short-tempered tone of voice. "Seems like I'll have to make you one then. Two o'clock or earlier, twelve."

"Two o'clock," said Caroline. She found herself rummaging in her bag, as if she had to pay for it, but when she stopped and looked round, there was her husband, Tom, standing there, the rain plastering his hair to his skull. He loomed over her, his round shoulders hunched. His long nose pointed at her and she noticed how his blue eyes seemed to have moved closer together, and to have become brighter, harder. Beads of rain dropped from his eyebrows, making him blink. "Tom," she said. "I was just coming."

"Not exactly difficult to find, are you?" said Tom. "The car looks like it's been abandoned by a bloody joyrider. Blocking the road."

"I was only planning to be here for thirty seconds, but . . ."

"I have been sitting at home and waiting for you, waiting, waiting, feeling like a right plonker."

Martin heard the raised voices and came through. "This is a doctor's surgery, not a marriage guidance service."

"You're in for two o'clock tomorrow," said Pauline helpfully.

Caroline felt a sudden rush of love for her husband, and a giddy danger that she might be about to lose him. Without thinking, she made a gesture that she'd used often during their courtship: she lifted a hand to the side of his face, just held it there, but only for a moment because he leaned sideways and pushed her arm away.

"I don't know if it's the drink or what it is," said Tom, "but you're just not *you* any more."

Caroline smiled nervously and a false laugh came as she glanced at Martin, at Pauline, and at Tom. "'Course I'm me. Heavens, who else could I be?" she said in a poignant tone. "It's just I . . . I . . ." She floundered and stopped.

Tom watched her for a while, and then said quietly, "I've packed a few things. I'll let you know where I am." Slowly, he turned away from the reception desk, and made his way to the hallway, looking slightly dazed.

"Well." Caroline smiled at each member of her audience in turn. First at Martin, then at Pauline. "This is brilliant, isn't it. What fun." She blinked back tears. "I mean. Christmas and the spirit of goodwill to all fucking men." She turned over Pauline's stapler on her desk with a thump, and then withdrew her hand and folded it back into the other one as if it were a naughty child that needed to be stopped from causing further trouble.

"Two o'clock all right then?" asked Pauline quietly.

"Yes, fine. Thank you. See you then." With stately good grace she, too, left Martin's surgery.

"See you then." Martin's frown followed her out of the room.

Outside, Caroline bent her head against the powerful onshore wind and rain, and she had a job to pull shut the door behind her. The cold halted her breath and she fought her way back down the path to where her car was parked askew in the lane. There was another car waiting behind her, catching her in the beam of its nearside headlight, which seemed to carry suspended in it many thousands of drops of rain. As she drew closer the driver's window rolled down and the man's cheerful voice reached her, "Wouldn't park there, love, if I were you."

She lifted a hand to shade her eyes against the headlight but then she gave up minding who it might be. She trudged up to his window and leaned closer. The rain poured down her grim face and made streams that looked like thousands of tears, but her expression was one of righteousness. "Really? Well if I were you, *love*, I wouldn't come out in the fucking daylight." She straightened, went back to her car and fought her way back in. The keys were impossible to control in her trembling fingers. When she did get the car started, she crunched the gears and lifted her foot off the clutch too quickly, which made the tyres slither on the wet tarmac. She took off down the narrow street, overcorrecting the steering in one direction and then in the other, clipping her wing mirror against the stone wall on one side. In two seconds she reached the bottom and lurched around to the harbour.

Here, through the pouring rain and darkness, the coloured lights strung along the seafront valiantly fought to spread their glow, and, through her rain-spattered windscreen, as she made two enormous uncontrolled swerves and slewed around the obstacle of the Crab and Lobster, they appeared as coloured stars. The drunkenness inside the Crab and Lobster created merriment and yet the same substance, alcohol, in Caroline created a despair that seemed only the deeper, worse, because Christmas pointed cheerfully in the other direction, towards happiness, a direction she found herself incapable of following.

The next day, Martin felt it was his duty to inform PC Mark Mylow that Caroline was regularly driving while drunk. He called in at the police station to find Portwenn's policeman leafing through a brochure. A small fake Christmas tree stood on the counter, and its fairy lights walked calmly and evenly around its dark plastic branches. Martin was sure he recognised it. Wasn't it the same one that . . .?

"Oh, hi, Doc."

"Mark, can I have a word?"

Mark waved the brochure. "I suppose I should ask you what you think about this," he continued, and read out, "'Pheromones at a molecular level are the tiny messages that attract women, whether they like it or not.'" He was excited. "That's the trick, isn't it — it's the pheromones. It's an animal thing, see. But it's a bit worrying, because does it mean she likes me for who I really am, or is it like a trick I'm playing on her? With the pheromones?"

"I haven't got time for this conversation," said Martin.

"'Rediscover your natural ability to attract the female sex'," read Mark. "Might as well hand Cupid his arrow, I tell you. But I don't dare stop using them, now."

"Mark, I think Caroline has a drink problem and is continuing to drive."

"Oh."

"I'm going to talk to her about it tomorrow, but what worries me is that she's an immediate risk to herself and to others."

"Right, I'll look into it."

"What does that mean, though, 'look into it'?"

"I need evidence, obviously. I have to have reasonable cause to suspect. That's the Road Traffic Act for you. After all, you might be an aggrieved neighbour. Out to do her down."

"I'm her doctor."

"Only joking, Doc, don't take it so hard. Come on. Christmas is a-coming. And love is in the air. More than in the air, I tell you. It's bloody everywhere. In the sitting room, in the kitchen, in the bedroom, of course. On the sea wall! Not kidding. Which reminds me — there's something I'm worried about, Doc. In your professional capacity —"

"Make an appointment."

★ ★ ★

When Martin pushed open the door of Portwenn's pharmacy, it was to hear immediately the by-now-familiar voice of pharmacist Mrs Tishell, talking to a customer.

". . . it's the bane of my life, is my neck," Mrs Tishell was saying, and she gave a corkscrewing motion of her head. "Always has been." She caught his eye and called cheerfully, "Morning Doc!"

"Yes," said Martin, in a disconnected way, because as usual he remained on the path that he was on, the one that concerned him the most.

Mrs Tishell hardly paused to find out if Martin was going to answer properly before she continued, "When I was a girl, if I didn't have the right pillow, my mother used to say to me, 'You're like the princess and the pea.'"

The words went past in a blur for Martin. "Mrs Tishell," he began firmly.

It had no impact. "Ooh, in the mornings I was like a bear with a sore head," she went on, in the grip of fervent memories of her own childhood.

"Mrs Tishell, my delivery? I have surgery." He was close enough now to observe his words strike home, and he watched her jump slightly.

"Of course, Doctor. I'll get it for you right away." She handed first one paper bag and then another to the customer she was serving. "Or a bear with a sore neck, more like," she said to the customer. "Ha ha."

Martin became aware of a man lingering near the till — a man he'd never seen in the village before. He wore some kind of uniform and from behind his beard he had a curious look, as if everyone and everything was of equal interest. Martin felt himself studied, looked over, and he saw that Mrs Tishell, also, was examined with interest, and the customer also, as she turned and left with her bag, was stared at briefly.

"Ooh-err — there you go, Doc." Mrs Tishell lifted the box across the counter.

"Thank you." Martin took possession of the box and smartly turned to leave, but the man leaned — sort of tilted — in order to put himself in the way of his exit.

"Excuse me?" said the stranger.

"No," said Martin and, without a trace of apology in his tone, he added, "No time."

The man wasn't put off; he persisted, "Graham Reynolds. I work for the Salvation Army." He drew a laminated identification card from his pocket and held it out.

"Well done," said Martin.

"And we're looking for a young woman, called Emma Lewis." The Good Fisherman said these words quickly — he was used to their utterance having the required effect. It wasn't often that someone turned away from him once he'd explained who he was and what he was doing.

"Never heard of her." Martin kept going.

Graham's expectations were disturbed, but he was experienced enough, and believed in the value of his work. After only a brief second of faltering, he carried on, "OK, but if you'd like to —"

"No thank you," Martin interrupted and carried on outside and down the street.

"— look at these photographs," finished Graham. By now he was standing inside the pharmacy door.

Mrs Tishell had overheard every word. "Oh dear," she said, glancing through the shop window at Martin's figure walking determinedly down the hill. She spoke up for him. "Don't mind our doctor," she said. "Underneath, he's a wonderful man, truly."

Graham came back to the till, and showed to Mrs Tishell the photographs he'd been trying to show to Martin. "Have you seen this girl?" he asked.

Mrs Tishell looked at a picture of a dark-haired girl, maybe in her late teens, her face a little plump, looking squarely, insolently, into the eye of the camera lens. The next was a glamour shot, of the same girl looking teasingly at the lens. And then a set of three passport photographs, the fourth one missing. "No," she said. "Sorry, I haven't. Have you tried the police?"

"Sometimes we don't like to get the police involved," said Graham. "Not when the missing person has . . . well, how shall I say, an unhappy relationship with authority figures."

Mrs Tishell leaned forwards as far as her neck brace would allow and examined the photographs carefully. "No," she said, "I've not seen anyone remotely like that here in Portwenn." She had heard about this man from Mrs Stringer, who worked for her in the pharmacy sometimes. And a couple of other people had mentioned him.

Graham swung his satchel around to the front, and took from an inner pocket a business card. "If you do happen to see her," he said, "perhaps you'd call me? We're the Salvation Army, not the police. We just want to make sure she doesn't . . . well, we're concerned for her safety. And the safety of those she comes into contact with."

Mrs Tishell was struck with a deep compassion and wonder at the fact that in this remote Cornish village, a stranger had turned up and was wandering from shop to shop, obviously looking for a missing person. She felt the warmth of the shop suddenly, and it was as if the roof had been newly built over her head and fresh food put in front of her. Despite her neck brace and despite the tedious nature of shopkeeping, which sometimes threatened to overwhelm her, she felt lucky, and well looked after, well fed and at home. "If I see her, I'll let you know," she said, taking the card he offered. Printed on it was the Salvation Army's motto, "Belief In Action". For Mrs Tishell, this motto, combined with the man's persistent kindness on behalf of another human being, meant that tears stood in her eyes. The feeling of Christmas, its generous spirit, had made itself felt in the village of Portwenn.

Caroline's descent into a dependency on alcohol had also been noticed by her old friend, Louisa. She too — as Martin had done — took a professional approach to the problem. The purely analytical part of her brain told her that the very first person she must talk to would be Caroline's doctor, and that happened to be

Doctor Martin Ellingham. It would be the first time she'd seen him since she'd got the post of headmistress, and she felt that even though he hadn't attended her celebratory drinks the night before last, they were on a good footing again, surely, after the misunderstanding during the job interview — after all, to all intents and purposes, her new job had been down to him.

As she walked up the path towards the surgery, she saw the front door open just the least amount possible and Martin's arm appeared and dangling from the end of it was the dog. The hand released its grip and by the time the dog had fallen, yelped, and twisted around to try to get back in the house again, the door had closed. When she went in, with Martin's help she was sure to keep out the dog, leave it behind in the damp, grey air.

They stood uncomfortably in the hallway. She unzipped her coat and pressed the sides of her ponytail, checking it was more or less in place. "So how are you?" she asked.

Her words collided with Martin's, "How's your new job?"

She answered first, chattering volubly because of nerves. "Yeah, great, but I'm glad it's the end of term soon. It . . . it's going to be hard, you know, I know that sometimes I will feel like a bit of a fraud. Like the governors will suddenly realise the huge mistake they've made and that I am, in fact, not really a head teacher at all. But I expect everyone feels like that, don't they? I mean, not you, because you're a proper professional. Which is why I'm here, actually," she finished. There was the softest of West Country burrs in her voice.

"You want to make an appointment?" They'd reached the doctor's reception room — Pauline's desk waiting tidily for her return.

"No, no, I wanted to ask for some professional advice."

"Of course."

She watched the familiar frown settle on Martin's face. She always wanted to soothe it away. The attraction of Martin, she thought, was that when the frown that so frequently occupied his expression cleared, it was like sunlight breaking from behind a cloud and suddenly everything was rewarding; and when the frown so quickly returned her task was to remove it again. "Thing is," she said, "it's Christmas, isn't it, and there's loads of parties and events in the Crab and so on, and everyone's drinking, aren't they. You know the saying round here, Portwenn's a drinking village with a fishing problem."

"I don't drink, so . . ."

"I know you don't, but there's this friend of mine. It's different with her. It's not just the Christmas spirit. She's drinking too much all the time, and her behaviour has become a bit odd. We're going to the Christmas fundraiser in the Crab, and . . . well, what do I do? Shall I just buy her a drink, or should I . . . How do I do the best for her? I don't want to buy her a single glass of wine."

"Well don't," said Martin.

"Fair point, but . . . well, technically speaking, how many units are too much? Every week, week in, week out?"

132

"Does it matter? You obviously think its too much or you wouldn't be here."

Louisa felt like Martin was throwing all her questions back in her face. "Er, I suppose, Martin, I'm asking you to give me a hand here. Caro — my friend is drinking too much and I don't know what to do."

Martin's tone of voice was offhand. "Well, if your friend is who I think she is, judging by my dealings with her, I don't think she wants any help."

"No, I know she doesn't, but surely that depends on the way you give it?"

"I don't know," said Martin. Resentment crept into his voice. "If I give people advice, they seem to want a prescription. If I give them a prescription, then they seem to want advice."

"Surely there are no fixed rules, you just have to feel your way and listen to your patients, I guess." As soon as the words were out of her mouth she realised she'd taken a wrong turn, because Martin's frown deepened. She held her breath for his next comment, which would push her away, she knew, and turn the room cold.

"Oh, right, that hadn't occurred to me."

Louisa felt a familiar sense of plummeting ill will. "Martin," she pleaded.

"What?"

"Am I doing something wrong? Whenever I try to, um, connect with you, you just . . . close down. Then I start doubting myself. When maybe it's you who should have the doubts, and then maybe you'd be more approachable and people would want to listen to your advice." She'd made it worse, but hadn't been able to stop herself. At least she'd got the message across that she wanted to connect with him, that she cared enough . . .

Martin said calmly, "Well, if you're so conversant with the finer points of my job, then you don't need my advice on what to say to your alcoholic friend Caroline when you buy her the next dose of alcohol with which to poison her liver."

The doors closed, the locks turned, the bolts were drawn across, the bars went up on the windows, the whole man closed down.

Louisa knew, in her heart, that she'd used Caroline only as a pretext to see Martin, to talk to him, test her mettle against his. It had gone badly, but she was still landed with accompanying Caroline to the Crab and Lobster's Christmas charity auction, on 12 December starting at 8p.m.

The village hadn't yet sucked in its quotient of Christmas visitors — those with second homes here, or those who came home to join relatives, and some who, over the years, booked into hotels and guest houses in order to escape from their own families. The Crab's charity auction was therefore an affair attended only by the winter-proven, full-time locals, with some of the lots on offer definitely more for comedy purposes, and some lots useful for Christmas gifts. Proceeds went to Portwenn's lifeboat and, as usual, the scale model of the lifeboat built by old Commander Graham during his retirement took pride of place on the Crab's bar.

The Christmas tree stood in the corner furthest from the danger of the fireplace and, as usual, was decorated with the same items as every year: fishing floats and lures, sections of differently coloured fishing nets, ancient bits of block and tackle from the boats. Instead of a fairy, a green-and-blue plastic mermaid was fixed to the top. From each corner of the room ropes of plaited fishing nets — black and orange — reached for the central light fitting across the tobacco-stained ceiling, and hooked into the twists of netting were colourful reminders of the creatures that lived beneath the waves: starfish, sea shells, dried-out sea urchins, unusual pebbles and flotsam. It was the Crab and Lobster's version of a Christmas tree, and was always up in time for the charity auction.

Louisa had arranged to meet Caroline an hour earlier, so they'd have time to talk, and the inevitable question, she knew, would arise almost immediately. Louisa arrived first, but had only just sat down at one of the smaller, round wooden tables when Caroline blew in like so much detritus from the storm. "Hey!"

"Boy, am I glad to see you," said Caroline.

"Bad day?" Louisa steeled herself for her friend's rush to alcohol. It was the season for drinking. Every other advert on TV was for drink; social occasions multiplied and intensified their spread of it, and here was Caroline . . .

"The world's going mad around me, I'm telling you."

"Is it?"

Louisa was determined to get in early with her idea of ignoring the spirit of Christmas and ordering soft drinks. "I was thinking, why don't we —"

But Caroline spoke over the top of her. "Oooh, have you ordered the wine yet? I could kill for some nice deep, dark red, wintery Rioja." Her eyes swung to the bar and noticed the chalkboard propped there. "Hey, or what about the mulled wine? Shall we share a jug of that?"

"Well, I'm not drinking tonight," said Louisa. "What about —"

"I definitely need a heck of a lot of wine," interrupted Caroline. She stepped towards the bar, unclipping her purse.

Louisa fumbled onwards with her plan. "I just thought that we all drink so much at this time of year, it's better to have a break, not have quite so much." It sounded clumsy.

Sure enough, Caroline was quick to see what she was up to. "How d'you mean, we all drink so much?"

"I'm just concerned," said Louisa.

Caroline's face twisted in that way it usually did. "Well I'm 'just concerned', actually. Because if you'd bothered to ask me, I'd have told you that Tom has just left me and I am feeling completely crap."

Louisa pleaded to be forgiven. "Oh, Caroline, I'm so sorry, I had no idea."

"So we . . . we could drink a . . . a barrel of wine together, because that's what old friends do, actually. And maybe, just maybe —"

It was Louisa's turn to interrupt. "OK then, as an old friend, I want to tell you with all the affection and concern in the world, that you don't sound yourself, and you're a bit shaky."

"So you just want to wish me a Happy Christmas and in the same breath tell me to sober up?" She sounded incredulous.

"No, Caroline, I just —"

"Well, thanks but no thanks. As far as I'm concerned, you can go and lavish your pastoral care on some poor nine-year-old. God help him. Or her."

The pub filled up with the buyers and sellers at the charity auction. Mark Mylow bid wildly for his new girlfriend, Julie, to sing a song there and then, on the spot, and the crowd sensed blood and the young men of the village — surfers who'd got stuck here, fishermen's sons, farmers' sons — pushed up his bid until, red in the face, he'd paid over a hundred pounds to hear the love of his life sing. She got up and suddenly all the rowdiness of the auction, all the drunkenness, dropped away and everyone listened to Julie sing "You are so beautiful", in as simple and as beautiful a voice as could be imagined, with, every now and again, a delicate, shy glance at Portwenn's figure of authority, its handsome local policeman, PC Mark Mylow, which gave an indication as to whom she might think was beautiful; and when she calmly brought the last note to an end it was Mark's hands that worked the hardest to applaud her, and his face was the most rapt.

Louisa wasn't the only one to warn Caroline about her drinking. A more official warning came the following afternoon from the still enraptured PC Mark Mylow, who, since the first of December, had tied a piece of tinsel to the top of his Land Rover's aerial. It had become rather bedraggled, since then, by wind and rain. He knocked at the door of Caroline's cottage, which had no sign of any form of Christmas decoration, so it stood out from its neighbours with an uncanny gloom. He called out in his best, most understanding voice, "Hello?"

Caroline was asleep on the sofa, when a voice called her up from the deeps. She thought it was her husband Tom and so when she twisted the Yale latch and pulled open the door she was dishevelled, and on the point of crying with relief. Instead of Tom there stood on her doorstep the figure of PC Mylow and her expression altered and settled into one of stony suspicion. She said in a complaining tone, "I'm asleep."

"Ah. Sorry to wake you." He looked at his watch: it was a quarter past three in the afternoon and she was fully dressed. "Just wanted to have a little chat," he said, in an even, steady tone.

"What is it?" she asked brutally.

"I just wanted to mention, I know it's Christmas time, but maybe especially because it's Christmas time, it's a good idea to be a bit careful about having one too many and then climbing behind the wheel of a motor vehicle." His hands wagged an imaginary steering wheel. "Deadly weapon?" He dropped the mime show when he saw she wasn't amused. "There's Christmas spirit," he continued, "in other words peace and goodwill to all men, and there's Christmas spirits, which is necking shots in the Crab. And as I always say, the thing is to know the difference."

Caroline peered at him. "You as well then." She sounded disappointed.

"You nearly ran me off the road a while back; I don't know if you were aware. And I've received comments in my professional capacity."

"What comments? I mean, who from?"

"I'm not at liberty to divulge my sources, but let's just say not from Father Christmas, put it that way. Forgiveness and all that Christian lark doesn't extend to drink driving, I'm afraid. And there's more police on the road; we're looking for it, obviously, at this time of year." He tapped the side of his head. "Not brain surgery to work out it's best not to."

"Oh bugger off," said Caroline. It looked like her eyes still hadn't opened properly.

"Caroline," began Mark, but the door swept shut and left him standing alone.

Inside the house, Caroline fell back onto the sofa and pulled over her the disorganised duvet, pushed the scratchy cushions under her head and closed her eyes. Standing on the occasional table was a half-empty bottle of Jura whisky, with its box standing next to it as if torn into by animals, and the Christmas wrapping paper a leaf of material resting brightly on the floor.

It didn't end there: blearily she slept the whole night through, but always feeling more tired, and drove to work still over the limit. In her little radio shack it came to the time — 8.30a.m. — for Danny Steel to give to the village his daily Christian message, Contact with Christ, in keeping with the season.

She put on her restrained but cheerful voice, and spoke into the microphone. "And it's time for Portwenn's very own spokesperson for Jesus Christ, whose birthday we'll celebrate in precisely fourteen days' time, so please welcome Portwenn's handsomest son, Danny Steel." It was about to become clear to Caroline that Danny had been coached, today, to offer a particular homily on the subject of alcohol.

Danny leaned closer to the microphone and used the same types of rhythm of speech as Terry Wogan, accelerating and lifting his tone, and then dropping and slowing it right down. It was a style of delivery he'd developed during a media-training weekend in Bristol.

"Thank you, Caroline, it's a pleasure to be here. Now of course, what is it, eh, this Christmas thing, if it's not a story of good news? Glad tidings, you might say. Christmas is a time of celebration. Wasn't there wine at the Last Supper, the end of Jesus' life? And I'm sure there would have been a glass of wine lifted at the beginning of his life, at Christmas time. But sometimes the celebrating can get out of control. When is the next drink the one that you shouldn't have? I remember when I was a boy growing up in Portwenn, I thought drinking and driving was when you were steering the car with one hand and, with the other hand, you lifted a bottle of water or a glass of milk, or suchlike, and drank from it, so guess what, you couldn't see properly around the side of the bottle, you know, and you'd

140

crash the car. So it was that I'd see my dad sip from his coffee after the stop at the service station. 'Dad, you're drinking and driving!' I'd say, and he'd reply, 'Son, it's coffee.' So that was a puzzle. Of course it wasn't long before I began to understand all the TV advertising that springs up at around this time . . . Don't drink and drive." He smiled at Caroline, who suddenly looked as if a bad smell had been put under her nose.

So, thought Caroline, Danny and Louisa were in this together. What a sanctimonious pair. And what horrible glittery eyes Danny has, she thought, forcing the smile to stay on her face for longer and nodding agreeably. Why hadn't she seen before that he was so unutterably pompous? She couldn't believe she'd thought he was handsome. That shirt collar was ridiculous with its little buttons. That springy dark hair was preposterous. And the smile — it was like a ghastly cut with a knife across his face. She blinked and realised her own mouth was twisted, and open. What on earth had Danny been wittering on about? She hadn't been listening. A story about a drunk Father Christmas rolling down a hill.

Danny finished off by reading directly from notes he'd made. His sugary tone of voice sang the words, up and down, fast then slow. "So our festival, our celebration of the birth of Christ, in this beautiful village, should be performed with the spirit of . . . joy . . . within us, and even, yes, with a bit . . . a bit of the spirit of alcohol within us. But if, in our joy and happiness, we find that our hands, at the same time, rest . . . on . . . the . . . steering . . . wheel of a motor vehicle, and the spirit of alcohol sings in our blood,

141

then one word should sound in our heads — no. And, by the way, I should end with a public service announcement: the number for Portwenn's taxi service is pinned up on the wall just on the right-hand side as you leave the Crab."

After Danny had left the studio, Caroline went straight into some music so she could once again howl and break down in tears; and the technician came out from behind his glass screen and once again held a comforting arm around her, and suggested that he should tell the same old funny story immediately, before the song ended, in order to steer her safely to a calmer mood. "Shall I?" he enquired.

"Yes," pleaded Caroline, "tell me again." She eyed the red diodes on the console. "We've got one minute twenty."

"Well, you know Bert Large the plumber? He went and put in Bruce Hanton's cistern and toilet bowl, didn't he?" He gave her shoulder a little shake. "But he plumbed it in with hot water, didn't he? And the cistern was hot as a radiator, wasn't it, and when you flushed it, hot water filled the bowl, didn't it? And made the most God-awful smell." With each little shake and hug that he gave Caroline, her tears moved more towards smiles, and when the song finished she was ready with her cheerful radio voice, although it was a little shaky. "A big thanks to Portwenn's handsomest son, Danny Steel . . ." The words stuck in her throat. Awful man. Portwenn's ugliest son.

When Caroline later rushed into Martin's surgery, without even greeting him, she took up a stance and looked at him from under lowered eyebrows and asked, "Please, please, please, can I have a prescription? I've got thrush. It's a pretty common condition I understand. Please don't examine me."

Martin was unfazed by anyone else's directness since he was so direct himself. "Thrush is common," said Martin, "but it's not common to succumb to it as frequently as you apparently do."

"Two or three times?" asked Caroline sarcastically.

"According to our pharmacist, five times in the last twenty-three weeks."

"Isn't that breaking patient confidentiality? I mean, I would be within my rights to go and get Fluconazole elsewhere, you know,"

"Yes, you would. Are you washing the affected area with soap and water?"

"I beg your pardon?"

"It's best if you don't use soap."

"I'll bear that in mind. Perhaps you'd like to check."

"Do you have any other symptoms? I don't know if you're aware but your speech is quite often slurred."

"I think I know what my voice sounds like. I work on the radio."

"I'd like to look in your mouth."

"What?"

"*Candida albicans*, the fungus associated with thrush, also lives in the mouth. Sit down."

For a while Caroline did nothing but stand and glower, but Martin's stare was so steady and unexcited that she felt her feet moving despite herself and she sat in the chair.

"Open," said Martin, standing over her.

Caroline's mouth opened as if she'd been hypnotised.

The fumes filled the room. "You've been drinking," said Martin.

Her mouth snapped shut. "That's what you wanted to know, was it?"

"First, I'll deal with the thrush and then with the alcohol."

Caroline shoved back the chair and stood up. "I don't drink any more than anyone else at Christmas time."

Martin was not aggrieved by the anger in her voice. He regarded her clinically. Her anger was merely symptomatic. "Do you ever find yourself drinking first thing in the morning to steady your nerves, or to get through a hangover?"

"No! I mean, certainly not."

"Do you often find yourself getting annoyed with people who observe or criticise your drinking?"

"Right, that's it!" shouted Caroline. She flung her bag over her shoulder. "I've had enough!" She stamped over to the door. "Who the hell do you think you are, asking inappropriate questions about something I have not even consulted you about!"

"So that's a yes then," said Martin.

She flung open the door so hard that it banged against her own toe and bounced shut, so she had to open it again. "Heard of patient choice? Well, here we go, I'm about to choose. And it's not you."

And then she was gone.

Pauline brought him the notes for the next patient. "You're such a people person, aren't you?" she said breezily.

Caroline climbed into her car, but the door slammed shut on the trailing seat belt, so when she gave it a yank it wouldn't pull free, and she didn't bother. She started the car and, with a jerk and another attempt at releasing the handbrake, the car started off down the hill. The tarmac was still whitened by cold; and the notion of Christmas stayed in her head. The season of goodwill. A slow-moving pedestrian, walking by the shuttered fish market, stopped in alarm at the sound of her racing engine, and, safely behind her windscreen, Caroline saw the person clearly enough, but imagined him as a bottle standing there. And the telegraph pole was a bottle. The familiar square shape of the Crab and Lobster was stuffed with bottles from floor to ceiling. The Christmas tree winking through a downstairs window had nothing but bottles in wrapping paper beneath it. The baker's shop on the right, she knew in her head, would have pastries and loaves in its glass cabinets and on its shelves, but she could not stop herself from imagining rows of bottles. In her hands the steering wheel became a pair of wine bottles and she was holding their necks, tilting them back and forth.

She realised she was turning a corner without really knowing where she was, and there was the Bevy of Beauties with their legs shaped like upside-down wine bottles. A seagull flew overhead and its harsh winter cry sounded like a warning as she sailed too fast around a right-hander; and, sure enough, as if arranged by a higher power, there was an aerial with a length of gold tinsel fluttering from it like a flag — she was heading fast towards the unmistakable royal blue front grille of the police Land Rover. Her feet stumbled from one combination of pedals to different ones, but she pressed hardest on the clutch and, at the last minute, she turned the wheel to avoid the collision by inches. The car came to a halt and she folded her forearms across the steering wheel, and on them rested her forehead, and wished she could cry, but she mustn't allow herself: without the story of Bert Large plumbing hot water into Bruce Hanton's cistern she might never laugh again, and only cry.

PC Mark Mylow felt the panic of the event subside and he climbed from his vehicle. He had recognised Caroline's face as it had loomed sharply closer during the emergency stop — her expression frozen in surprise. Now, as he rounded the back of her car, he could see her lifting her head from the steering wheel and wiping back the hair from her eyes. He gave a gentle knock on the side window. "Caroline?"

She looked at the kindly face of Portwenn's policeman and pressed the button to let the window down between them. "I know, I know, I wasn't concentrating, but I'm just not with it at the moment."

"I'm very sorry about this," said Mark, "but due to the manner of your driving, I suspect you might have been drinking." His tone of voice implied it was an achievement and she was to be congratulated.

146

"Mark," said Caroline sharply. "This is me. Caroline."

"We have to do this properly," said Mark, full of regret. "Please switch off your ignition and step out of the vehicle."

"Oh for God's sake, Mark." She bashed him with the door as she pushed it open suddenly. "I haven't been drinking. I mean, I've had exactly one glass of champagne. What is the matter with everyone?"

"When did you last have an alcoholic drink?" asked Mark, rather admiring her frank disregard for his official position.

"I don't know," said Caroline. "A couple of hours ago."

"Right. I now require you to do a breath test and I should remind you that failure to supply a breath test is an offence for which you can be arrested."

"I can't believe you're doing this, Mark."

"I'm afraid, Caroline, that during the Christmas season we are expected to be more than usually vigilant. How would you have felt if you'd come round the corner and a group of carol singers had been standing there, preparing to sing 'Silent Night'?"

"Don't be ridiculous, it's the middle of the day."

"Nevertheless." Mark unhooked the breathalyser from around his neck. "Now. This is the machine we're going to use. And I can show you how it works. This is the tube that you blow into." He gave it a go himself and then wiped the mouthpiece with his hand.

"Oh, just give it here." She snatched it from him and blew hard into it before he had time to issue a single other instruction or even switch it on, so they had to do the whole thing again, more slowly.

"Very good," he said, as if talking to a small child in a classroom. He held the monitor for a while. They both waited impatiently, so time passed slowly.

A bleep announced the machine had made up its mind.

Mark gave a low whistle. "Blimey," he said, again full of admiration.

"You've got to be joking." Caroline felt utterly drained of energy, and incredibly thirsty.

Caroline was obliged to leave her car where it was, ready for collection and transport to the police pound. Mark parked it more closely against the wall to allow traffic to pass, and then took her in the Land Rover back to the police station for her blood test. She sat wearily at the little table and allowed herself to be carried along by events, too tired to resist.

"Afraid we haven't got such a thing as a blood test machine here," said Mark. "But the test has to happen before a certain time has elapsed since the original offence, so Doc Martin — I mean Doctor Martin, um, Ellingham will be coming down shortly. He'll be here in just a minute."

"Oh well then, everything will be lovely."

"Can I get you anything?"

"Some water, please. Cold water."

"Hmm," said Mark, "I don't know if I should give you any water. It might . . . um . . . affect the blood test."

"Then what else is there that you'd like to get me, Mark?" she said with a peculiar, intent voice.

Mark was saved from an argument by the arrival of Martin. The familiar suited figure arrived in his usual brisk manner.

"Thank God you're here," said Mark. "She wanted some water but I thought I can't give her water, can I, because . . ." He was describing her as if she were a wild animal.

Martin lifted his medical bag onto the table. "Caroline," he began.

"Darling," she answered sarcastically.

"You all right?" He pulled open his bag.

"Is that some sort of joke?"

"Do you know why I'm here?" He snapped a syringe from the pack.

"For God's sake."

"I need to take a blood sample on behalf of the police."

"Hurrah." She flopped her arm on the table and pulled up her sleeve. "Get on with it."

Martin pulled up a chair and stripped the syringe from its sterile wrapping. "Are you decorating, Mark? I can smell varnish." He looked around the room.

"I noticed that," said Mark. "I thought it might be nail varnish, but . . . it could be my new aftershave. The one that goes with the pills. The ones I was telling you about. Pheromones. Sure did the trick."

"Which is surprising, if it smells like nail varnish."

"Guess where she is, right now. Julie."

"No, I don't want to."

"She's upstairs, waiting for me." Mark pointed at the ceiling and couldn't stop his smile. "God's truth." And then he added, "I was thinking of getting you some pheromones, Martin. Among friends you know. Looking out for each other. See if it does for you what it did for me. Honestly, they say love strikes like a thunderbolt but I didn't know they meant it literally."

"No thanks, Mark. I think I can do without your quack internet cure-alls." Martin inserted the needle into Caroline's vein and looked away. He couldn't watch the deep red colour swarm into the body of the syringe. He placed a sterile pad over the break in the skin and pressed down. "Hold that." His finger was replaced by Caroline's. "You can get her a glass of water now," he said to Mark, and then turned to Caroline. "You're not well. I'd like to do some more tests while I'm here."

"You're not my doctor," said Caroline vindictively.

"Nevertheless, I strongly urge you to let me examine you." He was conscious of where the vial of blood was, even though it was hidden from his sight.

"Well, you can keep your strong urges and point them somewhere else. I want to go home."

Mark placed the glass of water in front of her and watched her knock it back in one. "I'm afraid your vehicle will have to be towed," he said peacefully, "but —"

"Shut up, Mark."

He did.

"I want to go home now," she insisted, breathless from having drunk the water.

150

"I can't leave the station at the moment, I'm afraid," said Mark.

"I'll take her," said Martin quickly.

"No bloody thanks," said Caroline. "I'd rather crawl over broken glass." She stood, swayed, and steadied herself with a hand on the table. Then she launched off, made it to the door, pushed off from there and stumbled out.

It took her twenty minutes to walk home. Some of the houses she passed had miniature drifts of fake snow painted into the corners of the window panes, which only made her think of the bother of having to clean them after the new year. Some of the front doors offered wreaths, which were, to her eye, not cheerful and welcoming but funereal, as if someone had died.

As she climbed the hill she found it necessary to wait for periods of time, to rest and get her energy back.

Her own house boasted not a single Christmas light along its eaves or around its windows, and no wreath to decorate its door. When she let herself in, the interior was — as usual — empty and gloomy and cold. Along the hall and through open doorways there was no glimpse of a Christmas tree, there were no Christmas lights, no streamers. The only evidence of the seasonal celebration was an untidy pile of Christmas cards lying unopened on the hall table. The house was as if abandoned, and smelled of stale wine, and her only wish was to drink more water, more wine and go to bed and get the other side of this unaccountable tiredness.

As she stood leaning at her sink, still dressed in her coat, taking gulps of water, Caroline thought,

Christmas does this to you. It was Christmas that Caroline blamed for her powerful sorrow. Father Christmas didn't exist. The whole festival was an exercise in commercial exploitation and familial guilt.

She realised that for some reason she had opened the fridge, and couldn't think why. In this confused state, her thoughts appeared one by one, unconnected: there is an egg; the kitchen floor is dirty; the bottom shelf of the fridge is empty.

She tried to retrace her steps to find the argument that she'd been in the middle of. Something innocuous about Christmas. She groped for a sense of meaning and found herself in a fog, and a faintness entered her body before the gloom quickly intensified and took her into its darkness.

Caroline collapsed and lay motionless on the kitchen floor.

As soon as Martin returned to his surgery he asked Pauline to call the Police Forensic Science Service and tell them he must have, as a matter of extreme urgency, the results of a glucose test on Caroline Bosman's blood sample. When the call came through that same afternoon, he was suffering a tirade from a patient, Mr Abbot, about drug companies and how they peddle their wares and bribe doctors, bunging them computers, free lunches —

"Shut up," said Martin, covering the phone with his hand, but too late. "No, no, not you," he said into the phone. "Bosman. Yes. Are you sure? All right." He put the phone down and stared at Mr Abbot's aggrieved, shocked face. "Right, Mr Abbot," he said, "I'm very happy to be cutting short our consultation because I have to deal with an emergency. Go home, finish the course of tablets that I prescribed for you, drink plenty of fluids and by all means continue to read that moronic newspaper that you waste your money on." He stood up and moved quickly towards the door. "Pauline," he shouted, "call Mrs Tishell and ask her to prepare me a ten millilitre ampoule of soluble insulin. I will be there in four minutes."

"Hello," said Pauline, gazing at him critically but obediently picking up the phone. "You have patients." She indicated the people sitting on chairs in the waiting area.

"Reschedule." He was already on his way out.

At about the same time, Louisa and Danny were standing in front of Caroline's unadorned front door, pressing the buzzer for the third time. Louisa stooped to look through the letterbox. She could see the familiar, darkened hallway and, at the end, the kitchen door ajar. There were no lights on. Had Caroline not got the message that they were going to drop in?

"Obviously not," said Danny, handsome in his duffel coat with the collar turned up.

The air had that grainy quality of a wintery dusk descending.

Louisa stepped around to the next window and peered in. "I was pretty rubbish the last time we met. I wouldn't be surprised if she's avoiding me." She stepped further around and looked up at her windows.

"Probably down the pub," said Danny. "Come on, let's go."

Louisa looked at Danny, and the sight of his charming smile chased away the sense of unease she had at the ghostly emptiness of the house. She smiled and walked back and took his arm. "So how's life as a radio star then?" she asked.

They began to walk down the hill, while Caroline lay undetected on the chill floor of her kitchen, the amount of glucose in her blood so high that it would be off the scale, and with so much sugar in her blood that urine infections grew quickly and often — any infection would grow immediately and quickly — and her liver and kidneys had begun to close down, and it had caused her raging thirst. And yet none of that glucose was reaching her body cells and so, in effect, for the last few months she had been starved of energy. Her breath was shallow and, in her unconscious state, she didn't feel the hard, unforgiving kitchen floor. She registered no pain from the blow to her forehead or her twisted knee. Quietly, unseen, she was dying.

"Did you listen then?" asked Danny, as they walked away. "Am I any good?" He put his arm around Louisa's shoulders in a comfortable way, mostly to test whether she would answer by putting her arm around him. "Can't believe I've agreed to do a whole week of it. Obviously it's going to be a new career."

"A new career for you in Portwenn," said Louisa admiringly, and yet this conversation was effortful, automatic, because she couldn't shake off her unease at

154

that empty house. It didn't occur to her to put her arm around Danny, although she quite liked his around her.

"In Portwenn? A career?" said Danny smilingly. "I don't think there is such a thing, is there? Most people . . ." He trailed off when he realised he'd insulted Louisa. Her wooden silence confirmed it. "I didn't mean . . ." he began. Under his arm, he felt her shoulders stiffen, move away from him. "Obviously your job, I mean, that's fantastic. I mean, you've done brilliantly. Forging ahead. You're the new headmistress. That's a huge leap."

"Right," mumbled Louisa.

He had to take his arm from around her shoulders. "Look, I didn't mean to sound arrogant."

"No, no, that's fine." She noticed a sweep of headlights approaching — too fast. She and Danny pressed into the side of the alleyway and, as the car swept past, she realised it was Martin's car. At the same time she saw his determined, frowning face at the wheel, not even sparing them a glance.

She knew with a frightening certainty where Martin was going. Without a word, she turned and started running back up the hill. Behind her, she heard Danny's voice call, "Lou? I'm sorry . . ."

When she reached Caroline's house, Martin was peering through the letterbox and shouting, "Caroline?" She hurried to join him and, without a greeting or a preamble, she said, "She's not in, I was meant to drop by earlier —"

"She must be in," said Martin. "I dropped her off here myself not more than a couple of hours ago and she was in no fit state to go anywhere." He leaned on the doorbell and they could hear it sound inside, at length.

No answer.

"Tried the back?" asked Martin.

"Yes, it's locked."

Martin shouted through the letterbox, "Caroline!" Immediately, he made the decision. "We'll have to break in." He put down his doctor's bag, walked over to the wall and loosened a stone from the top of the wall, lifted it and threw it at the glass panel. He reached through the break and brushed the door jamb to find the lock, twisted it and pushed the door open, taking his bag with him.

Louisa followed him into the darkened interior. "Caroline?" she called.

Martin stepped through to the kitchen and, in the light thrown by the open fridge door, he saw the figure of Caroline lying unconscious. He already knew what was wrong with her and pulled open his bag to reach for the ampoule of insulin that he'd picked up from Mrs Tishell. "Call an ambulance," he said to Louisa. "Tell them it's suspected ketoacidosis and I'm about to give her ten millilitres of insulin subcutaneously."

"Right, OK."

"Too much sugar in the blood," added Martin, to make it clear. He held the ampoule upside down, slotted the needle through the rubber cap and drew down the insulin.

The light switched on, and Danny stood there. "Is she . . ." he began.

Louisa spoke into her phone: "Ambulance . . . Portwenn, Dairy Lane, The Gables. Yes . . ."

Martin leaned down and spoke slowly and clearly to Caroline. "Caroline, it's Doctor Ellingham. I'm going to give you an injection of insulin."

Danny was kneeling on the other side of Caroline's prone form. "Insulin?" he said. "But she's not a diabetic, is she?"

"Ambulance right now, please," Martin called to Louisa.

Danny rested his hand on Caroline's shoulder and rubbed gently. "I'm saying a prayer for you, Caroline."

"Little prick," said Martin, as he pinched the skin on Caroline's upper arm and slid the needle right in, beneath the layer of fat. He was aware of Danny looking at him and he pressed home the plunger, loading the insulin right into Caroline's bloodstream.

It was Danny who took over Caroline's slot on Radio Portwenn while Caroline recovered in hospital and learned about the new regime that was now going to affect her for the rest of her life. "Contact with Christmas" expanded from Danny's few minutes with Caroline to take over the whole programme, but interspersed with more music, which was chosen by the technician.

Danny's first broadcast in Caroline's place of course was centred around what had happened to her. Danny leaned close to the microphone and read carefully from the text he'd prepared the previous night. To write this address had brought to mind the sight of his father's back, the old jacket stretched tight across the shoulder blades, as he'd leaned over his desk and written sermons. The strange, unmoving quality of that back, for long hours it seemed in Danny's memory, had stuck with him, while his father's arm and hand moved carefully back and forth, writing a message to his congregation from God. It was moving, for Danny, to feel he was doing a similar thing, and to a larger congregation — to all the residents of Portwenn. "Christmas," he began, "is literally a gathering together to celebrate the birth of Christ. And that gathering together is of families, of course. At Christmas time we go home to our families, if we can. We think of the word 'family' and we picture a mother and a father and maybe two children. But there are many of us who live alone, who apparently have no families — and so, is Christmas a family experience, for us?

"Let me describe to you a particular situation and ask you, where does Christmas come into it? A woman collapses on the kitchen floor. She is all alone; her husband has recently left her and she has no son or daughter. No father or mother is nearby. She does not know it, but she's a diabetic, and her body is starving from lack of energy, even though she eats and drinks as much as she possibly can. Dusk falls, and she lies there alone. Where is her family, and where is the spirit of Christmas, in the life of this woman? And yet, outside the house, a woman calls out her name. Outside the house, a man calls her name. And another man. They break down the door: they are not going to let their friend die. They bring to bear all the resources that a modern society can offer the situation. One of the men injects her with insulin. The other man prays for her. The woman calls for the ambulance and exactly describes where they are so the ambulance can take her to hospital. This was the scene in Portwenn yesterday, when I saw, in front of my very eyes, the spirit of Christmas in action: the friends of Caroline Bosman became her family. The residents of Portwenn became her family, which was wonderful to see, and to feel. You know, the lifeboat is an emblem of this town — it's on all our postcards isn't it — and in some ways, each one of us individual souls is being carried along in the metaphorical lifeboat that is the village of Portwenn."

His radio was mercifully switched off and so Doctor Martin Ellingham, for one, didn't have to listen to Danny's "Contact with Christmas" broadcast. If he had heard it, he certainly would have left his toast and marmalade and stepped to the windowsill and clubbed the radio with a rock. Christmas was always to be avoided, as far as Martin was concerned, but this year — well, it was like a brick wall fast approaching, that he'd somehow have to crash into and hope to survive. There was no getting away from Christmas this year. Christmas was coming to get him. He should never have agreed. He shook his head. He munched steadily, and occasionally lifted the cup from its saucer and sipped his coffee, trying deliberately to sidestep the impending doom.

Louisa, on the other hand, did hear Danny's broadcast and her reaction was confused. She resented that her friend's medical crisis was being broadcast over the airwaves to be used as a Christmas fable, and yet she loved the idea of Portwenn as a family. Her attention snagged on the words, "The other man prayed for her," knowing that Danny was describing himself. She remembered him with his hand on Caroline's shoulder blade, his head bowed and his lips moving in prayer. It should have been a beautiful thing, a wonderful expression of hope, but there was something in the way that Danny promoted his own prayers that made them less the expression of a generous spirit, than a quest for approval, a step up the ladder of righteousness — the most important part of which was to be observed climbing. And yet he was kind, and attractive in his way, and successful. He was an effective man . . . She could love him . . .

Oh God, she hated him, didn't she? She wanted to swat him, to push him away . . . what was the use?

It was the last day of term, that descent into the Christmas holiday that she'd always loved, herself, as a child; not because it heralded going home, which for her had not been a welcome prospect, but because of the day itself — its fun and games. Today a host of pleasurable activities awaited her charges: the film showing in the morning was *The Grinch*; there were last-minute rehearsals for the school nativity play this afternoon and the performance this evening. This coming Sunday would be the school carol service, and the church choir would encompass three of her charges, and they would sing solo, unaccompanied, "Silent Night", during the Midnight Mass on Christmas Eve. It was a beautiful time of year.

After the school bell there was an unusual air of excitement in the building. On a normal day, the school would shut its eyes as soon as the children left, even with the footsteps sounding of the three teaching staff or the administrators going about their duties, but today the building stayed alive with the running feet, the bursting open of doors, caused by children staying behind, carrying costumes and props, testing each other's lines.

Danny appeared as good as his word, and Louisa was proud of him, and gladdened by his sense of wonder at visiting the school where he himself had been a pupil at the same time as Louisa. He went into their old classroom and touched the same radiator, the same windowsill. "This is the room we had to sit in when we had detention, d'you remember?" His eyes were almost supernaturally bright and he had a wonderful spring in his stride; youthful energy seemed evident in his curly hair.

Oh God — did she love him? Could she love him, or make herself love him?

She did remember all those years ago, yes. "You mean that time when we all got sent to the headmaster after we'd bundled what's-his-name into that wheelie bin."

"And then, we put that thing on the lid so he couldn't get out." Danny smiled and put his hand on his breast; "God, that makes me feel bad even now."

"He never forgave us," said Louisa mournfully. "We really frightened him."

"God forgive us," said Danny, looking skywards with exaggerated good humour. He turned to look at her. "I suppose *you* give detentions now?"

"Not really," said Louisa. "Well, I sort of try not to."

Danny stood much closer to her. "I only did that thing to Martin because he kissed you," he said, gravely.

Louisa was confused: the switch in subject matter, and from the distant past to the present, and from light-hearted matters to one of such emotional significance, stopped the words from coming easily to mind; she didn't know how to react. "Did *what?*" she asked, to gain a moment of time. "Has he said something?" she asked. She couldn't imagine Martin telling anyone about what had happened in the cab, that morning so many weeks ago. It seemed like another world. But she had — she'd kissed Dr Martin Ellingham in the back of a cab. It had been disgracefully forward of her. But she'd be furious if he'd told anyone. "Did he say something?" she asked again.

"Who?" asked Danny.

"Martin. You just said. Didn't you just say?"

"Martin Farry," said Danny. "In the wheelie bin."

"Oh. Oh, *that* Martin. Of course."

There was a moment of silence in their old classroom, although from beyond its walls came the sporadic cries of children released from school duties and allowed into the special time of imagination, of ritual, of generosity, that was the Christmas holiday. Louisa realised she'd committed a *faux pas* and had

162

given away something that she'd intended to keep forever buried. She could see the cogs turning in Danny's mind as he picked up what he'd now found out and looked carefully at what it meant.

In a smaller voice he said, "So that's why you've been so cool with me."

"Well, I've hardly been cool," she said. "And anyway, nothing actually ever happened. It was . . . nothing."

"Really?" Danny sounded hopeful, or maybe he was asking her to make it nothing, then and there, to discount it.

"No. Really. It was . . . you know, a moment."

He nodded woodenly. This secret event had suddenly shown itself and spoiled his reading of the possibility of a relationship with the girl whom he'd first loved during his childhood, and who he now found in the same rooms, but grown into a greater beauty — Louisa.

Throughout the rest of the afternoon, this revelation of a private event — her having kissed Martin — upset Louisa's enjoyment of the school nativity play. She went ahead on automatic pilot but with a preternatural awareness of where Danny was, what he was doing to help: securing the stage flats upright, hanging up the sign that said, STABLE, THIS WAY, carrying in the manger full of hay that would do for the infant Jesus' crib, scattering the straw on the stage, running extension cables for the lights, shepherding the shepherds, setting out the rows of chairs, arranging the blackout curtains along the windows, helping to push the piano into position, writing out the prices for the tea and cake, placing the photocopied programmes on the chairs. He was cheerful enough, but his mood had been altered, she could see, by the knowledge that she, Louisa, had kissed Doctor Martin Ellingham in the back of a taxicab early one morning a few months ago. It seemed an impossibly unlikely event now, but she remembered how, at the time, during the kiss, it had been like the most certain qualification — a certificate with the word "love" written on it — which she'd earned for the strange amount of hard work she'd found herself putting into her feelings for Martin — hard work that she would still, at the drop of a hat, take up again, although she couldn't bear to admit it.

When she had made her introductory speech to the audience — her first as the school's head, she suddenly realised — she took her seat in the front row, middle, next to Danny, and, as the first children appeared dressed as a donkey, a sheep, a lamb, a cow, a chicken and a goat, it seemed to her that all human beings, herself included, were walking around in silly costumes, with silly masks on, pretending things were happening that weren't really happening, and things weren't happening when they really were, whether they liked it or not. When the infant Jesus was lifted from the crib, she joined in the "ahhh" of appreciation, but the events happening on stage left her in a state of cold dread, nonetheless, because she felt that she herself was being fitted for the wrong costume, and if she let that happen, she'd never really get to play the role of her true self, in her real life, and that she'd be stuck for evermore, dressing up.

164

Martin had some medical housekeeping to do, following the crisis of Caroline's diagnosis as a diabetic. His first call was to Portwenn's homely police station, which had more of an air of a bed and breakfast with its kindly host, the incorruptible PC Mark Mylow. "Mark," he said. "We have a problem. How old is your breathalyser?"

"What? I dunno." Mark's frown cleared. "Before my time, though, I can tell you that."

"Right. Some of the older breathalysers picked up ketones in people with diabetes. Which gives you a false positive reading."

"Oh."

"You know that smell of nail varnish? That's ketones. Released when the body eats itself, when it can't get any energy out of the blood. That's what your device was registering. Not alcohol. Caroline's blood sugar measured so high that she nearly died. If you want my advice, I'd get rid of your old breathalyser and find something new that works."

"All right then, Doc. But," added Mark laddishly, "I tell you what does work, what darn well does work, and that's pheromones. Come on, jump in, join the fun." He pointed upstairs. "She hardly gets out of bed before three in the afternoon." He smiled and shifted easily from foot to foot.

"I'm not sure about the different models," said Martin efficiently, "but I would imagine any of the newer ones would have been designed to cope." He prepared to go, but found himself saying, gruffly: "That test. It probably saved Caroline's life."

"All in a day's," said Mark. "But can I ask, are my test results in?"

Martin shook his head. "Not yet." He remembered the policeman and his plaintive request for a sperm test. It would be the only way to escape, PC Mark Mylow had explained, from the terrible worry that small testicles and a bout of childhood mumps might have left him with a low sperm count. "No hurry I imagine," said Martin, "you've only just met."

"That's true," said Mark, but then a wise, concerned expression came over his face. "Except, I tell you what I never realised though."

"What's that?"

"That love . . . well, sex. Is like, the main thing, for the girl, is making babies, isn't it? That's what Julie feels when we make love, if that's not TMI."

"TMI?"

"Web-speak for Too Much Information. When the speaker divulges matters of a personal nature that disturb the listener. But Julie, right, when we are, well, being romantic let's say, for her, the excitement is making an actual baby. The nuts and bolts of it. It really is. One and the same thing. Sometimes she cries out, 'Baby', and it's not a term of endearment. We men are getting our end away, but Julie's making a baby. She is. She darn well is." The policeman stared fiercely. "So it's no wonder I'm a bit worried about the test, obviously" He rolled his eyes. "But, hopefully, no worries, because I love her to bits. I'm so far gone in love with her I'm not in sight. Really. And that little baby she wants, I want it too. True, I do."

166

"Mark," said Martin impatiently, "you shouldn't have anything to worry about. The size of the testicles bears no relation to sperm count. The mumps, is a factor, but only in a small minority of —"

"Shhh," interrupted Mark. "Confidentiality, Doc. Please." He gave a theatrical look up to the ceiling. "Big night out tonight."

"Did you hear what I said?" went on Martin. "The size of the testicles—"

"All right, all right, don't rub it in, I heard the first time."

Martin persisted. "You shouldn't have anything to worry about."

Mark pointed, dabbing his finger a few times. "I tell you something that will please your ears." The earnest, good-natured policeman looked full of love. "Size really doesn't matter in lovemaking, either. As it happens. That's one of the best things in my entire life, which I've found out from Julie. It's what you do with it." He grinned. "And we do a lot and, I tell you, there aren't many places in Portwenn and the surrounding countryside that haven't seen the—"

"Very well, then," said Martin. "I shall be in touch as soon as your test results are available."

"Great stuff, Doc. Just got to make Julie's tea now. But thanks for the vote of confidence re Caroline. Pleased to be of service."

The next piece of clearing up for Martin was a courtesy visit to Caroline in hospital. He waited for the following day, when she'd have got her energy back, and then drove to Truro during evening visiting hours.

As he walked the by-now-familiar corridors, he was stopped by a tall, owlish man whom he faintly recognised. "Doc?"

"Hmm?"

"Tom Bosman, Caroline's husband."

"Oh yes. I remember."

"I'm sorry about . . . everything. I was out of order. Causing a scene in your place."

"How is she? I am just on my way."

"Well, she's alive, thanks to you. Louisa told me what happened."

"Ah."

"So, thanks go to you for that."

"Good."

"Anyway she's in there. A whole lot of new paraphernalia to keep her going every day, now, it seems like. She's pretty bloody-minded about it. But there's no cure for that, I suppose."

"No. Afraid not."

"You'd be the wrong person to ask though, eh? No, I'm sorry, that was just a . . . that was a joke."

"Of course."

They parted company and Martin continued to the ward. A quick glance around the occupied beds — all faces he didn't recognise — told him that Caroline must, therefore, be in the curtained-off position at the end. He made his steady, purposeful stride towards it, but, as he went to draw back the curtain, a premonition warned him that maybe Caroline was asleep; in which case she wouldn't want to be disturbed. Instead of drawing back the curtain, he parted it just an inch and looked through. His eyes fell on Louisa's ponytail, her back, as she sat on Caroline's bed; and on that back, moving up and down slowly, was a man's hand; it was Danny's hand. Danny was sitting next to her on one of the plastic chairs.

For Louisa, the hand was unbearable. It was on the exact same place — her shoulder blade — where she'd seen it rest on Caroline's back. Didn't he have anywhere else to put it? Couldn't he move it here and there, instead of burning a hole in the same spot?

The last time Martin, too, had seen that hand stroking back and forth like that had been when he and Danny had been kneeling on either side of Caroline's unconscious body, and to see that same movement now, attached to Louisa, was like a terrible warning; and he had the unaccountable feeling that Louisa was in grave danger, if she actually . . . liked that. He was confused and disturbed by such a feeling that had no basis in logic, in reason, and he let the inch or two of curtain drop, then turned away and left the ward.

Inside the curtained-off cubicle, Louisa felt the presence of someone — just a second too late — and she turned round to see a pair of fingers let go of the edge of the curtain and disappear.

That night, Martin dreamed that an Action Man toy was given to him, and he was in loco parentis — instead of playing with it, he was to make sure no harm came to it. Without a word, the Action Man came alive; its mechanical joints swivelled and moved in a jerky, uncoordinated fashion and it crawled off down the

169

corridor — a featureless, broad, white square corridor. Martin followed, trying to call it back. At the far end of the corridor was a pair of swing doors but the Action Man changed direction and headed for the smooth vertical expanse of one of the walls. Just as Martin thought he could pick it up, it began to climb the wall effortlessly. It reached an opaque plastic box with the word "EXIT" written on it in green. Martin presumed it was for the emergency lighting. The Action Man stood on top of this box, its front close to the wall, and now Martin could see that it wasn't an Action Man at all, it was a baby in nappies, standing perilously high up on this narrow foothold, its legs wobbling. Martin held out his arms. He must be ready to catch . . . but the baby fell much faster than was natural, and he couldn't close his arms quick enough. The rush of the baby through his arms was the same as Martin's rush upwards, out of sleep, and he awoke with an intense feeling of anxiety, but no memory of the dream.

Twenty-third of December. The day before Christmas Eve. Here, right now, Christmas was coming to get him. His normal routine was going to be interrupted. He had shrunk the amount of time he would normally offer to patients to just five minutes each, so that he could take the afternoon off and drive to St Austell and pick up his parents from the station.

The rain coated his windscreen between each beat of the wipers. The tarmac had that feeling of having been sluiced so clean that soap and a scrubbing brush must have been used on the surface, while rivulets of muddy water ran at the edges. The comfort of the big Lexus isolated him from the soaked hedgerows, the sticky mud of the fields, the driving force of the rain.

At St Austell he stood grimly in the waiting room until the First Great Western from Paddington drew up, and then he moved onto the platform, looking in both directions. The Christmas season meant that the youth of Cornwall were pouring into the arms of their parents, or young families were greeted with enthusiasm by grandparents. Martin spotted his father and mother standing with their cases, looking brown and lean in comparison. As he walked towards them, he wondered if he might just continue and keep walking right past them. But then he saw his mother crack open a bleak smile and nudge her husband.

"Martin." She held his forearms as if she were restraining him. She smiled, another rare smile. Her grip dropped to hold both his hands, and she squeezed them.

"Mum. How are you?"

"I'm fine."

Martin turned to his father. "Christopher," he said. His father had always requested to be called by his name, rather than "Dad".

"Martin, good to see you at last!"

"How was the flight?"

"Oh, bit bumpy out of Lisbon."

He knew this would be the first of many uncomfortable pauses. He knew that for the next five days it was going to be up to him, as the host, to find a way out of the other end of such pauses. "Well," he said, "the, the . . . the car's this way."

They took their place among the throng that crowded out of the station. "So why Christmas in England this year? Your letter didn't say."

"We need a reason?" His father gave him a nudge. "To see you, of course. And Aunt Joan. It's been too long."

"Right. No, I was just . . . Well. It's been . . . It's been some years since we spoke."

His father frowned. "Really? Has it been years?"

"Seven," said Martin.

"Crikey. Well, we really did move abroad then. More than we realised, I suppose. Got carried away by the new life."

They passed through the entrance hall and joined the group of people milling about just before the exit doors delivered them into the pelting rain.

"Good of you to collect us," said Martin's father. "Hope you didn't have to reschedule any important patient care. I was wondering about your workload and I suppose it must be all sorts. Sore throats. Lumbago. And injuries, I imagine, from the fishing vessels."

Martin pointed through the doors. "My car is there. The grey Lexus."

"The silver one," said his father.

"We can make a dash for it," said his mother.

They hurried, heads down, through the rain. Martin lifted the two cases into the boot even as his father was folding himself into the front passenger seat, and his mother the rear. When he turned the ignition key the emotional intensity of Vivaldi's Concerto for Violin and Strings sounded ridiculous and he was quick to switch it off.

As he drove out of St Austell and gained the road for Portwenn, Martin became aware that his father was checking his movements — steering wheel, gear lever, indicators — which made him feel as if he were taking his driving test. Martin fought his way out of this silence by switching on the car stereo again — but not the Vivaldi, the radio.

"Beautiful *country*, Martin," said his mother from the rear seat as they caught sight of how the land met the sea.

Martin slowed down. In the lane in front of him a vehicle was parked up on the verge, making the space left for passing uncomfortably narrow. As he approached, the driver's door opened and a figure appeared, bent by the rain. The figure made a sign and Martin slowed to a halt and thumbed down his window. Even as he did so, he recognised it was Danny.

"Car's given up the ghost!" said Danny. "Thank heaven you came along. Would you have space to give me a lift into town?"

"Get in," said Martin and shut his window.

But Danny ran the wrong way, back to his car. He opened the boot and carried three loads of decorating equipment and tools back to Martin's car, putting them in his boot. By the time he slid into the back of the car next to Martin's mother, he was soaking wet. "Bless you, bless you," he said as he fitted his seat belt into place. "I'm Danny," he said, and held out a hand, which she shook politely.

"Margaret. I'm Martin's mother"

"Oh! Pleased to meet you."

From the front Martin's father said, "And I'm Martin's father, Christopher Ellingham."

"Right!" said Danny cheerfully. "So, a Christmas gathering, I take it. There's something wonderful about families travelling to be together at Christmas time."

Martin had started his engine again, and drove on towards Portwenn.

"All that equipment," said Christopher amiably, "leads me to presume you're a builder or painter and decorator."

"No, actually, I'm an architect. London based. I was just doing some work at my mother's place, which she's just handed over to me, which is nice."

"London based," said Christopher. "So you two have something in common."

Martin opened his mouth in order to say "No, he's an idiot and I'm a doctor," but Danny got in first. "Yes. Exactly. We both came down from London. Both looking for a more enriching way of life. Both found it."

"But not many major projects for an architect round here, I wouldn't suppose?" said Christopher.

"That remains to be seen," said Danny. "But, *cherchez la femme*, I suppose . . . I found when I came down here that an old flame was rekindled, and love should be at the centre of anyone's life, really. I suppose in that respect I've been very lucky. And a house falling

174

into our hands at the same time. God-given good luck really."

"Oh, that's lovely," said Margaret.

The car began the descent from the tops of the cliffs down into the village. It always seemed to Martin that his ears might pop, the fall was so sudden.

"Would you mind terribly dropping me off outside my place?" asked Danny. "All that equipment . . ."

"Certainly," said Martin. "I'll drop you off anywhere you want to be dropped off." For some reason he found the word "dropped" pleasurable to use in this instance and he felt inclined to use it again if he could.

Danny's farewell to Martin when he and his equipment was dropped off was, "Bless you, Martin."

"I didn't sneeze," said Martin, for the second time.

In the shelter of his porch, Danny didn't hear him. He clasped a hand against his chest and shouted to Martin, "Thankfulness."

Martin returned to the car and steered it down to the harbour.

"Nice man," said his mother from the back seat.

"If you like that sort of thing," said Martin. At the bottom of the hill, outside the Crab and Lobster, he pulled up. "Here we are. Shouldn't wait around too long, not really meant to park here."

"Which is your place?"

"No, I've booked you into here, into the Crab and Lobster."

Christopher said, "I thought we were staying with you?"

"Not enough room," said Martin. "So I booked you in for B & B. The Crab is adequate. You'll much prefer it."

"I'm not sure we can—"

"It's all right," interrupted Martin quickly. "I'm paying. We'll have to be quick." He opened his door and braved the rain to fetch out the two cases from the boot. They were marked with dust and dirt from Danny's decorating tools. He carried the cases quickly into the Crab's porch, and watched his mother and father step carefully towards him. He watched his father pause, and straighten, as a small trio from among the Bevy of Beauties went past, holding over their heads a shared overcoat. "What d'you think, girls?" asked one of them, and laughter arose from the group like birdsong.

Christopher said, "My word," and carried on. When he caught up to the others he said to Martin, "This is very kind of you. And entirely unnecessary. We'd have been quite happy staying with you, even though, as I remember it, Doctor Sim's old place is pretty tiny. Pretty much a doll's house."

"Well, obviously that's why I put you in here," said Martin.

"I remember taking you to Doctor Sim when you were bitten by that weaver fish," said Christopher. "Bawling your eyes out, you were, and I didn't have a clue what to do. But old Doctor Sim got out a bowl of hot water, plonked your foot in it and it was over. The pain left as if by magic. He was a credit to this place.

176

Just the sort of man who should have been a GP. Right man, right spot. Winning combination."

"Yes," said Martin.

"Shall we meet for cocktails at six?"

Martin wondered why his mother was staring at his lapel. Minute by minute she'd turned quieter and become more subdued.

They agreed to meet at the Crab at 6p.m.

Martin was sluiced by the rain on the way back to his car, and he drove slowly up the other side of the hill to the surgery. As he parked and hurried through the great drifts of rain that were coming in off the sea, he glanced at the Crab and thought he detected, for all its Christmas decorations — its flags and lights and the neon Santa hung on the seaward wall — a new, menacing aspect in its seaward gaze, as if the Grinch, instead of Santa Claus, looked out to sea from its accommodation. The truth was, it was inexplicable that his parents had turned up at all, let alone at Christmas time. Dinner in the Crab and Lobster, with his parents sitting at the same table, would have seemed inconceivable as a social event a month ago — yet here it was, about to happen in a few hours' time.

Even more remarkable would be tomorrow evening, when, on Christmas Eve, he would drive his car up to Haven Farm and he, his parents and his Aunty Joan would all sit down to a Christmas dinner. That was an impossible idea. Never before had Christmas done such a thing to him.

★   ★   ★

177

Shortly before 6p.m. that same evening, 23rd December, Martin changed into a fresh set of dry clothes and returned to the Crab and Lobster to have dinner with his parents. First, he was invited up to see their quarters. A carved four-poster dominated the room, with a television fixed to the wall giving the highlights of a rugby match between a team wearing dark blue and a team wearing red and white.

"Gowarnnn," said Christopher. His face reddened and a vein appeared in his temple as he stared at the television. He broke off with, "Sorry, can't help thinking I'm playing again myself. The rough with the smooth, that's rugby football for you. Nothing like it, if you've done it before."

Martin remembered how he and one other boy, a huge fat boy, had stood forlornly shivering in the middle of a rugby pitch at school while both teams had thundered back and forth doing something inexplicable with an oval-shaped ball.

Christopher stood and tugged his jacket. "We going down then? Margaret? Ready?"

"Yes." Her voice sounded odd, from the bathroom. Martin had the impression she might have been crying.

"I've booked a table in the dining room," said Martin. It was, he thought, likely to be the most hellish meal that he'd ever had the misfortune to sit down to.

"Start in the bar though," said Christopher.

"We can order drinks from our table," said Martin.

178

"Page one, Martin," said Christopher. "First time in a new place, buy everyone a drink." His gaze flickered back to the television screen and he frowned. "No, don't . . . don't kick!" he groaned. "Possession, man, that's the thing." He cupped his arms and pulled them into his chest. "Keep *possession!*"

Downstairs, in order to cope with increased numbers in the bar, the Christmas tree had been moved to the pub's reception area. It reached to the roof, and it carried its freight of fishing objects — floats, pieces of fishing nets, plastic lures, antique fishing reels, toy sharks and dolphins and swordfish, streamers of coloured lines — with a pertinent sense of style for a fishing village, and the fairy lights threw this collection of paraphernalia in a glamorous yet homely light. Both Martin and Christopher were tall enough to brush their heads against the paper streamers that looped from the corners of the room to its centre. Sprigs of red-berried holly decorated the tops of the picture frames and strands of ivy were arranged around the doors that led onto the terrace and to the dining room. A fire burned vigorously in the grate and already the bar was half full, with people's coats taken off and gently steaming where they hung on the pegs or over the backs of the chairs. There was the sense that the voices would become louder, more numerous, as the party spirit would only grow.

Among the people that Martin knew in the bar, it was the figure of Portwenn's policeman, PC Mark Mylow, who loomed closest.

"Ah, Doc," said Mark. "Good to see you. Season's greetings. What can I get you?"

"I'm not . . . um, I don't—"

Christopher interrupted. "Let me get these. Christopher Ellingham."

"Ah." Mark's honest face brightened as he took in the figures of Martin's mother and father. He pointed. "Are you—"

"Correct," said Christopher. "Martin's parents. Down to see what he's up to, hidden away down here. What's your poison?"

Mark smiled agreeably. "Oh. Well. That's very kind of you. I'll have a pint of Extra Smooth please. I count myself as not only a colleague of the doc's here, as Portwenn's police officer, but also a personal friend. Are you a doctor, too, then?"

"No. I'm a surgeon," said Christopher.

"Retired," added Martin.

"Margaret?" Christopher didn't look at his wife, but pressed forwards to the bar. "What d'you want?"

"I'll come with you." She moved to follow him.

Martin only caught the beginning of his mother's sentence as she spoke in a low voice, "You know, you really don't need to buy . . ." The tone of voice was weary, dismissive.

His attention switched to Mark, who stood uncomfortably close, swaying slightly.

"Doc," said Mark in a quiet voice. "Must have a quick talk with you, before your dad comes back with the drinks."

"What is it?" said Martin.

180

"Hey, you kept that quiet, your mum and dad coming down for Christmas, how about that?" He gave Martin's arm a gentle punch. "Oops, sorry, I forget sometimes. Deadly weapons." He blew across his knuckles and went as if to put his fist back into a holster hanging from his belt.

"Mark, I'm not in the mood." Martin could see his father standing at the bar, collecting drinks orders from everyone around him.

"Sorry my old friend," said Mark. "Can't help being in a good mood myself. Because . . . well, you'll never guess."

"I don't have to."

"Go on. Try."

"No."

"Pheromones. Amazing. Result is, I'm not only in love. Not only having the time of my life. I'm engaged to be married." Mark brought a small blue box from his pocket. "At least. I'm about to be. Going to ask her tonight."

"Mark, this is—"

"I know, I've been a bit of a dark horse on this one, didn't want to spray it all over the village."

"Did you find her on the internet? Russia?"

"No. Met her in the village. Whirlwind romance." Mark snapped open the box to show off a gold band with a single diamond. "And you'll remember my old problem of being too 'gentle' and all that. Well, no complaints in that department from her. The opposite of complaints, in fact." His smile was huge. "So it's time to let everyone know."

"Her name is Julie Mitchell." Martin felt dread on the policeman's behalf.

"Yes, Julie. How did you know? Well, she's the only new girl in town, I suppose. She's great, isn't she? You know, I was trying to think of the word. The right word for her. She's a woman. I should know, eh? Well, made it my job to know." Mark tapped the side of his nose. "Made enquiries. Extensive enquiries. In that department. If that's not TMI. And very *successful* enquiries. No problems, you'll be pleased to hear. No complaints on my side, either. Yes. So. The opposite of complaints. On both sides. But I need to know for certain I can give her a baby. That's everything to her, you see? It's all she wants, a baby. Be unfair to marry her and not give her that. And I had mumps as a child as you know, plus there's the size issue. So I was hoping you had the results of —"

"You've known her for how long exactly?"

Mark was about to answer when Christopher returned, carrying a tray of drinks, and followed silently by his wife. "Ooh, jumping into the fire, eh?" said Christopher, nodding at the ring.

"Well, I . . . I hope so," said Mark. "If she says yes."

"Brave man," said Christopher and handed him his pint of Extra Smooth.

"Thanks."

While Mark burbled on about his new girlfriend, Martin looked carefully at his mother, wondering why she was hardly saying a word to anyone, or even meeting anyone's eye. He studied her face — a face he hardly knew, he realised. It was as if she were a stranger to him, and she was behaving as if none of this was anything to do with her. He couldn't yet believe his parents' visit was anything to do with Christmas spirit, or at least not on her part. Maybe, thought Martin, as he half listened to Mark, it was his father who was, in his bluff, crass manner, trying to mend the hurt and the disappointment that had stretched over so many years, and she didn't want to do any such thing? At any rate, Martin was becoming increasingly sure that at some time during their visit, their purpose would become clear. He wondered when that might be, and what it would reveal.

Mark's voice interrupted his thoughts, "Talk of the devil, here she is!" His face brightened and he lifted an arm to hail her. "Julie, over here."

Julie Mitchell pressed through the gathering throng. She was smiling, her oval face a picture of prettiness, the blonde hair beautifully cut and arranged. Around her neckline was fixed a thread of gold tinsel and on her head was a playful pair of felt antlers.

"Now then, meet some friends of mine."

"Hello, Doctor," said Julie and offered her hand.

"Miss Mitchell." Martin shook the offered hand, briefly. His tone was cold, offensive.

"You two know each other, then." Mark was amazed. His arm lay heavily along Julie's shoulders.

"Yes, we've met before," said Julie. "Only once, though."

"Patient confidentiality forbids me from saying more," said Martin. He made a mental note to take

183

legal advice about this situation. It was impossible to have his hands tied, to remain silent.

"Ah, right, of course," said Mark.

Julie smiled seductively. "The doc here accused me of bewitching you." Steadily, she met Martin's stare. "Didn't you, Doc?"

"Ah. Quite right. Good old Doc." Mark smiled easily. "But you don't know his dad . . . and his mum—"

"We should go in to our table," interrupted Martin.

"We certainly can't do that yet," said Christopher. "Not until I've met this exciting young woman." He picked up Julie's hand and kissed it. "Christopher Ellingham. Delighted to meet you."

"He's a surgeon, too," said Mark. "Like father like son."

"I'm not a surgeon," said Martin abruptly.

"'Course, I meant, you *were* a surgeon," said Mark amiably.

"Well, I don't think anyone's ever kissed my hand before," said Julie, impressed. She held up the back of her hand for everyone to have a look.

Martin noticed — and disliked — how his mother had been forgotten. It added to his intense feelings of discomfort. Yet it was as if she was deliberately asking to be excluded.

"Now, now," said Mark, tucking Julie closer under his arm. "Back off, menfolk. She's spoken for." He wore a proud smile and then turned and kissed her.

"I realise I don't stand a chance, of course," said Christopher smoothly. "Look, why don't you two join us for dinner?"

Martin was quick to answer "No, I don't think Mark . . ."

And Mark took his cue and helped out, "No, I don't think the doc, I'd imagine —"

"Oh, now, now come on," said Christopher and chuckled. "We need to get to know my son's circle of friends. Hmm? Don't we, darling?" He glanced at Margaret. "Let's all go in together. My treat. Why break up the party?"

Julie looked shyly at Mark and gave the sort of sigh, and the sort of shrug, that showed she was excited at the idea. "Thank you. That would be so great. I don't know that many people in the village yet, so . . . wonderful."

"Been keeping her pretty much hidden away. Hard at work." Mark smiled owlishly.

Everyone started to move through, carrying their drinks.

"I'll get some menus," said Martin, and turned away. He wanted to halt everything, so great was his frustration at not being allowed to speak out. Instead he had to pick up the menus and walk back towards their table. It was an incredible sight: Mark Mylow and Julie Mitchell, along with his preening father and silent mother . . . organising chairs to sit down together to a dinner that he, Martin, was obliged to attend all the way to the very final word. He had a grim feeling, also, that somewhere along the way they were all going to have to witness Mark's marriage proposal to Julie Mitchell.

CHAPTER
FOUR

The sea in the harbour looked iron-coloured. The cliffs on either side of the bay became giant repositories of cold. Just as in summer they became hot as radiators in the sun and you could hold your hands close and warm them, now the opposite was true: the rock face held on to the coldness of the previous night, and chilled the daylight hours.

Most of the holiday cottages along the front were now inhabited by their quota of families who chose to come down here for Christmas, and the decorations had thickened in this more charismatic quarter of the village where the centuries-old cottages stood on top of one another with a ramshackle crowdedness that gave, in effect, an effortless charm to the narrow, chaotic alleyways. Cascades of silvery fairy lights, strung along the eaves, gave some of the houses the appearance of being festooned with icicles, although the truth was, snow and ice were rare this close to the water and so far west. The windows of other houses were garnished with tinsel around their edges and, through many, the glittering lights of Christmas trees illuminated tree decorations kept carefully from one year to the next and, underneath the trees, piles of extravagantly

186

wrapped gifts, which had already been picked up and shaken, or small corners of their wrappings picked at, by enchanted and curious children. Portwenn's kitchens were stuffed with more luxurious brands of ingredients; the shelves of its larders spilled over with Christmas cakes and Christmas puddings perhaps made months ago, as well as tins of biscuits and dried fruits and large saucepans of mulled wine ready for heating through; the fridges couldn't cope with the size of the turkeys ready to be cooked on the following day, and were crowded with unusual cheeses and white wines and champagnes more expensive than usual. Every bedroom had its occupant, children were shoehorned in, grandparents found themselves having to deal with the narrow, twisted staircases once again, and everything that was said in one room was overheard by the occupants of the next one along.

Portwenn was full; and it was Christmas Eve.

Early that morning, before breakfast, Martin's father turned up unexpectedly to look around the surgery.

"Oh," said Martin, irritated.

"Your mother begged to be excused," said Christopher, stepping into the hallway and unwinding the yellow cashmere scarf from around his neck. "Got a bit of a head on her. Probably the red wine."

"I see."

"Well, this is homely," said Christopher, stepping into the reception area. Pauline's desk waited, neat and tidy, for her return.

Christopher wandered, looking here and there, as if visiting an art gallery. Abruptly, he swept behind Martin's desk and sat down. "So this is where the great man sits!" he exclaimed.

Martin frowned, confused at the feelings of dislike towards his father, who, it seemed, couldn't deliver a compliment without it seeming like an insult. "Indeed," he said.

Christopher slapped the desk. "It was entertaining, last night, wasn't it. That marriage proposal was priceless. How often does one get to witness one of those? Never."

"I'm glad you enjoyed yourself," said Martin.

"Possesses a wonderful naivety, your chum, the village bobby."

"Yes."

"And his girlfriend, dressed as a reindeer. He's going to have his work cut out there."

"How do you mean?"

"Well, the only way he's going to keep her is if he shuts the stable door now, and keeps it well and truly bolted at all times. Otherwise —"

"Dad."

"What?"

"What is the matter with Mum?"

Christopher straightened his shoulders. "She's tired," he said eventually.

"Oh, right. She's so tired she can't speak?"

"That's right."

"She's not ill? That's not what all this is about?"

"No, good grief. She's fit as a fiddle. Still wagging her tail in every way. You know your old mum."

"Not really, no," mumbled Martin under his breath.

"We going to have some breakfast, then? Is that possible?"

"I've got some eggs. Come through." Martin led his father through to his living quarters, to the kitchen. "Coffee, I presume."

"Long as it's decent." Christopher took off his overcoat and hung it up. He looked suspiciously into all the corners of the room. "What are you doing in this place, Marty?" he asked, as if it were impossibly beneath him.

"I prefer Martin, nowadays." Martin charged the espresso machine and turned on the heat for the eggs.

"Sorry, Martin. But, I mean . . . why here?"

"What? It's fine. I like it."

"Still got the flat in Kensington?"

"Yes."

Christopher gave a wry laugh.

"What?"

"Oh, nothing. Well. This whole Cornwall thing. It's obviously some sort of midlife crisis."

"No, it's not." The coffee machine began to make its slow hiss as the steam was pressed through the ground coffee.

"Then why d'you keep your place in London? Bolt-hole for light relief? Or are you heading back there as soon as you can?"

"I kept it on as an investment."

"I'm told house prices are rocketing up in Cornwall, as well."

Martin picked up two glasses and poured some orange juice. He pushed down the toast, and prepared to break the eggs into the frying pan. Was he really frying eggs for his father? It was incongruous. This one simple act, making this breakfast — a slice of toast, an egg, an orange juice and coffee — added up to a greater and more useful act of simple generosity than had ever travelled the other way, from his father to him. "Er, yes, I understand they have. Risen just as fast."

"Well, what are you waiting for? You think prices are going to fall? You should buy something decent before it's too late. Ah, you never did have any financial nous, Marty."

"Martin."

"Sorry, Martin. You used to drop your pocket money on the way to the shop." He gave a little laugh. "You should buy yourself a little farmhouse." He pointed to where Martin was emptying the eggs into the hot oil. "Free range eggs outside the door then. Fresh as you like." He paused. "What would that cost you, these days, d'you think? A place like Joan's?"

"Joan's? I don't know. Five hundred, six hundred thousand?"

"Hmm. See, there you go. Your whole flat would fit into her living room, and the flat's probably worth a bit more than half a mill."

"Breakfast is served," said Martin. He drew the eggs carefully onto the buttered toast, ground salt and pepper on the top, and set the plates on either side of the table.

"*Bon appetit!*" Christopher pulled his chair closer to the table. With the tip of his knife he lifted a corner of the egg as if something were hidden underneath. "I don't doubt," he added, "that it's going to be *bon appetit*."

"She's looking forward to seeing you, of course," said Martin. Whenever he made that first incision across a beautifully cooked egg, he liked it for innocently bleeding yellow and not red.

"Who?"

"Joan."

"Ah yes. Of course. Well, it's very decent of her to host us after all this time." Christopher chewed solidly. "I hope we can make a connection again, like we used to have."

"I'm sure she'd approve of that."

"I very much hope so. It's Christmas Eve. Spirit of goodwill."

Martin frowned. "One thing though."

"What's that?"

Don't expect anything much to do with Christmas, this evening. It's more likely we'll have to serve ourselves a bowl of soup while she heads outside because the pony's lame. And then she'll go to bed early to listen to the World Service."

"Well, too late, I'm afraid," said Christopher solemnly. "We've already bought her a fairly enormous Christmas gift."

★   ★   ★

In the days before Christmas, the population of Portwenn grew with the influx of visitors who came for the holiday. At the same time as visitors appeared, a proportion of the residents left the village in order to spend the holidays with family members elsewhere. There was one individual who also left the village. Graham Reynolds, from the Salvation Army, had made himself known to many of Portwenn's residents. He had even stopped outside PC Mark Mylow's police station, where the woman he was looking for was hidden away upstairs, and contemplated breaking his instructions not to talk to the police. He had decided in the end not to. He knew she was in the area somewhere, but he was going to have to give up and return home to his own family for Christmas. In the B & B up on the hill, he packed away his clothes and wash things, and laid the envelope containing the photographs on top, before zipping his bag closed.

Downstairs, he paid his bill, and walked to his car.

And then one, last minute, idea occurred to him. The doctor's surgery was one of those places — like the pub, and like the Spar grocery store — where people came and went, and where it could be assumed this girl might have reason to visit. He had left copies of the photographs with the pub and with Spar, pinned up on their noticeboards. He would make one more attempt to talk the village's doctor, and leave a set of photographs at their reception desk.

He walked down to the harbour, and up the other side to the doctor's surgery. There was no reply to his knock, and although he'd already talked to the receptionist, and tried to talk to the doctor, something told him that he shouldn't just accept defeat. It was rather like the feeling he got when he went fly-fishing, and was about to dismantle his rod and pack his reel and his fishing flies in the respective compartments of his fishing bag — just one more cast, he'd always tell himself. It's not that he ever caught anything, but he could never forgive himself for not trying, having had the thought. He took the envelope containing the photographs and wrote, on its front cover, a long message to Doctor Martin Ellingham. He explained the situation, and asked for the photographs to be left at the reception desk, together with his telephone number. And then he turned away from the closed door and left the village, heading for his own Christmas, in his own home.

The traditional, out-of-the-blue accident has no respect for a human ritual such as Christmas; and an accident, sometimes, doesn't wait to happen, and there are no combinations of circumstances that have all lined up and wait only for the final instruction. Some accidents leap out of the water, invisible until they snap up their victims.

Portwenn's fish and chip shop stood, like most of Portwenn's houses and shops, on a steep slope, and it seemed miraculous that the floor was level, with one end of the shop being so much lower than the other, and it seemed a miracle, as well, that the back wall of the establishment didn't topple over the cliff and fall into the sea, so close was its footing to the edge. This impression of instability was also evident inside, in the increasing age of the equipment, with the linoleum squares lifting in some places and the pattern worn in others, and, while it was clean and well run by Mrs Cronk, Peter's mother, the consistent dropping of white envelopes containing accounts of deficits from her electricity company, from her cooking oil supplier, from the council (business rates), from the equipment leasing company, from the insurance providers — all these together meant that the business itself clung to its viability only by a thread. Therefore, each time Mrs Cronk opened the locks, top and bottom, holding shut the glass door, she feared that this would be the session that would, instead of earning her enough to live and feed and clothe her son, push her over the edge into bankruptcy. Her chest tightened each time she turned the dial on the deep-fat fryer to 6 and yet she knew it was no good turning it instead to 5 — the speed and quality of her cooking was the first requirement of this establishment. She searched in vain for other areas where she might cut costs, but she knew her business depended on using the local fishermen's catch directly not least because they and their wives and children were her customers. She wished there could be, for once, a lift to her heart as she filled the tanks with oil and charged the basin again with her gloopy batter mixture that she so enjoyed the feel of. She so wished, as the heat behind her counter began to warm her through and bring a charge of blood to her complexion, that her house was this warm.

194

The practised movements would begin to take hold: fish into the flour, into the batter, into the oil, a swish of her hands in the soapy water to clean the gloop from her fingers, lift out the chips to inspect, tap the basket to leave behind as much of the hot oil as possible, lift the chips over and leave them to drain . . . And now she recognised the plumber, Bert and his son Al, coming in. Look, they were always kind to her son, Peter, talking and joking with him, admiring how he helped his mother. She knew their order in advance and she repeated the same actions: two fish into the flour, then draw them through the lovely silky batter, drop them into the deep fryer, swish her hands . . .

Except today, during the lunchtime shift on Christmas Eve, of all times, she swished her hands not in the basin of soapy water but — a terrible, stupid mistake — in the boiling hot oil, and the fiery heat tore at her nerves instantly and with a cry she pulled out her hand but it was too late: her fingers were flaming red already and she felt the terrible pain of the burn occupy her whole arm all at once and then course around her body. She nearly fainted.

Bert was there, holding her up, and pointing her hand under a cold tap. Her son, Peter, was already calling the doctor's surgery. Mrs Cronk found that she was standing in the firm embrace of Bert and she was repeating the same words, "I can't close the shop, I can't close . . ."

"There, there," Bert was saying, "'course you won't have to. Breathe now, breathe, don't forget to breathe."

But the air was stopped up tight in her chest and even when she sucked as hard as she could it felt like her throat had narrowed to a tiny filament and even that narrow passageway, with the odd convulsion now and again, shut tight. As soon as she'd taken her hand out from under the cold water it was on fire again and so, standing in Bert's embrace, she held it back under the cold water — and at the back of her mind she wished with all her heart that the water supply wasn't metered. This was like chucking pennies into the sea.

It didn't seem more than a few minutes before she heard Doc Martin's voice and the sound was a blessed relief. This was the man who had saved her son's life after all. She heard, "Right, give me some space," and then he was there, frowning at her injury. "I just need a moment." She fought with her breath. "To recover."

"Try not to speak," said Martin calmly. He glanced to one side. "Peter," he asked, "do you have any cling film?"

"Yes." Peter reached down to a shelf underneath the counter.

"Got to keep the air away from this," said Martin. He was already holding his mobile phone to his ear.

"That's a nasty burn, that is," said Al.

"Nasty," repeated his father, Bert.

"This is Doctor Ellingham," said Martin into his phone. "Portwenn surgery. I need an ambulance at the fish and chip shop on Rose Street."

"I can't leave the shop," Mrs Cronk tried to say, but there was no breath to carry the words out.

Martin carried on regardless. "Patient with acute asthma attack and burns to her hand." There was a pause. "Not quick enough," said Martin. There was another pause. "You sort it out," said Martin and dabbed the phone, dropped it in his suit pocket. "Ambulance on its way."

"I can't leave," hissed Mrs Cronk, "we need the money."

"You have to go." Peter's voice was certain.

"Can't go." Mrs Cronk shook her head.

Martin circled her hand and wrist with the roll of cling film.

"Hey, we could run the place for you," said Bert. He shifted his hat back on his head and peered into Mrs Cronk's face. "Don't worry, Mrs Cronk, I'll keep your business afloat for you. Just till you get back, like."

She was trying to say "For God's sake, no, no," but her breath only came in tiny sips and she didn't have time to load them up with any words. Instead she shook her head.

"It's all right, we will," said Bert, "we will." He put a hand on her shoulder. "We're not going to ignore someone in trouble, are we?"

Mrs Cronk shook her head repeatedly. It would be a disaster. It would. But she couldn't get the words out.

"That's right," said Bert, "we're not going to allow you to go under. We'll run the place for you. Me and Al."

Mrs Cronk gasped, but the next breath refused to come.

"Eh?" Al was mystified at his dad's offer. "How we going to do that then?"

"Well, I have some experience in the catering trade."

"Dad, we're plumbers."

"I know, I know that." He leaned closer to Mrs Cronk and spoke into her ear as if she were mentally sub-normal. "We will keep the place ticking over for you until you're better, OK? I don't suppose you were going to open on Christmas Day, anyway, were you? So we'll keep the show on the road today, and we'll open again on Boxing Day, and then you'll be back here yourself, I dare say. How's that?"

Mrs Cronk shook her head vigorously. Her hand burned like the fires of hell and her whole arm throbbed, but it was worse news if Bert took over the fish and chip shop during one of the busiest periods of the year, Christmas time. She was so frightened by that thought, on top of all the anguish and pain, that she couldn't speak.

"What's that?" Bert looked carefully into Mrs Cronk's pain-stricken face and he knew for certain that all this anxiety and panic, her breathless struggle for words, must be her attempt to thank him. What a good woman she was. A bit nervy, but salt of the earth. With great kindness, he squeezed her arm and smiled affectionately. "No, don't you worry. You're very welcome, love. Very welcome indeed. The least we can do. After all, it's Christmas time, and so, like, it's time for us to remember the parable of the Good Samaritan, isn't it? You won't catch Al and me walking past on the other side, let me tell you." And in Bert's good and generous heart, it was almost as if music sounded. "It'll be fine," he said. "Off you pop to the hospital, and get yourself right as rain, and we'll run the business for you." And now was the time for a little boast, maybe, and he'd do his best to make it come true. "And guess what, let's say we'll have enough money, I bet, by the time you come back, for you and little Peter to go on holiday, and all."

At the hospital, it was Peter who looked earnestly at Martin and told him what was what. "They're keeping her in for a couple of days," he said. "They've put her on a nebuliser for the asthma, Salbutamol. And for the burn they've just put her on morphine. Where have you been?" Peter was having to walk fast, now, to keep up with Martin.

"Talking to her doctor, but clearly I didn't need to," answered Martin. Half of Martin's walk was a run, for Peter.

"Mum's worried about where I'll sleep tonight."

"What's wrong with your house?"

"Nothing apart from the fact that I'll be all by myself. Which I'm guessing is against the law. So I'll have to stay with a responsible adult," he finished meaningfully.

Martin stopped abruptly and frowned at the boy whose life he'd saved, not many months since. "Um, no. Out of the question. Not with me."

"Why not?"

"Because it's simply not possible, obviously. And in any event I have to attend a family dinner with my mother and father at my aunt's house and it isn't something I can invite you to attend."

Martin drove Peter back to Portwenn, and from the passenger seat Peter talked about infections, skin grafts, scarring, psychological trauma and acid reflux until, just as it was getting dark, they returned to the seasonally decorated village. Most striking was the train of coloured light bulbs that was hung along the junction where the houses met the cliffs and the beach, the dividing line between the persistent timelessness of nature and the ever-changing human geography — the houses changing ownership, the births, marriages and deaths, the money made and lost, the desires and disappointments of its residents burning like so many lights in the eyes of Portwenn's resident souls. Christmas, somehow — the very notion of dressing up the home, of giving gifts, of celebrating kindness and generosity and forgiveness as opposed to intolerance and greed — gave the human side of this chain of lights a convincing victory, for a while, over the darker side, where nature's cruelty waited, forever patient, for the celebration to dwindle away into the new year.

The silver Lexus negotiated the narrow lanes from the top of the village down towards the sea. In the passenger seat, Peter Cronk noticed they didn't drive on down to the bottom and up to the surgery as he might have wished, but instead they stopped on the eastward slope and parked in the car park. He had a good idea where they were going and he shouldered his school bag, which he'd kept with him all this time, and followed the doctor's march down the narrow twisted alleyway to Louisa's house.

Martin rang the bell and they both waited.

Peter had run out of things to say, and it was obvious his strategy hadn't worked. He'd hoped, during the drive here, that if he'd said enough interesting things then Martin would have just carried on to the surgery, and they'd have continued to talk while sitting at either end of the supper table, and afterwards during the washing-up, and then, with great mutual respect, they'd have gone to their separate bedrooms like a pair of working doctors; and the next morning they'd have risen and spent the whole of Christmas Day discussing the most interesting case histories. He'd have his own stethoscope around his neck.

The door opened and Louisa was there, standing over him, immediately alive with sympathy. "Peter, I'm so sorry," she said. "I heard what happened to your mum. It's awful. Christmas time and everything. But I'm so pleased she's going to be all right."

How forlorn the boy looked, she thought. She could hardly bear to look at Martin standing there.

Martin's voice was stern and cold, compared with her sympathetic one. "Peter was hoping he could stay with you."

"No I wasn't," said Peter.

"Well . . ." said Louisa, very conscious they were standing on her threshold, and the words "no room at the inn" sprang to mind. This was hardly the time for turning someone away. "What an amazing idea. Christmas Eve night with me, Peter Cronk? Are you sure you'd like that best?" If she were to say no, it would feel like the start of a fairy tale in which she was the wicked witch.

"Of course he'd like it best," continued Martin. "As I've just explained to Peter, you're a woman."

"Glad you noticed," said Louisa.

"Years of medical training," said Martin. Something passed between them. A smile? No, the possibility of a smile. "Good. So that's settled then."

Peter looked up at Martin. "Please," he said. "I'll be dead quiet."

"Shushh," said Martin.

"Oh. Well, it looks like Peter would rather spend Christmas with you, Martin." She turned to Peter. "I'd love to have you, Peter, 'course I would, but I'm sure Martin would like to have you just as much as I would. So you can choose, can't you?" She looked at Martin boldly. It would do him good to have the boy she thought. It might actually turn him into a human being. In fact it suddenly seemed quite important that Peter should stay with Martin; he must. She had a sudden image of the two of them wearing paper hats, sitting at either end of a table with an enormous roast turkey on it. "I don't mind giving you up, Peter, if it's what you want," she finished.

Martin, under a guise of politeness, said, "It's out of the question. I have my parents staying with me for the first time in many years and this evening—"

"I thought they were staying at the Crab," interrupted Louisa. "So you've got a spare room."

202

"Yes, but they are, in effect, staying with me, and I am duty bound to give them my full attention. There is a family dinner that Peter can't possibly attend."

"Well, I'm hosting a Christmas party this evening, Martin, to which you were invited if you remember, and I'm duty bound to give a lot more people than that my full attention."

Martin turned to Peter with a stiff, courtly bow. "I'm sure you'll have a wonderful time with Louisa." He turned and walked quickly away.

Louisa's heart turned cold. So much for that vain hope then. She put a hand on Peter's shoulder. He looked solemn, as always. "Right," she said cheerfully. "D'you want to come in? It's good to see you, by the way." She shepherded him into the house. This was her enclave, her private space, and suddenly to have the school, as it were, or a figure representing the school, her working life, Peter, here in these rooms, during the holidays, was disturbing. And yet the cheerful decorations she'd made — streamers looping to the corners of the rooms, lines of Christmas cards, holly around the picture frames, tinsel draped around the door frames and of course the Christmas tree — seemed to offer themselves in a more optimistic way, with an actual child, Peter Cronk, walking among them, his rucksack still on his back, looking around to observe the place as he entered the sitting room, where the Christmas tree was aglow with fairy lights coloured in red and green and gold. Yes, to have a child in her care, tonight of all nights, gave her the sensation of living

203

inside a parable. His mother injured. His own house bleak and cold and empty. And yet here . . .

She realised with a lurch of responsibility that she would have to play Father Christmas.

Underneath Portwenn's houses, the channels of water that ran in stone-built gulleys spilled more loudly at this time of year, chock-full of winter rains and carrying a heavier freight of debris onto the upper stretch of the beach.

With its curtains closed against its view of that cold, inhospitable beach, the Crab and Lobster worked hard for its guests and for the town's Christmas Eve revellers; the stoves and ovens burned fiercely and the pumps pressed the beer from the barrels in the cellar up to the bar at three times the normal volume.

Two more senior figures, a man and a woman, waited in the shelter of the pub's porch, guarding a large square parcel wrapped in silver paper. Unlike everyone else, who was heading into the pub, Mr and Mrs Ellingham waited to be taken out. They wondered why their son Martin was late.

Martin, the adrenalin from the afternoon's events still in his system, and dressed as always in a fresh, clean suit and tie, steered the Lexus down to the harbour and picked up his parents, who said nothing about their ten-minute wait. Seconds later, they were driving up through Portwenn's narrow streets to the cliff top.

Next to Martin in the darkened interior of the Lexus sat his father, also dressed in a suit and tie, but sensibly wearing a jersey of fine maroon wool under his jacket. In the back seat was Martin's mother Margaret, wrapped in a warm coat, which hadn't seen a day's use during their retirement in Portugal. Silently the vehicle gained the main road and turned towards Haven Farm.

Martin could never perform small talk; the empty space left by this deficiency was dutifully filled by Christopher who related an incident from the childhood he'd shared with Joan, his sister, at Haven Farm, which had involved the loss of her pet tortoise, and it being discovered again in the garden two years later, completely unharmed. "She never once stopped looking for that tortoise," he finished. "If she hadn't found it, I dare say she'd still be out there in the garden every day, looking for it still."

The headlights swept over the gateway to Haven Farm; the entrance had been left hospitably open, which was unusual. The light over the porch was on, too. Martin expected Joan to appear from a shed covered in mud, but there was no sign of her.

Christopher moved to the rear of the car and lifted out the large square parcel.

Margaret tucked herself on his other arm, and the trio walked to the porch.

Christopher paused to look up at the house, which stared confidently from its lighted windows over the same farmyard as ever was, during all the years he'd been alive. "It's smaller than I remember it," he commented.

Martin, for one sharp, unfair moment, hated the awful, punishing silence of his mother. Frustrated, he had flat out asked her, the previous day, "Mum, is something wrong?" She'd answered a plain, "No." This was obviously untrue, and therefore he'd tried one further question. "Is there anything I can do to help?" She'd given the same answer, "No," which of course had implied there *was* something wrong, but she wasn't offering him her confidence. All he could do was put up with it, and watch his father gamely try to further whatever it was that this visit was about.

As they gained the porch, Martin noticed the flagstones were freshly swept, and around the door knocker was wrapped a strand of gold tinsel.

Their knock sounded against the ancient door, and shortly it opened to reveal Joan wearing something he'd never seen before: a smart woollen skirt and a sleeveless puffa jacket for the cold, an item of jewellery at her throat, and a touch of eye shadow and lipstick. Her sheep's wool hair had been tamed. She said to her brother, "Is this the olive branch then? After all this time?"

"Ah! If you'd softened up in your old age, I'd have been very disappointed," said Christopher. He thrust forward the square parcel. "But yes, it is."

"I suppose this is me accepting it then. Apparently it is. But don't expect me just to forget. Come in, anyway." She ignored the gift and it was left to Christopher to carry it in.

Martin indicated for his mother to go before him, and then he followed his parents into the house. He immediately noticed the differences: the overhead light was switched off and instead a lamp stood on the side table, which gave the hallway a cottagey glow, helped by a candle — and another — standing nearby. There was tinsel looped across the top of the mirror and over the top of the picture. A smell of cooking filled the air.

"I sent you some letters recently," said Christopher. "Well, several." He slid the silver box onto the hall table.

"I know," said Joan. "I didn't open them."

"Well, just to say, I was trying not to make it such a surprise that we wanted to come and share Christmas with you."

"Well, I'm sorry about tomorrow, but I have to stick with my friend, Mrs Steel, as it's her first in the old people's home. But I hope this evening will do just as well for us."

"It's better," said Christopher. "I always prefer Christmas Eve to the day itself."

They went through to the kitchen, which had been transformed. It was uncommonly warm. The table had been cleared of the usual clutter and a white paper tablecloth overlaid a red one. Along the centre of the table, the flames of five candles moved gently. A Yule log gave the table its centre decoration. Gold and green Christmas crackers lined up alongside the place settings. Hanging from the roof beams were strings of glowing fairy lights. On each place setting were a knife and fork and spoon, plus a side plate, although they were all mismatched.

"Joan. You've gone to such trouble. This looks lovely." It was a rare comment from his mother, and Martin felt a sense of dread. It was slightly embarrassing, this amount of effort, from his Aunt Joan. Martin had never seen the like.

"Well," said Joan, "welcome to Haven Farm."

"It's a beautiful table," said Christopher, removing his jacket to reveal the maroon jumper underneath. He slung the jacket on the back of a chair, as if he were about to start work. "Thanks ever so, Joan, for such a welcome. You are a great host."

Joan put on the apron that she'd only just removed to answer the door. "A drink for everyone? Martin, would you do the honours?"

"Damn," said Christopher in dismay. "We bought some champagne but left it in the hotel room."

"There's plenty of wine here," said Joan quickly.

Martin noticed that Christopher and Joan, brother and sister, had hardly looked at each other. And yet they'd spent their childhood holidays here, just as he had. He tried to picture them as children, but only ended up remembering the family photographs he'd happened to see, over the years.

"It's so great to see the old place." Christopher strode around, rubbing his hands. He pointed at the curtains drawn across the kitchen window. "D'you remember? Out there is where Uncle Dick used to have his sheds. Joan and I smashed this window, once, playing football. Remember, Joan, the rollicking he gave us?"

"You played the football, I got the rollicking, if I remember rightly." Joan looked hot, lifting out the roast potatoes and turning them over to brown on all sides.

Martin set out four glasses and poured red wine, and an orange juice for himself.

Margaret sat daintily at the table and smoothed her fingertips over the cloth, as if impressed with the texture.

Christopher edged the curtain to one side and looked out. "This farm," he exclaimed. "So many memories, for both of us, Joan."

"Mmm?" Joan wrestled the tray of potatoes back into the top of the oven.

"How long have we been coming here?"

"We? Well, to be honest I haven't counted. I was four years old, wasn't I, when we came for our first holiday? A long time ago."

Martin carried around the wine glasses.

"But why exactly have you come back?" asked Joan in a typically straightforward way. She lifted the greens into the steamer, and then onto the stove.

"Must be like a salmon upstream," said Christopher. "Just seeking to consolidate the old roots."

For a while they indulged in childhood memories, and Martin and his mother listened. The turkey was lifted from the oven and sat there for ten minutes, wearing a coat of silver foil. The steam from the greens worried away at the lid, and the gravy jug warmed through in the bottom oven.

"Martin," said Joan. "The turkey's rested. Carve it, please."

"Cheers to all of us," said Christopher and gave his glass a lift. "To the family."

"Cheers," said Margaret dutifully.

Martin lifted his empty glass of orange juice. "Yes, cheers," he said in a tone that told of his curiosity — what on earth were they all doing here?

Joan banged open both the oven doors and fetched out the roast parsnips and the roast potatoes. "Right," she said. "Time to eat." She barged the potatoes aside with the parsnips. "By the time we've served it out, the greens will be cooked." She gave the impression she wanted to hurry this meal along.

Martin considered the effort Joan had gone to with her dress, and the food, and the room's decoration; he hoped his mother and father realised how unusual it was.

"I've got you a present that should do ideally well for this kitchen," said Christopher, "seeing as you're such a cook."

"Greens to be served," said Joan. "Gravy on the table." She pointed. Martin did her bidding. He was glad to have something to do so he wouldn't have to look at his mother, who sat strangely composed, as if she were in a church. He realised, then, that all of them around this table had the same agenda: just to get through this.

Christopher was on the track of his childhood memories again. "Strange to think of us as kids, being in this very room, isn't it? Joan?"

"Hmmm?"

"And Mum and Dad, and Uncle Dick . . . Like ghosts."

"I hardly think of those days," said Joan. "Perhaps I'm just too busy, too much to do." As if to prove it, she

210

banged the warmed jug down on the surface and poured the gravy out from the saucepan. "It's sit where you like, really."

"Yes, must be a bit of a burden, the old place." Christopher drew back the chair with his jacket hanging off the back, and sat down. He glanced at his wife. "Lot of work. Always was."

"Oh, yes, of course." Joan sounded hassled. "It's a farm, after all. Bottomless pit of work."

"Too much, d'you think? For you?"

"Oh much too much," said Joan cheerfully. "Ridiculous, really. But, luckily, I do love it quite a bit, which makes a huge difference."

This was strange, thought Martin. There was a hint that his aunt and his father were about to get on. As he began to serve food onto the plates and position them on the table, Martin watched his father's expression, which was one of concern, as if he were a psychotherapist rebuilding a fragile patient.

"Too many animals, I suppose," said Christopher.

"Not really the animals," said Joan. "I never seem to mind them. It's the upkeep that causes me the bother. The hedging, the fences, the strimming, the topping, the broken slates on the roofs. Maybe because I always have to ask for help in doing a lot of that stuff, and it's a major drag on expenses. The old iron water pipe is going to have to be replaced this year — it's rusted through. The rust literally has filled the pipe, there's just a little channel this big, like a wormhole, so there's only a trickle of water getting through, and what with supplying the troughs as well as the house . . . you can see . . . I wonder, sometimes, if I'm going to survive another year. But I have to, I simply have to."

And as they all worked with knives and forks to eat the food she'd put in front of them, Joan continued, like a tap that had suddenly been unstuck. "And maybe part of that is being alone, you know, up here. I mean, of course, I have many good friends, and thank God for that, and they come running if I call them. They do. Completely marvellous. At the drop of a hat." She frowned and they could see she was remembering all the occasions when her friends had done just that. "But it's still, you know, wake up and alone you face the demands of the lovely animals for water and for food and for shelter. And they look at you with their lovely faces. Do you know how lovely . . . are the faces of animals? Sheep and cows and dogs and cats and chickens. They wear this expression on their faces and do you know what it is, that expression? It's trust. Isn't it? Even if you're about to . . . maybe especially when you're about to . . . kill and eat them, for heaven's sake." She pronged a bit of the breast meat from the turkey she'd raised herself, one of around thirty or so that she farmed for the local butcher. She chewed with a look of sorrow, suddenly. "And I have become pretty good at mending things. Not bad with a hammer and nails. Not too bad with a screwdriver and a drill. But the heavier stuff: I can't tension a wire fence. I certainly can't lift up a hundredweight sack like I used to, so thank God they don't use hundredweights any more. But I can't even lift the half-hundredweights, now . . . I can't for the life of me mend the tractor, unless it's just

212

to fix the wobbly seat. Hydraulics and engines are double Dutch to me." She lifted the wine glass, but it was empty. She stared into it.

Martin poured more for her, and for his parents. They had all finished eating, while Joan was only halfway through because she'd been talking so much.

She didn't want to hold them up. She picked up her cracker and crossed her arms across her chest. "Quick now, we have to do the crackers, so we can all wear ridiculous paper hats and tell jokes." She immediately saw there was no way they could reach all the way around the table with only four of them, so she uncrossed her arms and simply pointed her cracker at her brother, while snapping her fingers at Margaret. "Come on, Margaret. Buck up."

Carefully Margaret lifted her cracker and offered one end of it into Joan's waiting hand.

"That's the spirit," said Joan.

Martin didn't hold with any kind of group entertainment or organised jollity, even on such a small scale, so he was having to work hard even to stay in his seat, but for his Aunt Joan he would go with it. He offered his cracker to his mother, and accepted the other end of his father's.

"Pull," said Aunt Joan.

They leaned and pulled clumsily; the crackers went off. Christopher was the quickest to get in among his stuff and find the paper hat, and read the joke. "'A man walked into a bar. Ouch.'"

Joan said, "One for you, Marty. "'Doctor, I feel so unfit,' said Father Christmas. The doctor replied, "You need to go to an elf farm.'""

"Ha ha," said Christopher.

"'What do you call two happy mushrooms?'" asked Martin lugubriously. "'Fun guys.'"

"Urrrr," groaned Joan.

Margaret took her time but was obliged to read hers out, too. "'Why couldn't the skeleton go to the Christmas party?'" She waited, while the others tried to dream up an answer. "'Because it didn't have anybody to go with,'" she finished.

"Gawd," said Christopher and guffawed loudly. "Why do we do it to ourselves, eh?" And then he turned to his sister and put his hand over the top of hers. "It has been a complete privilege to hear about your work here, Joan," he said. "And I can see how very hard it must be."

"Sorry, didn't mean to bang on." She was the only one with food left on her plate, so she spoke and ate at the same time.

"No, no, I can't tell you, it gives me such intense pleasure to hear just what you've achieved, what you've done with your life."

"Sometimes . . ." Joan had swallowed too early, and she laid down her fork in order to hold a knuckle against her mouth and wait for the food to go down. "Sometimes," she went on, "I think someone's going to come and pick *me* up by the scruff of the neck, and knock me on the head, and it will turn out . . . that I am just a creature on someone else's much bigger farm,

214

a farm so big that I can't see where it ends or begins. Ridiculous notion, of course. Anyway, I'm far too old to be worth anything, for the pot." With the cooking, and the wine, and the anxiety at her brother's visit, and the business of the paper hats, her hair was beginning to come apart, to revert to its usual sheep's wool look, and Martin saw that her laugh, her smile, suddenly was a smile from her youth. "And every day," she said, "the mud feels heavier on my boots." Suddenly it looked as if she might be about to cry.

"Here's to mud on our boots," said Christopher.

They lifted their glasses and repeated, "Mud on our boots."

How odd they all looked. It was as if the paper hats defined both the event itself — Christmas Eve — and their personalities: the magenta one on Joan's head was bashed in and slightly torn by her habitually running her fingers through her hair and resettling the hat; the crisp golden one sat rather primly on Christopher's head, still with its creases; the purple one that was meant to be on Margaret's head lay, still folded, next to her plate, signifying her refusal to join in; Martin's green hat was so uncomfortably, dutifully worn that it was going to be swept off and screwed into a ball at the earliest opportunity.

Christopher, his golden hat worn sombrely and with a sense of occasion, was obviously worried about his sister. "I think you have to consider getting somewhere smaller," he said. "Don't you? More modern. Less work. You shouldn't be working so hard."

"But I love it, you see."

"We love our place in Portugal. Something like that — you would love it too."

"Portugal?"

"I don't mean Portugal, obviously. I mean something around here. I mean something smaller, all on one level. And still a few animals about. A cat, a dog. But not a whole farm. Good idea, given your age, as you say yourself."

"Good grief no," said Joan easily "I'd die of boredom."

"You ought to think about it. Seriously."

"What are you talking about, Christopher?"

"Well, only that this might be an opportunity for both of us to reorganise. I know I want to."

"Reorganise. What do you mean? I thought you were happy in Portugal?"

"It's only idle thinking. Thinking out loud. But you remember that Uncle Dick left this place . . . left Haven Farm to both of us."

"Well, yes, of course. Of course I know that, but—"

"And my half of the farm has sort of . . . well, *sat* here, hasn't it. Sat here quite happily, I should say. Very well looked after by you."

"But . . . but you said that Phil and I could have it."

"Live in it, exactly, yes."

"Live in it? I don't understand. You said this farm was small change for a surgeon."

"Yes, exactly, it is, or was, but I suppose I'm only having this conversation because we're both so much older. It's like we're returning to childhood, isn't it, into who we were before, and, just now, seeing your distress at living in this place—"

Joan interrupted, "That wasn't distress . . . at living in this place. It was *love* of this place."

"Well, circumstances change. We've all changed. We've got older. And there might be the opportunity for both of us to get what we want, if you take your half, and I take my half . . . and . . . a new life beckons." He picked up his glass and twirled it.

"You want to take your half? Oh." Panic crept into her voice. "But . . . I don't have any money. I mean, I don't know how much this place is even worth."

Christopher leaned forwards. "Martin . . . Martin estimated it was round about the six hundred K mark."

Joan stared at her nephew. She sounded incredulous. "*Martin?* You are in on this?"

"Hold on a minute, I said that only after—"

"So you *did* say that?"

Christopher interrupted, "That's what he judged the house to be worth. The land as well . . . sixty-three acres I understand."

Joan stood up sharply and sent her chair tipping backwards with a crash. "Oh God. Oh God." She held both hands over her mouth, like she'd made a dreadful, fatal mistake. She stared at her brother with a look of incomprehension.

Martin rose to his feet as well. "I didn't mean—" he began.

Joan interrupted; and suddenly her voice was strong again, and certain — although she talked to the ceiling, to the walls, to the table; she couldn't trust herself to look anyone around that table in the eye. "I couldn't raise half that. I couldn't raise a quarter or an eighth of it, not at my age. We'd . . . we'd have to sell the house. It would be impossible." But then she glared full bore at her brother. "You have got to be bloody joking."

"Well, I think you're forgetting the conversation we've just had, when you talked so movingly about the stresses and the difficulties of living here, which was the very thing that led me to making the offer."

"The *offer*!" Joan pulled at her sheep's wool hair, finally knocking the magenta paper hat carelessly from her head. She said loudly, "Get out." She ducked and roughly blew out the nearest candle. "Out!"

"Joan—"

"Get out, you bastard!" Her violent shout was followed by her scraping the leftovers from one plate to another. There was a clash of crockery, clumsily handled, and knives and forks dropped to the floor. Her face was reddened by anger.

"Aunty Joan," began Martin, "there's no way that you—"

"*And* you, Martin!" She picked up a gnawed leg of the turkey and threw it back down on the plate.

"What?"

She glared at him. "Well. How dare you?"

"I didn't *dare* anything. If you'll just listen, I didn't . . ."

Joan flung out an arm, the forefinger pointing accusingly at Margaret, and she said to him, "I've been more of a mother to you than she ever was. And now you collude with these poisonous . . ." Words failed her.

218

It was Margaret's turn to rise. She said in a tired voice, as if this whole scene was nothing to do with her and she was only in a hurry to get away, "Martin. The car. Please."

Martin felt a sense of dread. This was what the visit had been about. At the same time he was horrified — at the misunderstanding, and that he had been unwittingly recruited by his father. "Aunty Joan, I want to explain."

"I don't want to listen, I don't want to have been made a fool of, I don't want this visit ever to have happened, I don't want . . . any of you, ever again, in this house. Go, get out!"

"I was in no way aware that the sale of the house was even under consideration," began Martin.

"Enough!"

Christopher was unhooking his jacket from the back of his chair. The golden paper hat made it difficult for him to be taken seriously, but he looked grave, self-important. "I think now's not the time, Marty. Your mother's upset. Joan's upset. We're all upset. Best to separate ourselves off." He began to walk towards the hallway, where his wife waited, staring at the front door as if she were waiting on a station platform for a train to arrive that would take her away. "Let's all spend some hours apart, and speak again in a day or two."

Martin's green paper hat was a compressed ball in his hand. He stayed behind to make another attempt to explain to his aunt that he wasn't part of this initiative and had known nothing about it. "Aunty Joan—"

"OUT!"

"It was part of a different conversation; I had absolutely no idea that he—"

"Martin!" She stamped her foot. "I shall scream and go mad if I am not left alone!"

In the car on the way home, it was as if the whole visit was equivalent to a boil that had been lanced: the ugly truth was plainly there, but there was a measure of relief, in Martin, that the purpose of his parents' visit had been revealed and he could go back to disliking them as plainly and as utterly as he'd always done, safe in the knowledge there was no need ever to contemplate a reconciliation. And everything that was to be said, now, on this journey home, would confirm this.

Christopher attempted to claim the moral high ground that he seriously believed was available to him. "I know you're fond of Joan," he said to Martin, "but you should keep out of things that don't concern you."

Martin was so angered by this instruction that he wagged the steering wheel, and mismanaged a gear change. "It *does* concern me. She's my aunt. And I live here, in the same area as she does."

"It's between me and my sister," said Christopher.

"What are you doing with Joan? It can't really be about the money. You've got a private income, haven't you? More than one pension."

"It is about the money. Isn't it always? I have a deal pending. There's a bridging loan. It's complicated. And I don't have to justify myself to you. Look at you. What are you doing here, buried away in the middle of

220

nowhere? Wiping people's noses and cutting their corns. Playing at doctors in Portwenn. It's ridiculous. Who are you trying to kid?"

"There's nothing ridiculous about it. I am responsible for the health care of this community, and that's a duty I take very seriously indeed." Just as he was saying this, the car headlights pointed over the rise and downwards and there was Portwenn, dressed in its Christmas lights, and with an avenue of moonlight leading from the moon's disc to the village's small harbour; and the rise of pride in him, at his work, and at all that had happened here, caused an uncomfortable constriction in his chest.

"Oh, please," said his father.

There would never be any need for a reconciliation, Martin realised. Ever. He wondered at his mother's descent into silence the previous day. What did she think about all this? Come to that, what did she think about anything? But he needn't mind about either of them any more.

When they pulled up outside the Crab and Lobster, the smokers could be seen gathered around the doorway, coats and collars fully buttoned against the cold, and the sounds of revelry from within could easily be heard — the Christmas cheer of Portwenn's residents in stark contrast to the glacial chill that presided over Martin and his parents. Christopher was first out of the car with what sounded like a ridiculous statement, "See you tomorrow," before striding between the smokers and into the porch. Martin had the good manners to open the car door for his mother to get out.

"Listen, I've had enough of this, of your silence. I want you to tell me what exactly it is you want with Joan's money."

"You're not like your father at all, are you?" Her mouth twisted and she looked tired.

"What?"

"No, you're not like him, not one bit." She began to walk towards the pub and Martin kept alongside. She appeared to be talking to herself, or to the pavement underneath her feet, or to the dark Portwenn sky, but at least, finally, she was talking. "He reached the very top of his profession," she said. "He is charming. Still a handsome man, even now. We were happy, you know, before you were born."

Martin felt the cold truth slide in like a knife. Happiness, before he was born — and then he'd come along and ruined everything. By now they had reached the gang of smokers, most of whom he recognised even if he couldn't remember their names. They blew smoke like dragons, and competed with one another to give the funniest lines; they flirted with one another and leaned into their friendships, and they celebrated Christmas. And they were close enough to overhear, should they have wanted to break away from their revelry and good humour. His mother, who had aroused in him nothing but panic and dislike his whole life long, turned and looked him in the eye and in a very quiet voice she gave a summary of his childhood years.

"We had a perfect marriage, your father and I. He was always touching me under the table in a restaurant, in the car, or . . . it was like electricity. Then you came along. I knew it was all over. He never saw me as a woman again. Instead I was your mother. A deflated balloon. So I tried to make things just as they had been before, just him and me together. I put you in boarding school, and sent you to spend the summers here with Joan. But it didn't work. Somehow you were always there between us. Always needy. Always bullied and teased and wetting your bed. When I couldn't get his attention, there was always his money. Then we lost everything. Did he tell you that? Lost it on some bloody fictitious golf development in the Algarve. We only have the villa because he put it in my name for tax reasons. That's when I realised what our marriage had become. A marriage of convenience. A tax arrangement."

Suddenly, Martin didn't want to know any of this — the less he knew, the easier it was going to be to forget about his parents, and escape. "I don't want—" he began.

She carried on regardless. "I've met someone else. Someone who looks at me and sees . . . a bloody *woman*. He's moving in with me. That's why your father needs somewhere else to live. Forty years. Forty years of clinging on to your father. Forty years of my life wasted. There, is that enough of my speaking, my *talking*, for you?" She started to head into the pub.

"I'm . . . sorry to hear you've been unhappy," said Martin formally. He felt like he was escorting a foreign delegation from an unknown country into their overnight accommodation.

"Because of you," confirmed Margaret.

Martin wasn't quite sure where his next words came from, but he said them very simply and was glad to say them, because he meant it, as an instruction, something that was going to be good for her, and for him. "Then we must say goodbye," he said.

He turned on his heel and walked back to the car. He climbed in and, when he shut the door, he felt no wish to glance back and see if she'd made it through the wisecracking smokers and into the pub. He had no desire to see either of his parents ever again.

The headlights illuminated the mouth of the beach, the sand more tumultuous and untidy in winter, scattered with debris and inhospitable. The enormous darkness yawned out to sea, out of reach of the village's Christmas brightness. Next, the headlights caught the shuttered doors of the fish market, with its red-and-white sign, JUST SHELLFISH — PORTWENN CRAB AND LOBSTER — ORDERS TAKEN. In summer, the aquarium had been open, but not now. And then the car and its searching headlights filled the narrow lane between the stone wall of the fish market and those of the shops and houses, which leaned up this westward side of the cove towards the surgery.

When he'd parked and walked to his house, he was glad to be back so early, to gain the sanctuary of privacy. He unlocked the door and walked in, and felt, without consciously expressing it in lucid thought, that his relationship with the world had changed and he'd severed a connection with his parents that had lingered, and troubled him, which had kept him, in fact, like an intemperate child.

Behind him he could feel the stirring of the village as it moved towards Midnight Mass, towards the extended opening time of the Crab, towards the time when hundreds of different versions of Santa Claus would manifest themselves in the bedrooms of all Portwenn's children.

But all that was for other people. For himself, though, he now gained the much-needed sanctuary of his private, solitary home. He would listen to the radio and read, before the rituals of bathroom and bedroom. He was beginning to appreciate the silence of the cliff into which his home was built: its unquestioning acceptance, and its shelter, its comforting weight and solidity. Most perfect of all was that within the four walls of his modest home there was not a single other human presence.

For Louisa, Christmas Eve had passed on a separate track, and in a very different mood. At around 5p.m. Peter Cronk had been delivered to her house like so much lost luggage and somehow, at the last minute and with only a few hours to spare, she'd have to find a Christmas stocking for him, as well as suitable things to put in the stocking, and she'd have to wrap them, and put a gift for him under the tree. She would need to do this secretly and quickly, and yet it was a tiny cottage, and he was right there, under her feet.

It was warm in Louisa's cottage and Peter unshouldered his coat and his hoodie, but he found that with one arm still left in the sleeve, Louisa suddenly stopped him.

"Peter," said Louisa, "you haven't got anything to stay the night with, right? So why don't you quickly walk on up to your place and pack some stuff in a rucksack, clothes for tomorrow, your toothbrush and all that, and quickly come back? Then we can relax and not think about a thing. And it will give me a chance to get your room ready, make up your bed. You happy doing that on your own? Do you have your own key?"

"Yes." Peter shrugged back into his coat. "OK." He was aware of the glow that shone from Louisa's skin, the youthful quickness of her speech and her actions, compared to his mother, who was old enough and tired enough to dip her hand into boiling chip fat by mistake. Louisa's ponytail swung energetically, whereas his mother's hair hung limp as an old flannel on her head. There was a fresh youthfulness to Louisa's clothes, as if they'd been freshly unwrapped, worn for the first time. His mother's clothes were as tired and grey as she was. Louisa's shoes moved deftly across the carpeted living room of the low-ceilinged cottage, whereas his mother's . . .

"Come back as quick as you can," she said.

"Will do." He hoped Louisa wasn't going to expect him to attend this Christmas party; he didn't want to be fobbed off with any kind of Christmas gift, or Christmas stocking, either — or any other kind of celebratory item. Hopefully, he prayed, it would be too late for any of that nonsense. It would suit him best to sit down with a plate of fast food and watch a horror movie, all alone, late at night, with a bowl of mini Mars bars to get him through the small hours, with neither help nor interruption.

He stepped out into the cold December air, which was laden with the salty moisture of the sea. Cries of revelry had already started to carry on the air, even though it had only just gone 5p.m.

He started walking towards home. With each step he was aware of the Christmases of others, and not having, nor wanting, one of his own. Behind every door a fire was blazing or a bottle was being uncorked. There wasn't time for anyone to remember his mum in hospital with her burned hand.

When he reached his own house, the glass panel in the front door was dark. He turned the Chubb and the Yale locks and walked into the chill and silent hallway. The decorations were a ghostly commentary on the absence of his mother and himself. The light switch clicked underneath his finger, and the gloom, the emptiness, seemed even more powerfully present, having been illuminated by such a harsh light. Quickly, he climbed the stairs and went into his bedroom, which suddenly didn't seem to welcome him at all; he felt like a stranger. He unzipped his rucksack and walked to and fro to put together a spare set of clothes, some wash things, some books, but his instinct was to leave as quickly as possible. On the bed — put there by his mum — was the enormous red-and-white knitted sock that she brought out every year for Father Christmas.

He couldn't quite remember where this giant sock had originally come from; it had always reappeared as if by magic every Christmas Eve. On Christmas mornings — tomorrow morning — it would have been filled with chocolates and sweets, perhaps some tricks from the joke shop, a silly mask, some writing pens and stuff for school, usually a second-hand paperback or two that he had to pretend to read.

Well, he wasn't going to have to put up with that part of Christmas morning this year. He was escaping from the whole nonsense.

And yet, when he came to leave his bedroom, he found it difficult to leave the giant knitted sock behind. It looked so forlorn. What would happen if his mother, for some reason, was discharged from hospital and came back here and saw it? It would seem to take away from all her efforts to keep life going as normal, to keep life good for him.

With a grumble of frustration and bad temper, he snatched it up and stuffed it into the top of his rucksack.

While Peter had gone back to his house to collect his overnight belongings, Louisa rushed to the drawer where she'd only just packed away the remnants of this year's wrapping paper. She pulled out the last dregs of several different rolls and chucked them on the kitchen table. She snatched scissors from a drawer, and the Sellotape dispenser from its cupboard above the fridge.

Of course it was all very well to have the wrapping, but what could she give Peter as a gift? She sorted through the parcels under the tree, to think if there was anything she could claw back from somebody else. She walked around the house, staring at Christmas tree decorations, at her book shelves, into her food cupboards, to see if there was anything that would make a good present. Her eye fell on her chessboard, on the shelf next to the television, and never used. It was quite a smart travel set — magnetic — and it looked in perfect condition. There was a good chance Peter might like it. She slid the box from between the other games and took it to the table to wrap it. For a label, she cut out a picture of a Santa Claus from one of the Christmas cards hanging from lines hung across her kitchen. She wrote on it, "For Peter, who came to stay for Christmas — lucky me. Much love from your head teacher and your friend, Miss Louisa Glasson." In five minutes it was under the tree with the others. She felt powerfully pleased. One down and two to go — a Christmas stocking for Peter, and keep the Christmas party on track.

She glanced at her watch — not long until her guests arrived. She would have to be quick: what on earth could she put in a Christmas stocking for Peter? Her hand closed on a satsuma from the bowl . . . but what kind of sock could she find? Some people used a pillowcase instead of a sock, but how on earth could she find enough to fill a pillowcase? She carried the satsuma at a trot up the narrow, crooked staircase, cursing Martin because this was a bore to have to do, just when she should have been getting ready. She turned over the contents of her sock drawer and saw her red pair — longer than ankle socks and they would stretch long enough. She took one of them and dropped the satsuma into it; it landed with a heavily satisfying "thump" at the bottom. A quick tour of the kitchen and she found a bag of mixed nuts and a luxury tin of biscuits. With each back and forth from the kitchen to the living room, she glanced at the Christmas cake which stood under its tinfoil shield on the kitchen surface, wondering whether or not to do it — was Peter old enough? In some ways he was older than she was . . . She lifted off the tinfoil and looked at the cake. Specifically, she examined the three tiny plastic figures arranged on top: a little Joseph, with his long brown beard, leaning on a staff; a Mary with a halo of yellow plastic hair, her hands folded over her midriff, her eyes cast down; while underneath Mary's gaze rested a crib containing the tightly wrapped body and the tiny pink face of the infant Jesus. These were among her most valuable and cherished items, made in the 1960s — and yet the spirit of Christmas, surely, demanded from her such an act of generosity.

Peter Cronk was as good as a surrogate son to her, after that conversation they'd had last summer on the cliff top while eating ice-cream cones. She could explain the importance of the figures — how they'd come from Christmas cakes that her grandmother had made, during her own childhood. It was important, suddenly, that Peter Cronk had them, even if he kept them locked away at home until he had children of his own. She enjoyed the thought of an adult Peter Cronk using the decorations for his own family, and remembering his old head teacher from that little town in Cornwall, where he'd grown up. His memories would be full of affection for her, an old lady now, with children of her own . . . and a husband . . .

It was no longer a bore to fill this Christmas stocking for Peter Cronk, but it was as if she had physically to lift aside the image of Martin Ellingham and replace it with Danny Steel, surely — the younger man, and a man who loved her, and whom she . . . No, she didn't love Danny Steel. She couldn't — she wasn't allowed — to love Martin.

She plucked each figure in turn from the top of the cake, washed and dried them carefully, and wrapped them in leftover bits of the most glamorous paper different from the pattern she'd used for Peter Cronk's travel chess gift. Then she pushed the figures into the red sock, followed by foil parcels she neatly made containing three or four of the choicest types of biscuits taken from the Christmas tin. It was a small Christmas stocking, but a powerful one. He'd remember it forever. She carried the bulging red sock upstairs and hid it under her pillow. It was going to be the first time she'd ever played Santa Claus.

Now she was behind with preparations for the party and, just to remind her, the doorbell went as she tripped downstairs. It was her cousin, who could be press-ganged into helping. The extra rush and hurry caused by Peter's sudden arrival had added to the feeling of Christmas, she realised — someone in trouble taken in, given shelter. Her own life, and this small Christmas Eve party she was hosting in her even smaller cottage became more valuable, more spirited.

She hurriedly pulled her cousin from the cold outside into the warmth of the house, and admired her dress when the latter took off her coat. And then it was straight through to the kitchen, to set out the glasses on trays, to peel back the cling film from the dips and set them in various places around the living room, accompanied by jars holding carrot sticks, bread sticks and cucumber sticks. She rested her fingers against the bottles of champagne in the fridge to see how cool they were, and moved three of them to the freezer; she unlatched the heavy door of the log burner and threw in two more logs and wriggled the poker in the embers to make the logs sit down in the heat and catch fire.

Louisa felt pleasure at the thought of people making their way through the cold towards her warm cottage, where they'd find laughter, she hoped, and good feeling, and food and drink . . .

By the time Peter returned to Louisa's house there were already six people present and from the moment he stepped over the threshold he felt the inevitable discomfort at being among members of a different species — grown-ups. To start with, he managed to escape by going upstairs and unpacking all his stuff and laying it out in her spare room. The knitted Christmas stocking he kept stuffed in his rucksack: he didn't want Louisa catching sight of it and having ideas. But then he had to go downstairs and, as he wandered to and fro, he responded politely to Louisa's explanations to her guests as to who he was and why he was there. He had the usual feeling of plummeting despair — grown-ups were so addicted to their habit of small talk, and so manically overexcited in each other's company, and so resolutely committed to the drug-taking that they disguised as a life-giving necessity — "drinking" — and always so garishly and inappropriately dressed. The women especially wore all sorts of get-ups and were plastered with make-up that seemed deliberately to exaggerate how old they looked, while the men dressed with . . . well, here he was, shaking hands with Danny Steel, who Miss Glasson had the misfortune to think might have to be her boyfriend. He was dressed as if he were a member of the Rolling Stones.

"Hey Peter, so sorry to hear about your mum, but I'm glad she's OK. Welcome to our humble home."

"Hi," said Peter. "Thanks." Even as he shook his hand, Peter could have told Danny it was pretty much a mistake, to have said "our" home when it was Louisa's home, every brick and every piece of furniture paid for by Louisa, and Louisa alone having lived here for the last five years, but he didn't say anything. Grown-ups, thought Peter, were so incredibly clumsy and stupid and untruthful and vain and, when they got together in parties, like this one that thickened around him now, in the warm and comfortable cottage, that clumsiness and stupidity became magnified.

Only Louisa, he thought, was lovely. And yet even she wasn't clever enough to realise, Peter thought soberly, that she didn't love that shiny-jacketed religious fanatic Danny Steel, while really, all along, just across the bay . . .

As the party began to trap him in smaller and smaller corners, Peter became unhappy. He nodded and shook his head at various polite questions that came at him from people he'd never met before and would never see again, but he began to lose any connection with Louisa, who seemed to be permanently taken up with either saying hello or goodbye to people. The party became a thicket of strange men and strange women. Every now and again there was a comforting swoop from Louisa, who would bring someone for him to talk to. He grew weary and at the same time restless and anxious to escape, to escape from Christmas, from everyone. He realised this was, in fact, an intense, emotional, overwrought form of *boredom*. Which was quite an interesting idea, and he went to consult Louisa about it. He struggled through the press of people who stood or sat on every available perch and he mumbled to her in a surprised tone of voice, "I think I might be bored." As soon as the words were out of his mouth, he realised it was the wrong thing to have said.

"That is not my fault," said Louisa. "I didn't ask for you to be here." And she felt the cruelty of her words the instant they'd left her mouth, but it was hurtful to be told he was bored when she'd gone so far out of her way to give him a good Christmas in spite of what had happened to his mum. "Peter, I'm sorry," she said, "I didn't mean that in the way . . . I didn't mean that."

"You're not like this in school," said Peter.

"What am I like in school then?"

"Kinder," said Peter.

She knew this was a ploy, but she had to answer it anyway. "Peter, in school, it's my job to give you my full attention. Here, now, look — there are loads of other

234

people, other things I must do, all these guests to whom I must pay attention. I've invited them, after all." She took him by the arm and shook it just a little bit and smiled at him. "It's Christmas time, Peter. It's Christmas Eve. You've got to expect a bit of a party or two."

"No, you're right," said Peter simply. "I'm sorry. It's my fault."

"But it's a grown-up party; I completely understand it's boring for you," she said. "Why don't you go on up?"

Peter nodded. "I think I will just go," he said.

"I'm sorry. But you tried your hardest. Thank you for that. Even if you didn't enjoy it much, I loved having you here. I could get quite used to it. Your mum should watch out or I'll keep you forever." She gave him a hug. "You know where everything is?"

"Yes, I know where everything is."

"And don't forget to brush your teeth."

"All right then, I won't."

"OK. I will see you in the morning. I am right here and, when the party is over, my bedroom is right next to yours."

"Thanks, Miss Glasson, for everything."

"Louisa, you must call me Louisa when we're not in school."

"Louisa When-we're-not-in-school."

"Very funny. Goodnight, Peter."

"Yup. Bye then."

She watched him thread through the chattering people who were all crammed into her cottage. She felt proud of her friends, and she felt proud of him, and proud to be sheltering him under her roof. She liked the way everyone ruffled Peter's hair, or spoke to him, as he passed by and out of the room.

It was slow going: Peter worked his way through the cosy, crowded sitting room and across the hallway and up past the guests who were sitting on the stairs. As he gained the landing, he glanced into Louisa's bedroom and saw everyone's coats lying in piles on her bed. The chatter from downstairs filled the whole house. He continued further along the landing and into the spare room, and shut the door behind him. The volume of the party decreased, and it felt peaceful.

And then he packed into his rucksack everything that he'd only just unpacked, including the stupidly empty knitted Christmas stocking from home, and he hoisted the bag onto one shoulder. He opened the door again, meeting the increased noise of the party. With some trepidation he trod down the stairs — carefully, slowly — past the people sitting on the bottom steps. When he twisted the latch on the front door and pulled it open, several people asked curiously, "Hey, where are you going?"

"I'm off to the North Pole," he said, "to collect my reindeer and my sleigh."

Several people offered cheerful goodbyes in return; and he could hear Louisa's laugh coming from the living room. With painstaking slowness he shut the door behind him and threaded through the gaggle of people who were smoking cigarettes.

It didn't escape his observation that both drinking and smoking were banned at school, and yet so-called grown-ups threw themselves into both these activities more vigorously than into any other. It would make for an interesting experiment, he thought, to ban grown-ups from drinking alcohol and smoking, and see how terrifying would be the resulting misbehaviour.

He put up his hoodie against the blast of cold December air that invaded every gap in his clothing, and put his other arm through the rucksack to make it sit more comfortably, and then he headed off into the night.

On the other side of the bay, Dr Martin Ellingham went from room to room, downstairs, turning off the lights. He always left on the hallway light because, should there by any chance be someone who faced a medical emergency and came in the middle of the night arid knocked on the door, he would need to be downstairs to open up as quickly as possible, without having to struggle to find a light switch.

Even as he idly indulged in these habitual, banal thoughts, in an attempt to banish the fraught evening he'd just suffered, and make his way peaceably upstairs in order to forget, forget utterly, both his parents, the doorbell rang. He stopped with his foot on the bottom stair and turned back. Already he was calculating the weather conditions. He moved swiftly, ready to engage with whatever crisis, but when he pulled the door open he had to lower his gaze a little, because standing there in the yellowy porch light, his face round and white and anxious, the breaths coming out as puffs of smoke in the cold night air, stood Peter Cronk.

"Miss Glasson had other fish to fry," said Peter. The sight of Martin blocking out the light was awe-inspiring. The whole idea of a doctor's surgery was like an adventure story, with missions undertaken which might lead him to the wildest regions of the human body. He knew it was likely that he'd be turned away, but he'd give it a try. "Any room at the inn?" he asked.

For a while nothing happened: Martin stood there, frowning, and Peter waited, his eyebrows quite high on his forehead.

Martin thought about all that had happened: the dreadful meal; the revelation of his father's crude attempt to extort money; his aunt's distress; the ghastly outpouring, eventually, from his otherwise silent mother.

This boy, Peter, standing on his doorstep, appeared in comparison like an angelic figure. It was nothing to do with the Christmas spirit, Martin told himself. It was not. It was merely the accidental collision of certain events. As for Peter's use of the phrase, "Any room at the inn?" — he should ignore its effectiveness. It was merely a cultural reference making itself known. In the event, for a price, of course, there had been room at the inn. His parents were sheltering from the storm in the Crab and Lobster. He himself was paying the bill. He said to Peter, "Well, you'd better come in for a minute, and we'll call Miss Glasson, shall we?" He stepped back.

Peter was over the threshold; as far as he was concerned that was the main thing. He unshouldered his backpack and went through to the waiting room.

"No, this way," said Martin, and walked through into his kitchen. He checked his watch. No doubt Louisa's party was still in full swing. He would phone her. He searched for the handset.

Peter followed Martin into the kitchen. This was the inner sanctum. These were Martin's private quarters. Here they would spend time together, and ignore Christmas. He saw the pegs holding the coats, and he hooked up his rucksack and began to take off his coat. It was warm in here. Suddenly he felt tired.

Martin stood with the handset against his ear. He could imagine that Louisa would have that ridiculously pompous man's — Danny's — arm around her waist. A glass of wine in her hand, no doubt. He counted the rings, and the answer machine picked up. He remade the call. This time the phone was picked up and a babble of noise came from the receiver. He could hear laughter and high spirits. "Is Louisa there?" he shouted. He couldn't hear any reply, just more laughter and loud conversation. Then a man's voice said, "Hello? Hello?" Was that Danny Steel? He repeated, "Is Louisa there?" There was no answer, just the babble of the party. One or two voices were nearer to the phone, at the other end, and he could make out a word or two of what they were saying: "Fetch . . . let her know . . . through there . . ." It sounded like they were discussing what to do. He waited patiently, but instead the line went dead.

Martin was impatient and dialled again, but was put through to the message service. This happened three more times. Maybe the phone had been left off the hook.

He looked up, and realised that Peter was no longer in the kitchen. He walked through to the living room to look for him and there on the sofa lay Peter, curled up, facing away from him, still fully dressed, except for his shoes neatly positioned, side by side, on the floor.

Martin stood over the boy, looking down. He observed the gentle rise and fall of Peter's ribcage, the closed eyes, the hands curled loosely near his mouth. He felt like he was looking at him from a long way off, from a distance of many years. His mouth set, grimly. He said, out loud, "Oh God, he's fallen asleep." He realised he'd been saying those words to Louisa, in effect, but there was no one in the room. He was alone on Christmas Eve with Peter Cronk asleep on his sofa.

He trod upstairs and lifted the duvet off the spare bed and walked it back down again. Without taking much care — after all, it would be in his interests if the boy woke up so he could be despatched back to Louisa's — he arranged the duvet over the sleeping Peter Cronk. For a moment he remained there, looking down on the inert figure of the boy whose life he'd saved not that long ago. It didn't bear thinking about: with his own hands he'd held shut Peter Cronk's artery during that journey in the ambulance. He had had to curb the instinct to check the scar and see how neat a job he'd made of the cut, performed in the back of an ambulance driving at high speed along a country lane.

And yet here the boy was, the breath moving evenly in and out of his lungs, his heart beating easily, the damaged spleen removed, the fragment of secondary spleen developing slowly no doubt.

He left Peter Cronk asleep on his sofa; and, with the chimes striking midnight, he could pick up again his usual routine: change into pyjamas, bathroom, glass of water and reading, light off and calmly asleep.

It would be the first time he'd not slept alone in the house.

Louisa was taken with how her party had turned out; she'd enjoyed it, herself. As she carried the used glasses through to her kitchen she felt affectionate towards them, the strange places the glasses had been left, as if they impersonated, still, the people who had been drinking from them: a group sociably gathered around the table lamp; a solitary one on the floor at the foot of the curtain; a curious one on the windowsill; a line of them on the bookshelf; a half-full one on the cistern in the downstairs loo; a crowd politely waiting on the draining board next to the sink. She was proud of all her friends, and she loved her cousin. Her cottage had been full of good cheer and when she'd seen friends of hers talking to other friends whom they'd never met before, she'd felt a glow of achievement: she'd known so-and-so; and also she'd known so-and-so; and of course although they'd never met they'd got on famously; and thus friends of hers had become friends in their own right. Surely that was the best, most life-enhancing effect of a good Christmas party.

Like so many in Portwenn, Louisa's house was so small that even the twenty-five people she'd invited meant the place was crammed, and when Danny started trying to corner her in a private place, they'd bumped against Caroline, or she'd stepped on Richard's foot, or they'd been interrupted by Francesca.

Danny had to make a joke of it and opened the door onto the cold, cold balcony. As he'd closed the door behind them, it was the natural thing for her to step into his arms, just to keep warm. "Hurry up, what is it?" she said jokingly. "Else we'll freeze to death."

"This whole Christmas with you," said Danny, "it's really got me thinking about how precious life is, and how you've got to seize the day. Or seize the girl."

"What?" She'd pushed against him a bit.

"Seize the girl," repeated Danny meaningfully.

"Oh. Right. I've been seized, have I?" And yes, she thought, she was standing in his arms, even if it was only to keep warm.

"Look, I've been thinking."

"Go on, then." She was determined to be in a good mood.

"I've been doing up Mum's place, as you know, to sell it. You've been out there, and I've seen how much you love it."

"It's a gorgeous house."

"I know. And it's like . . . the house has been talking to me, whispering in my ear. So what about — let's say we move in? Keep the house, not sell it, and you and me move in? I've been thinking about this all night. I was going to tell you tomorrow, Christmas Day, but I just couldn't wait, and here you are, looking so lovely, and your smile . . ."

"I smile at lots of people," she said teasingly. "I smile at him, and I smile at her . . . smile at anyone, me—"

"Louisa, shush a moment."

"What?"

"Listen."

She could hear the cold, cold sea, its work never done. She could hear a car zooming loudly down by the harbour, its exhaust popping, a young man's car. She'd heard a dog bark, and someone's cheerful call. "What?" she asked.

"Will you marry me?"

"Whaaat?" The truth was, she'd wanted to laugh — just from the shock — but she knew she must not; it would be a fatal kind of cruelty, to laugh, for whatever reason. She didn't have time to interrogate her feelings; she only wanted just to cope. "Wow," she said. "Where did that come from?"

Danny had pressed on. "You could sell this house, or maybe rent it out. Keep it as an investment."

Louisa felt ashamed — on his behalf — that she could not bring herself to grab him in a tight embrace and cry out, "Yes," because that was the part that no doubt he wished she would play. But also she felt confused and resentful and flummoxed. She'd stalled for time. "I'm flattered," she said, "but I'd . . . I don't know what to say."

"Say yes." His face was pale in the near darkness.

"Danny," she said, and there was a pleading, whispering quality in her voice. "This is a big thing, Danny. I'm going to have to think about it."

"No," he said, charmingly shaking his head. "Don't think, just say yes, say what your heart tells you . . ."

"Don't rush me," she said. "Let me have my party. Come on, let's go back in." She'd broken away from him, taken his hand and dragged him back inside.

And yet the marriage proposal had floored her, a little bit. When she was saying goodbye to everyone, she was aware of him lingering next to her, saying goodbye as if he, too, were the host. As the numbers dwindled to three, two, and then just him, she'd pleaded with him to give her time, a day or two, to organise her thoughts. Without saying a word, she'd managed to sort of organise Danny towards the front door, and then she'd zipped up his jacket for him, and then he was on the front step, and then he was gone, his leather jacket disappearing into the night. She knew already that she would say no to him, in the nicest way she knew how — and that meant stringing it out for ages.

Everyone had gone. The house was her own again.

How it seemed dear, to her, that the lively popularity of her house hadn't completely ended with her guests' departure, because Peter Cronk was upstairs. She could picture him asleep in her spare room. She remembered what it had been like as a child to go to sleep while adults partied downstairs: the comfort of their voices, fully alive and awake, their going about their adult business while she, a small girl, had closed her eyes and slept, however unhappy she'd been, with the darkness

244

taken care of, made benign, by the adults' confidence and noise.

She sat on the side of the bed and allowed waves of tiredness and satisfaction to overtake her. However, there was one more task left — perhaps the most pleasing duty of any Christmas that she'd ever known. She lifted her pillow and drew out the bright red sock, stuffed to bursting, which she would now deliver to Peter, just as Christmas stockings were being delivered to all the other children in Portwenn, in the small hours. By giving Peter his childhood, perhaps she could mend her own. Peter would feel the unexpected weight of the stocking lying across the foot of his bed; he would hear the crackle of wrapping paper when he nudged it with his foot. Perhaps, if she wasn't quiet enough, Peter would half wake up, and glimpse the strange figure of Father Christmas as she slipped back out through the door.

Mother Christmas, she thought.

She lifted up the sock and carried it with both hands. She tiptoed as quietly as she could across the landing and stood listening at Peter's door.

Not a sound.

She let the stocking hang from one hand, and placed the other on the chill steel of the door handle, in order to press — quietly, slowly — downwards. The door gave inwards an inch. She stopped and listened again, but there was absolute silence.

Louisa couldn't resist smiling — almost laughing — for a moment now. Both she and Peter knew there was no such person as Father Christmas, yet here they both were, playing the Christmas game, pretending Santa Claus did exist. She felt a marvellous complicity and sympathy with Peter Cronk.

Stealthily, she pushed the door further open.

On the other side of the chilly, wintery bay — where the sea made its continual licking of the shore, its continual moving of tons of sand, its lifting and dropping of the fishing boats moored there — Peter Cronk was awake in Martin's house, and he, also, that night, not many minutes later, looked through a gap in a bedroom doorway, and pushed the door carefully open. Doctor Martin Ellingham lay on his back, peacefully asleep, his arms folded across his chest. He looked like an effigy on top of a tomb in a church. It was daunting to have to wake him.

Peter stole closer, carrying the phone handset. It was scary to approach the sleeping doctor in the middle of the night, but there was nothing else for it. "Doc?" he said, quietly, and then a little more strongly, "Doc?"

Martin opened his eyes and sat up: it was one and the same movement. He was used to being woken in the middle of the night, by his pager or by the phone, and it always meant one thing: an emergency of some description that he would be required to answer to. But he wasn't expecting the solemn, pale face of a ten-year-old boy, Peter Cronk, right there, in his bedroom, standing next to his bed and looking at him.

"Peter, what is it?" he asked curtly.

"Sorry . . . It's all right, I'll deal with it; it's OK." A touch overawed, Peter turned to leave, carrying the phone with him.

Martin cleared his throat and woke up an inch more. "Peter, come here. What is it?"

"There's a phone call for you." Peter held up the receiver. "I thought I'd better answer it because it might have been an emergency, but don't worry, it isn't."

Martin took the phone. "Hello?"

Louisa's heart lurched when she heard Martin's voice. She said, "Martin, you could have rung and told me that Peter had come over to your house."

Martin's expression relaxed. "I did ring. I couldn't get through."

"I nearly died of fright. I went into Peter's room and his bed was empty." Unaccountably, her hand went to check her ponytail, and to tug down the hem of her jersey, as if she could be seen.

"That can hardly have been a surprise to you, given you threw him out."

"I'm sorry?" Her ear burned hotly against the receiver. "What?" She stood up.

Martin's voice came down the phone. "Peter says you threw him out."

"Well, the little . . . That is not true. I did not throw him out. He said he was bored and so I said it was time for bed, that's all."

"Well, finish scrubbing the wine stains out of your carpet and come and get him. He's dressed and ready to go."

"Martin, it's one o'clock in the morning."

"The quicker the better then. I don't have a bed for him here."

"Your parents are at the Crab. You must have a bed for him."

"The bed's not made up."

"Peter told me he was asleep on your sofa. He said you'd given him a duvet. So you've made a bed for him, haven't you." She pleaded, "It's very late. Couldn't you let him stay there with you?"

"No." Martin pressed the phone harder to his ear and glanced at Peter's glum face. "I'm simply not equipped."

"You obviously *were* equipped. He was asleep when I rang. And . . . ask him where he'd rather stay." Her voice suddenly had a note of triumph in it. "I think you'll find it's with you. Goodnight, Martin."

The phone went dead.

CHAPTER
FIVE

Of all the houses in England, Wales, Scotland and Ireland, Christmas Day was perhaps the least celebrated, the most ignored, in a small house which also doubled as a doctor's surgery, halfway up the side of a cliff in the small fishing village of Portwenn.

The two inhabitants, Doctor Martin Ellingham and Peter Cronk, aged ten, rose at approximately the same time, at around 8a.m. Peter folded away his duvet and made the sofa once more presentable. He unpacked his rucksack of its few possessions, but left inside, unused, the giant knitted sock that had been customarily used by his mother as a Christmas stocking. It was not that he'd expected or even half wished it could have been used; it was the best news in the world that he didn't have to pretend to be impressed with — and forever grateful for — a Toblerone, a pair of nail clippers and a fart balloon.

Christmas, for Doc Martin, was traditionally an opportunity to catch up on back issues of *The Lancet* and to have a day that was perfectly his own, measured out in cups of coffee and two delicate pieces of cooking for himself: lunch and dinner. He enjoyed observing from a distance some of Christmas's rituals without having to take part. Like all cultural events, he thought, Christmas was an exercise in self-hypnosis leading to mass hysteria, and he was quite happy to explain to anyone who asked his diagnosis as to how the condition had come about, how it had spread and how such a widespread illness managed to keep and extend its grip on a large proportion of the world's population over such a long period of time.

Martin and Peter thus enjoyed a largely silent breakfast of toast and tea, with the best wholemeal granary offered by Portwenn's bakery. Martin had thick-cut marmalade; Peter preferred Marmite. Their conversation was confined to practical matters: the butter, the knife, the washing-up. And yet both Martin and Peter quickly found that charmed place where time passes in a comforting silence; and such silences can only become comfortable if both parties are happy with the insides of their own minds — in other words, if there is enough going on in there to keep them agreeably occupied, without feeling any pressure to shore up, rescue, amuse or validate the other person in the room.

Such was the case with Peter and Martin.

Martin, without a word, fetched to the kitchen table a pile of the year's back issues of *The Lancet* and began to soak up the papers written by colleagues that he hadn't had time to read fully after his quick scan on the magazine's first arrival. This offered him intense pleasure and involvement for hours.

Peter, with the solemn pride that comes when an intellectual mind stoops to something lowbrow, plugged the headphones into his Game Boy and attempted to increase his score on "Alien Hominid".

Martin's only duty was to take a moment to call his Aunty Joan and repair the damage from last night. He explained the circumstances in which he'd given a valuation of her house — and how his father had manipulated the situation to make it look as if they'd been discussing the sale of Haven Farm, rather than Martin's purchase of a similar property. Joan was so pleased to hear his voice, and so grateful to have the situation explained, that she managed to laugh, even, at the ridiculous Christmas present that her brother had brought for her. "D'you know what it was, Marty, when I ripped off that horrid silver paper?" Her voice came down the phone. "It was a pasta making machine. For God's sake! How little does he know his own sister?" Martin finished by promising her he would do everything in his power not to allow his father to force her to sell Haven Farm.

Before lunch, Martin and Peter both agreed to put on coats and gloves and take a walk along the cliff top; and no sooner were they on their way than Dog appeared and trotted at their heels. The cold was biting, but they were appropriately dressed and the uphill effort warmed them through.

During their walk they deconstructed the notion of Christmas. Martin was interested to hear from Peter that the myth of Father Christmas flying his reindeer through the sky originated from a remote tribe in Russia, or somewhere, whose members had learned, at a certain time of year not too distant from mid-December time, to drink the urine of their reindeer, because during this season the reindeer keenly ate a variety of mushroom which contained an hallucinogen. The erratic behaviour of the reindeer, along with the visionary hallucinations of the drugged tribe members, combined to invent the fantastical notion of teams of reindeer flying through the sky, dragging a sleigh in which a bearded man . . .

"Very interesting, if true," commented Martin, walking with his hands behind his back.

"It's a pretty big if," replied Peter. "But it's a compelling theory and has the *ring* of truth, at least."

"Indeed it does. Makes Christmas truly visionary, in a way," offered Martin.

"It's more romantic than thinking the whole idea was made up by the shops in order to sell more gifts," said Peter. He felt ashamed of his mother's ridiculous knitted sock lying at the bottom of his rucksack. With Martin, he breathed the clean, uplifting air of reason.

When they turned and walked back, the village of Portwenn lay beneath them, clinging to its cliffs, sheltered in its cove. In every house, thought Peter, people were glued to their Christmas dinners, to their paper hats and the mottos found in their Christmas crackers, glued there by convention and by ritual and by habit, whereas he and Martin were free to stroll along the cliff tops and do as they pleased. His stomach rumbled emptily.

Martin, as they looked down at the town, wondered whether his parents were still at the Crab, or if they'd left early. He was determined never to see them again.

252

They went back to the house and there was a low spot when Peter realised that although Martin had a video player, he didn't have any videos.

The crisis passed at 4p.m., when Martin made shepherd's pie, which turned out to be Peter's favourite dish. Several times he phoned Louisa in order to hand Peter over to her; however Louisa's phone remained unanswered.

The evening passed with a handful of games of backgammon, all of which were won by Martin. It so happened that alongside the backgammon board, on the kitchen table, sat the envelope containing the collection of photographs left by Graham Reynolds.

Suddenly, much quicker than expected, it was bedtime.

The next morning, on Boxing Day, Martin wasn't going to trouble with the phone. He would simply deliver Peter to Louisa, like a parcel.

"You don't have to walk me over there," said Peter. "I know the way."

"Peter, you're my responsibility until I hand you back to Miss Glasson, at which point you become her responsibility. Finally." He said it curtly; and he saw the hurt cross Peter's face.

"I don't want to stay with Miss Glasson."

"Well, I'm afraid that's what is going to happen, so brace yourself." He had tried to say it in a kind way and to his own ears it sounded perfectly reasonable and straightforward, but all the cold-heartedness that had been delivered to Martin as a child couldn't help but infect his dealings with other people, leaving him in a world of his own making, cut off from other human beings, who often found themselves as if waving at him from a distance.

But when they walked over to the other side of the bay, there was no answer to his summons at Louisa's door.

"Can I have some crisps?" asked Peter, as they walked back.

"No. The shops aren't open on Boxing Day."

"Some of them are. The pub sells crisps."

"No."

"I'm hungry."

"Tough. You should have eaten more breakfast then, shouldn't you? By the way, I'm going to check on your mother's progress again today."

"Can I come with you?"

"I suppose you must, yes."

Later on, when Martin was walking through the town, it was the newly happy and satisfied policeman, PC Mark Mylow, who pulled up alongside him in the narrow street and asked to have a word. Mark's smile was permanent: he could have been delivering news of a fatal road traffic accident and still he'd be unable not to wear his smile. His new woman — and such a woman — was on his arm at all times, whether she was actually there or not, for he carried her presence with him; she was a gift from the Gods, it had seemed, with a heavenly singing voice, which made her categorically an angel. And now this . . . superb, golden news that was impossible to hold on to. He was telling everyone.

Martin didn't stop walking; Mark drove alongside, slowly. Martin was aware that the Bevy of Beauties was nearby, huddled together and shivering, dressed in bold contrast to the demands of the weather, all bare legs and goose pimples. "Guess what, no need for that sperm test, after all, Doc," said Mark.

Martin stopped, and so did the police Land Rover.

The Bevy of Beauties had caught the words "sperm test" and they were in fits. It was like a pack of hounds, the way they seized on stuff and tore it to shreds. "I'll test him," said one, hands on hips, parading back and forth in front of her mates. "I'll test his bleedin' sperm. Come on." Her mates dragged her back to the group and shushed her.

PC Mark Mylow carried on blithely, "Don't know what I was worried about. Because I've got the results already." His open expression was one of pleasure.

This was the news that Martin had been expecting. "Oh?" He was filled with dread.

"Yup. Julie's pregnant. We're having a baby."

Martin said nothing. His frown deepened.

"So you can chuck the envelope away when it arrives," said Mark cheerfully. "How about that?"

"I shan't do that," said Martin, but Mark didn't hear.

"Christ," said Mark. "Talk about jumping in with both feet. But you just know when it's right, don't you? I didn't know life could move this quickly. Never has before. But I can't be surprised. When we've been doing what we've been doing, stuff's going to happen, you know?"

255

Martin was groping around the edges of the situation to try and think what to do. He'd never in his professional experience known patient confidentiality to throw up such a situation as this.

He remembered his first encounter with Julie Mitchell. He had thought it was going to be a very routine pregnancy appointment. Her words, and his answers, sounded in his head.

"Thanks for seeing me, Doc." She had wiped back a strand of hair and smiled.

"I'm on the phone."

"Sorry."

"Shut the door. No, not you."

"Right. Thank you."

"Come in."

"Thanks. It's just that, um, I've done a test, and, um, I'm pregnant."

That had been the start of the whole affair: just an ordinary woman, whom he'd never met before, coming to find out what she should do about an unexpected pregnancy. He remembered the way she'd moved — quite slyly as if trying to make the least possible noise. Catlike. With strange pauses. And always those steady blue eyes — amused and engaging — focused on his.

He'd asked, "How many weeks pregnant are you?"

"Can't be that pregnant. Not long."

"I'll examine you."

"Oh, I hadn't —"

"You can get changed behind there."

There had followed a standard examination and health check. Still, he believed he was dealing with a straightforward pregnancy. He'd finished with standard advice. "You need to get plenty of rest before your scan."

"Right."

"Which I suggest should be soon. Fundal height is an inexact measurement, but I'd say you're a good twelve to fourteen weeks pregnant. Is that right?"

"Oh."

That, he remembered, had been the first warning sign — her tone of voice had changed. Her manner had changed. "What?" he'd asked.

Her movements had become quicker, more abrupt. She no longer had that sly, curious look about her. Instead she looked anxious. She'd plunged a hand into her bag, and had withdrawn, of all things, a packet of ten cigarettes.

"No smoking," Martin had said sharply. "And certainly you must give up those things completely."

"Of course," she'd said, dully. And yet she'd taken one cigarette from the pack and held it between her fingers. Martin had noticed the cigarette trembling, slightly.

"Is there a problem?" he'd asked.

"I didn't know you could tell." Her voice had lost its warmth, its draw.

"Tell what?"

"How many weeks gone I am."

"It's quite accurate, but the scan will tell you precisely."

She'd looked at him in a resentful way and said, "Mark doesn't need to know."

"Mark?"

"Mark Mylow. My boyfriend."

"You're going out with Mark?"

"I am now," she'd said meaningfully.

And Martin had seen what she was up to. For a long time there had been silence in the room. Martin had looked at her; and she'd looked insolently back.

Martin had said carefully, "He'll find out sooner or later."

Her words suddenly flowed quicker, more sharply. "How will he find out? I'll just tell him the baby's a bit early." And then she'd slowed down, and time had slowed down as well for Martin, in his memory, when she'd said, "And if you tell him, Doctor, I'll sue you."

Martin had stood up. "This consultation is over," he'd said in a quiet voice. "You need to find a new GP to manage your pregnancy." He'd handed her his account of her examination. "Your notes," he'd said, and he let them go before she'd properly got hold of them, so she had to pick them up from the floor.

Martin had held the door open for her to leave.

She'd said, as she walked past him still holding the cigarette and with the lighter in the other hand now, "Mark is happy with me. I'm happy with him. And he's going to be a great dad. And no one's going to rock the precious little boat."

Martin was brought back to the present moment by Mark's words, and by his benign face smiling at him from the window of the Land Rover.

"And you know what," said Mark cheerfully, "your wise words came back to me." He lowered his voice.

"The size of the testicles —" he shook his head "— nothing to do with the sperm count. You told me that, and I didn't believe you. Well, you were right as always, Doc." He crunched the gears on the Land Rover and prepared to move off. "Invites to the wedding will be in the post shortly. Costs an arm and a leg, all this, doesn't it, but you want to pay don't you."

"I can't really offer my congratulations," said Martin in a voice of steel, but Mark didn't seem to take it in.

"Well, cheerio for now." Mark set the Land Rover going, and Martin started walking, but the Land Rover jerked to a halt and Mark's head popped back out. "Hey. By the way. I was pleased to see you've put your name down for the Nuddy Jump. Bit of community spirit. Joining in. Good to see that from the old village doc."

"What?" Martin chose to keep walking.

"In the Crab," said Mark, trailing the Land Rover alongside at the same pace. "You know, the list. On the wall above the bar. You put your name down. Brave man! Not for the faint-hearted, that isn't. 'Course — I'm not eligible any more. Not being a single man, nowadays."

The Bevy of Beauties followed, as well — laughing and repeating the words "Nuddy Jump".

"I haven't put my name down for anything."

"Definitely your handwriting," said Mark. "You won't be allowed to wear a wetsuit, mind. The clue is in the title. And with your name down, you'll definitely have an audience."

"I have no idea what you're talking about."

"Seriously though, just tear up the envelope when my test results come in."

"I will call you when they arrive," said Martin.

"Right y'are. Thanks for that. Bye for now. See you New Year's Eve, if not before, eh?" The Land Rover picked up speed and bounced around the bend in the alleyway and was gone.

After they'd finished giggling at the words "Nuddy Jump", the Bevy of Beauties moved on, like a school of fish, bottom-feeding on good humour.

When Martin reached the bottom of the hill, in between him and the sea stood the Crab and Lobster, its Christmas decorations looking suddenly forlorn now that the day itself had passed.

The Nuddy Jump? What was this list behind the bar in the pub?

But Martin didn't want to go in. He remembered his father in the bedroom upstairs, watching the rugby. "Possession!" his father had shouted at the TV, the vein standing out in his forehead. And so it had turned out — that had been his strategy all along: possession of Haven Farm.

He hadn't heard from his mother or father, and had only spoken to his Aunt Joan by phone. Everyone had been licking their wounds after the ghastly Christmas Eve dinner. He would have guessed — if he were to put himself in his parents' shoes — they'd have fled from the village as quickly as they could, which meant they were probably no longer staying here. And yet, Martin had booked them in until tonight, and it wasn't as if they had a home to go to in the UK. If they were short of money it might have led to their making the decision to stay at the Crab until the bitter end . . .

And then he glimpsed his father in the interior of the pub — just a snapshot framed by the window — fast enough to have him think he'd imagined it.

He didn't want to see them. He continued on his way.

A few paces later, he stopped and turned. He would not let his parents affect one single decision he made. He returned and walked into the Crab fully expecting to see them after all, or not — it didn't matter. But as it turned out his father stood there, bags in hand, like on a stage set.

"Your mother and I are leaving," said Christopher.

"Goodbye," said Martin.

His mother appeared and looked steadily at Martin. Without greeting him, she said quietly to her husband, "I'll wait for you in the taxi."

Christopher squared his shoulders and set down his bags on the floor. "Regrettable," he said. "Hasn't been a great trip."

"Where will you go?"

"She'll fly back to Portugal in the morning. I'll stay at my club in London. Talk to the solicitor and be back down here in a few days. Sort out this business with Joan."

"No, you won't," said Martin. And suddenly he knew what was the right thing to do — the only thing to do. The idea arrived fully formed, and there wasn't a shred of doubt in his head; it was as if he'd already done it. "Here's what's going to happen," he said. "I will sell my flat. I will instruct estate agents immediately. I will also obtain a valuation of Haven Farm based on the mean of three different valuations offered by three different estate agents. The money which I will raise from the sale of my flat will pass to you in return for your half of Haven Farm. You won't get it straight away, but you'll just have to wait. In the meantime, you can go and stay in your ghastly club or wherever else they'll have you. But don't come back here."

Christopher was profoundly puzzled. "You'd sell your place — to pay Joan's debt?"

Martin was impatient. "Don't tell Joan. Just say you've changed your mind or something."

"Why on earth wouldn't I tell Joan?" His eyes narrowed. "What's your game? Are you on to something I haven't thought about?"

"I don't want her to feel grateful to me. She doesn't have to. She's my family."

For a while Christopher looked into his son's face, trying to recognise any sign of himself in that wooden expression. He couldn't. He picked up his bags again. "Well, goodbye," he said.

Martin didn't answer. "Goodbye" was a figure of speech used to bestow goodwill on the recipient, and he wished nothing for his father.

A moment later, he remembered why he was here — the list that had been pinned up in the bar, a list with his name on it? He walked through and quickly found it among the flyers pinned up for other entertainments. "The Nuddy Jump" was written in comic-book writing at the top of the page, with an illustration of stick figures leaping into thin air. A subtitle prescribed, "Bachelors only". A list of signatures unfolded below this headline, some of them heavily crossed out. Various comments such as "Jack can't swim", were scribbled alongside the names. It was obviously some kind of primitive local ritual to mark the passing of the old year and the coming of the new.

And there was his name — in his own handwriting. Someone had copied it from a prescription, no doubt. Alongside someone had written, "In it to win it — the doc". He reached into his breast pocket, brought out his fountain pen and drew a line both through his name and the comment. The Nuddy Jump would have to do without his entry.

An A4 square of paper Sellotaped to the inside of the glass door leading to Mrs Cronk's fish and chip shop announced that service would be resumed on Boxing Day at 5p.m., and so it was an hour earlier when Bert Large parked his van, took out the set of unfamiliar keys and let himself in. The grey stainless steel surfaces waited quietly, the fridge hummed out the back, and the oil sat coldly in the frying tanks. The whole place had remained untouched since Mrs Cronk had carelessly dipped her hand in boiling hot oil; however Bert Large immediately brought life and vigour and optimism to the premises. He started to twiddle the buttons on the fryer, and his practical, plumber's eye made several quite good guesses as to how the arrangement of electrical switches worked. Soon a new heat began to warm the fish and chip shop; it began to assume its customary aroma of hot oil and vinegar.

A few minutes later, Bert was joined by the tall, languorous figure of his son, Al, who looked more dubious about their volunteering to keep the shop going on Mrs Cronk's behalf.

"Come on," said Bert, ripping open a half-hundredweight bag of potatoes. "How can I teach you the secrets of fine cuisine when you're standing over there?" It was true that Bert liked cooking, and he enjoyed making anything work, whether it was a baling machine or a switchboard.

Al was different: he looked like he thought the kitchen equipment might bite him. "Plumbing's what we know, Dad," he said gloomily. "We're just going to make it worse for the woman."

Bert lifted out the cages for the chips and for the fish, banged them experimentally to knock the oil off, and hooked them up so they were out of the tank. That's how it worked: dunk the cages into the boiling fat, time them for cooking, lift them out and hook them up, serve. He said to his son, "I got my merit badge in food preparation before you were born." It was true, as well. Or was it food hygiene? He couldn't remember. Anyway, what counted was that he was qualified.

Al didn't agree. "You don't have a clue what you're doing. You don't even know whether to use engine oil or sunflower oil."

"Eh? You what?"

"Is that oil safe to use, when it's been standing there for two days?"

264

"'Course it's safe."

"How hot does it have to be?"

"I'll turn it up high when we've got a customer or two," said Bert. "You've seen their electricity bill, it's a whopper."

"Dad, to heat that amount of oil will take ages. Your customer will be out the door and in the pub down the road if he has to hang around for the oil to heat up. You've got to keep it going at full bore all the time so you can fry the stuff like now. It's a takeaway, Dad."

"All right, all right. I know that actually."

"We're never going to make any money for her," groaned Al. "And we're supposed to start on Mr Bakin's cesspit tomorrow. We're in the shit whichever way we turn."

"I'm a man of my word," said Bert proudly, rubbing his hand back and forth over his crown in a habitual gesture. "When I say I do something, I do it, and what's more we're going to do well for her. Coin, my son." Bert rubbed his fingers together. "We're here to help, remember. Good Samaritans and all that."

"Oh sure, it's really going to help, isn't it, running her business into the ground?"

"Who says I'm running it into the ground? Taking flight, more like."

"Awww . . . Dad. I . . . I can't watch this happen." Al loped to the door and pulled it open.

"Hey!" called Bert. "Where d'you think you're going?"

"You stick to your gourmet cuisine, and I'll do the plumbing."

"Don't be such a teenager. Come back here and muck in. We're family."

"Teenager? I'm twenty-five. And sometimes I feel like I'm a lot older than you are."

"Well, so, where's your community spirit?" Bert stood there, a pair of fish tongs in his hand, and he sprang the jaws of the tongs together twice — click click — as if he would pick up Al's community spirit and serve it, if only he could find it. "Come on, we're a team aren't we? Father and son. Working together. Facing down the world, we are."

A certain look came over Al's face — it was a wooden expression that he wore, as he came back into the shop and approached the counter. "OK," he said. "Let's just say I'm our first customer. I'll have a bit of fish, please. Doesn't matter which kind. So. What fish have you got?"

"Fish?" Bert's lips were turned down a bit like a trout's mouth as he remembered what he'd forgotten. "Ah. Yes. Well. Come on, then. Fish. Next challenge."

Mrs Cronk had slaved for years behind the stainless steel surfaces of the fish and chip shop, cooking and then rolling up the portions in squares of paper and then in more squares of newspaper, taking the cash and giving out change, refilling the ketchup and mayonnaise bottles, topping up the salt cellar, mopping down the floors, keeping down the vermin, mending the fridges, repairing the broken window out the back, carrying sacks of potatoes and boxes of fish, gluing down the vinyl flooring, cleaning over and over again the same panes of glass — especially those corners — in the door and in the shop window, polishing the brass door plate . . . It made her exhausted just to think about it. She lay injured in her hospital bed, her hand throbbing still from its burn, but it wasn't until the day after Boxing Day that news was brought to her, from her own son, of how Bert and Al were getting on.

It ended up being Martin who drove Peter to see his mother in hospital, and they'd both had a chance to see Bert and Al in action in the fish and chip shop. Peter sat on the bed next to his mother, while Martin stood at the foot of the bed, glancing at the chart.

"Are they doing a good job?" Mrs Cronk used her good hand to squeeze her son's.

"Definitely," said Peter and nodded firmly.

"Will you thank them for me?"

"Of course, I have already," said Peter.

"Both of them."

Peter nodded. "Yup. Both of them."

"I feel all right about it if Al's there. He's got a sensible head on his young shoulders. Is he enjoying it a bit, maybe?"

"I think so." Peter frowned.

Martin said abruptly, "I think what Peter's trying to say is that Al is no longer there. He didn't think it was a good idea."

It was as if a steel band tightened around Mrs Cronk's chest. "What?"

"It's nothing, Mum. Al just left the shop for a short while. Nice flowers these. Who brought them for you?" He fingered the unseasonal blooms.

"If you ask me, it will be a while before Bert and Al work together again," said Martin bluntly.

Mrs Cronk found that she was holding her breath. She lifted up her bandaged hand as if to demonstrate what could go wrong. "Bert's on his own?" she managed to say. "He'll burn the place down."

"No he won't," Peter soothed her, and turned to Martin. "Will he, Doc?" he said meaningfully.

"What?" Martin glanced at both of them. "No. 'Course he won't. He can't even turn the fryers up to the right temperature."

"So he's serving my customers uncooked fish?" A whole new raft of possible disasters opened up in front of Mrs Cronk's eyes. Poisoning. Lawsuits. Health and Safety. The licence from the council . . . With each imagining, her throat tightened. She could feel the pressure building in her chest and behind her eyes.

Peter shook his mother's shoulder gently. "Mum? You all right?" He could see little blood vessels actually breaking in the whites of her eyes.

"I'll get the doctor," said Martin with professional simplicity, and strode off.

Peter held up the glass of water for his mother and spoke earnestly, trying to press his words right in, past her panic and confusion. "It's all right," he said. "The shop is perfectly all right. The fish is cooked all the way through, piping hot. I tried some, and I poked my finger into the middle and it was burning hot." He nodded as if to encourage her to believe him. "And all the surfaces are clean. The windows are clean. The floor is squeaky clean . . ."

268

In the car on the way back to Portwenn, Peter asked Martin, "Why did you say those things to my mother?"

"I was just trying to put her at ease."

"Maybe next time just put her in a coma or something." They were descending into the town, now, and some of the shops were open again, in the gap between Christmas and the New Year. Peter's eye was caught by the familiar posters in the window of Spar. "Hey," he said, "can I get a video?"

"What's wrong with a book?"

"Nothing. Just that I've been reading non-stop for the last three days."

"When I was a child I didn't watch videos," announced Martin. And yet he'd steered the car into a parking space next to the harbour.

"Had they invented TV by then?"

"Oh, very funny."

They climbed from the car and walked back to Spar, which had a collection of videos for hire. Peter greedily soaked up the garish images. He turned to Martin, who browsed the food shelves. "I'll get an educational one," he said reassuringly.

When they returned to Martin's house, Dog was waiting in the hallway and Peter, as was natural, knelt and stroked him repeatedly from the top of his head all the way down his spine. "Wash your hands after touching that," said Martin.

"We need constant exposure to bacteria and to other microscopic organisms in order to build up a healthy defence system," said Peter. "Did you know that the average human body has over a kilogram of bacteria living somewhere in it? That's like a bag of sugar."

Martin removed the grill tray from the cooker and on one side he laid a freshly unwrapped trout and on the other side he shook out four Bird's Eye fish fingers. He chopped up yesterday's baked potatoes (he tended to make half a dozen for later use) in order to fry them. The peas would add colour and make up the necessary balanced diet.

He heard the television go on in the lounge, and he took a moment to rest, to keep his own company in his kitchen and read the newspaper.

Without giving it a moment's thought, he had in fact become used to having another human being living in the same house.

He turned the trout over, and each fish finger. With a fork he turned over each piece of fried potato, so they were evenly brown on both sides.

Some minutes later his doorbell sounded. His mind was occupied with other matters so he didn't even try to guess who it was. He was surprised to find that it was Louisa standing there. For some inexplicable reason, at the same time as he saw her wrapped in her sheepskin coat and sheepskin hat, a glow on her complexion from the cold, the unwelcome idea — or image — of Danny Steel came to mind. He frowned.

"It's customary to ask someone to come in, Martin," she said in a threatening voice. Behind her, the village of Portwenn made itself visible as pinpoints of light crowded on the hill opposite, lights that were

270

themselves reflected, and therefore doubled, in the measureless deep of the ocean.

"Come in," said Martin and took a pace back. It was as if he was admitting Danny Steel, also, into the house, which felt like an unfair imposition on his hospitality. This was ridiculous, he thought.

Louisa stepped through to the familiar kitchen. "I just wanted to come round to see how Peter was, and to find out about his mother." She swept the hat from her head and unbuttoned the sheepskin. From the living room came the unlikely sound of the television. Peter was parked in front of the TV, she thought, and she felt a moment of ill will against Martin but then she admonished herself for making that judgement — everyone's kids watched TV and it was the Christmas holiday for heaven's sake. And here he was, cooking — the potatoes in the frying pan made their comfortable sizzling; the aroma filled the room.

"She is progressing," said Martin.

"Er, Martin," began Louisa, "I do realise there's such a thing as patient confidentiality, but I think you can do better than that. What's 'progressing' mean?"

Martin divided his attention between Louisa, the grill and the frying potatoes. "Right, yes, um . . . she should be home in a couple of days. Her asthma's under control, more or less. I'm going to refer her to a respiratory physiotherapist."

"Oh. Right. Well, that's good. Isn't it? And, thanks for looking after Peter. It's funny the way he looks up to you, isn't it?"

For a moment a silence descended between them, while Martin turned down his grill and turned up the heat under the peas, for them to catch up. Louisa watched this operation with a strange longing to be invited to stay, to sit at the kitchen table and eat with them. "I'll just go and say hello to him before I go, if I may?" Her optimism made her believe that without doubt he'd see the possibilities, he'd notice the little door that was open here, with, on the other side, if only he pushed it open a bit, the chance of complete, life-long happiness, no less. All he had to do was say, "Why don't you stay for—"

"Go ahead," replied Martin. He pointed with his serving spoon. "Through there."

Louisa swallowed her disappointment. At the same time from the television came the sound of a blood-curdling scream. She stepped through to the living room. "Hi there," she said to the back of Peter's head.

"Hi," said Peter, without turning round. He was leaning forward, glued to the screen, which showed a naked girl writhing on an altar, held down by a variety of powerfully built men dressed in leather masks and capes, carrying various weapons. More screams came from the girl. Her head, which had been raking back and forth, was now held still by several strong hands. The blade of a knife appeared on the screen.

"What are you watching?" asked Louisa quickly. She turned to call back, "Martin?!" And then she turned back again. "Peter, switch it off please."

272

Peter leaned forwards in his seat more intently. "They're just about to eat the virgin's eyeballs."

Louisa took the several fast steps it needed to take her to the television. A red diode told her where she could switch it off and she did so. The screen shrank rapidly to nothing and the screams stopped.

Louisa repeated her call, "Martin?" When he appeared she asked, "What on earth was he watching?"

Martin looked at Peter. "You told me it was educational," he said.

"He just said the words, 'virgin's eyeballs'," said Louisa.

"Is that bad?" asked Martin

Peter, for once, couldn't think of anything educational to say about virgins' eyeballs, so he kept quiet. The room seemed full of portent, like something was about to happen, but he didn't know if it was going to be bad, or good.

Later that night, Bert Large dangled a fillet of cod in the air, and walked it over to the tub of batter mix. He swam the cod back and forth in the gluey mix and then lifted it in the air again, to walk it to the fryer, but the cod's tail had become slippery and it dropped from his fingers and fell to the floor. "Darn," he said, gently, but there weren't any customers in yet so he picked up the cod and dropped it in the fryer. He was happy enough in his work actually to hum. This was top class, he thought, this line of work.

The bell tinkled and he looked up to see his son Al enter the shop.

"Dad," said Al.

"Son," said Bert.

"Bit quiet."

"Just you wait," said Bert. "Word is out, how good the hands of Bert Large are at frying good quality, fresh fish. I've been run off my feet up to now. Just time to get one or two pieces in hand, for the late rush after the pub shuts. I mean, I don't know how she does it, old Mrs Cronk. Another night like the one we've just had and I shall have to purchase a bigger till." He squared his hands, exaggerating the size of the cash till he'd need.

"That's good. So you'll have change for a fifty then, won't you." Al handed his father the huge denomination note. "Cod and chips, please."

"Surely." Bert took the oversize note and sprung the till, lifted the tray and laid the note respectfully in the bottom. He whizzed the cash tray shut. "Large chips or small?"

"Large," said Al.

"Large by name, and look at that, large chips," said Bert affectionately. He folded the paper over and handed the portion to his son. "And this is how we do the fish for eating now." He took a well-battered cod from the hot cabinet and chopped it into four pieces, then wrapped them in paper, with an opening in the top. "Easier to deal with." He handed it over to his son. "Ketchup, mayo. Salt, pepper" He pointed at the row of condiments. "I recommend ketchup for the chips, and mayo for the fish."

"Aren't you forgetting something?"

274

"What's that then? There's no bleedin' salad, if that's what you mean. Nothing green allowed in here."

"No, not salad."

"What then? You can't have barbecue sauce, not with fish." He pointed suddenly. "Hey, good idea, though — tartar sauce. That would be excellent. We'll have some in ready for tomorrow."

"No, not that. What about my change, Dad? I gave you a fifty, for heaven's sake."

"'Course you did." Bert dabbed the till, but nothing happened. "Sorry 'bout that." He dabbed the till again, but the drawer didn't open. He looked up. "Soz, it gets stuck sometimes."

"Your own bloody son," complained Al in disbelief.

"No, it's stuck. Really, it is."

"Like hell, come here." Al put down his wrapper of fish and his chips, and stepped behind the counter. He took a careful look at the till. With the second button he pressed, the drawer sprang open.

"Oh aye, I get you. That's a different way of doing it. Nice one."

Al lifted up the tray of coins to look for the notes, but there wasn't a single one, apart from his own fifty. "You been robbed?" he asked.

"Wednesday's a bad night for fish," said Bert. "It was yesterday we had the busy night now I come to think of it."

"How many customers, Dad?"

"Well, yesterday was, like, I was whirling the fish round me head, you know, that busy. Tonight . . ." He shrugged.

Al picked up his portion of fish, took out a chunk, and bit into it. For a moment or two he chewed. And then he asked in a voice like a TV quiz master, "What is batter made of, Dad?"

"Egg. Any idiot knows that."

"So this is fish, cod, right, with fried egg on the outside. Isn't it."

"If you don't like it, you know where you can go," said Bert.

"Yeah, like, where everyone else has gone, and all."

The next morning, with the return of normal service by the Royal Mail, Martin tore open the envelope and unfolded the square of paper within. A keen observer might have noticed, at a certain point, it was as if some of the energy had left his body — there was a slight slump in his posture, a defeated look. He stood up, and carried the letter with him around the room. He read it in different places. He put it down, and picked it up again. He opened a drawer, inserted the letter carefully and closed the drawer again.

Extraordinary. One little figure printed on a page. A chance in a million. Strange how it changed everything. Suddenly, he, Martin, had the means to point PC Mark Mylow in a different direction. The truth would . . . erupt. There was no other word for it.

Mark Mylow sat with a pen and paper to one side of his keyboard, and typed in the trade name. "Mothercare". He knew it was bad luck to order things too early, but he wanted to find out how much money he would have to save. In his rounded, well-organised handwriting he made several columns: "Maternity"; "Nursery"; "Car seats/buggies"; "Clothing"; "Toys"; "Bathing and changing"; and "Feeding".

Under these columns he made lists of the items he thought they'd need, how many of them and their cost. He became familiar with trade names for buggies that sounded like racing car manufacturers, such as Britax, Silver Cross, Maclaren. He investigated *Which?* reports on the combination car seats and buggies, the combination prams and carrycots. He worked out the total cost of the discount scheme, "My First Wardrobe". He wrote down unfamiliar words like "playmats" and "bouncers" and "cot top changers". He preferred the look of the Tutti Bambini range of cots, especially the Louis IV fixed side cot in walnut, with underside drawer, until he saw how much it cost. He spent far too long in the toy section of the website, and scolded himself for presuming that he was going to have a daughter that looked just like Julie.

When Mark looked at any computer screen, his face always assumed the same expression. His eyebrows lifted half an inch and stayed there. His mouth dropped open just a touch, and his eyes took on this curious, grazing look, feeding off the different parts of the screen in front of him — gathering, gathering. In some ways it was the face of a handsome, curious and excited child.

Their baby was going to cost them an arm and a leg, he decided. Quickly, he realised they'd have to depend on getting everything second-hand from charity shops, or as gifts from relatives. He tore up his list into squares. Hopeless. No one would have a baby, ever, if they made lists like that. He was going to have to be big, brave, bold. Different. He was going to have to be a man. There was no need to worry any more about his . . . equipment. Size didn't matter. Nor did the size of his testicles matter. So what, he'd had mumps as a child. It hadn't affected his fertility as he'd thought it might. All those anxieties were behind him now. It was like they belonged to a younger version of himself. He began to look forward to the conversation he'd have with Julie — how they'd get there, how they'd do it together.

The footpath ran up the westward side of the town. In summer, a flow of people climbed this side and walked the cliff-top path, to gain the views, but today, despite the rain, Louisa wanted to be up there, to walk fast and hard, to hope the height, and looking down on the village, would give her perspective, would allow her to think about all that was happening in her life, to think about Danny. She zipped her raincoat up to her neck and pulled the fisherman's cap firmly down to keep the rain off her face. She quickened her pace. It would be good to go up there alone . . .

Even as the idea of "alone" passed through her mind she heard her name called — it was Danny. She felt a plumb depth open in her stomach. The very person she wanted to think about. It was like a sign. She watched as he came hurrying up the path towards her. That Barbour coat — the sort of thing people wore who

278

thought about the country as an idea, the branding of the countryside.

"Hey? How's my girl?" he asked, but she didn't answer. "Where you going?"

"Come with me," she said simply, without thinking. "Just up the top."

"We'll get soaking wet."

"So what," she said.

"Great," he replied.

He fell in alongside her and they climbed the stile. They had to drop back into single file to pass through the drenched greenery where the path narrowed and then they were on top of the cliff. The wind caught in their mouths and stopped their breathing and they had to work hard to overcome the pressure of the air that pushed them backwards and troubled every loose bit of clothing.

"I've been thinking," shouted Louisa.

Danny walked backwards in front of her. "So have I!"

"When we got together, you know, way back. When we were boyfriend and girlfriend."

"I love thinking about that!" shouted Danny.

"And we split up, didn't we?"

"I know, my fault. It was my . . . mistake!" he shouted happily. "It's just at that point, in my career. Men are programmed." He pointed his thumb at his own chest. "Success. Like hunting with a spear." He swung around to walk forwards again, beating his chest like an ape. "Man as hunter. Providing. Dragging home the kill. We're programmed like that when we're young."

"That's rubbish though, isn't it?" said Louisa into the wind, which tore the words from her.

"What?"

"Rubbish. Do you really think we're programmed? We make our own decisions, don't we?"

"The point is, I've changed. That's what I've been trying to tell you." He looked happy, the rain pouring down his face.

"I know, I know."

"So?"

"I just don't want to rush into anything. And you've only been in the village for five minutes."

"You're not saying no?"

"No." She shook her head. "No, I'm not."

"That's fannnn-tassstic!" Danny shouted, as if she'd said yes. Even as his cry went up into the emptying clouds — into the big, fast-moving air — the insistent trilling of Danny's mobile phone sounded. He scooped it out of his pocket and protected it with his hand. He turned his back to the wind, pressing the phone to his ear. "Hello? This is Danny Steel? Hello? Can you hear me?" He unzipped his Barbour and tried to lift one side to shelter the phone and his ear. "Can you hear me now?"

Louisa stood on the windward side to protect him.

"Hello?" He stared at the phone's screen for a second and then held it to his ear again. "Hello?" He looked at Louisa. "Lost them," he said. "That was work. We'd better head back if that's OK. I need to take that call."

"You go back, that's fine," said Louisa. "I'll carry on for a bit."

"OK," he said. "Sorry sorry. I'll see you later. That might be exciting news." He pecked her cheek and trotted back along the cliff top towards the village.

As Louisa watched him go, she thought he looked like a puppet, with someone else pulling the strings. In a little while she would get to pull the strings again, before someone else would have their turn . . .

She walked onwards, bowing her head against the weather, until the land started to dip under her feet. She'd told herself she'd get as far as the next bay along. She liked this cove because it was the opposite of Portwenn — not a sign of human presence, no road, no cars, just a footpath, which in winter was deserted, and with only the detritus from the sea turning up on the shore. Only for half a minute, because of the wind and rain, did she stand at the top of the cliff and look down on this solitary spot, with its green carpet of moss covering the boulders where the stream slid noisily to its final destination, the ocean. And then she turned and, with the wind at her back, she walked up to the top, heading back to Portwenn.

And here, with a pleasing symmetry she saw Danny again, this time running towards her. As he came closer she could see that he was smiling, and out of breath.

"You've run all the way back," she said amazed. The wind pushed at her, blowing her forwards, and him backwards.

He turned and walked alongside, took her arm and threaded it through his. "That phone call," he said. "You know I told you about that project?"

"Which one?"

"The art gallery conversion in the East End. The old warehouse, remember?"

"Oh, yes, yes."

"I went for the job ages ago — usual thing, a competition, five architects, and I put loads of work and effort into it — and I didn't get it. Anyway, their first choice, the architect who did win, just pulled out. So I'm back in the frame. They want to talk." He squeezed her arm tighter under his. "I think I might get it, Lou. We can go back to London."

"We?"

"This is the one, this is the type of job it's worth hanging on for."

"In London."

"Yes. Louisa, marry me, and come and live in London."

"Danny I live here in Portwenn. I work here. I am the head teacher of Portwenn primary school."

"God, Louisa," he said in a daring tone. "Imagine, right, imagine *you* showing up at *any* East End primary school." He continued emphatically, his stride lengthening so he could round on her, "They would get down on their hands and knees and kiss the ground you walk on."

It was her turn to be emphatic. "You don't get it, do you, Danny? My life is here, it is wholly and completely here."

282

"Well, I thought mine was, too, but . . . things change." In order to defend himself he added, "I didn't plan this." He showed his mobile phone to her as if it, the machine itself, were in charge of their lives. "I didn't know I'd get that call. It suddenly happened." In a more generous voice he went on, "I understand . . . you need time to think, think carefully—"

"Go to London, Danny, take the job." She quickened her pace, pulling her arm free from his.

He kept pace with her. "That's a bit of a sudden turnaround, Louisa."

"It's not sudden at all, actually."

"If you don't mind me saying, you're being perverse now."

"No, Danny, I just know who I am. But you don't seem to have a clue who you are or what you want. One minute it's London, next it's Cornwall and your mother's house. You're all over the place. And I'm sorry I haven't said this before, but all this finding religion. I mean, where did all that come from? It feels like you're trying it on, like a suit of clothes handed down to you from your dad. I'm sorry if that's rude. There is no substance to you. I'm afraid that's what I truly think."

"I don't believe you mean that, Louisa."

"Don't tell me what I mean."

"Because if you did mean that, I can't see how I can recover from that. How *we* can recover from that."

"Let's not 'recover', Danny."

He stopped in his tracks and called out, "*Not* recover?" He sounded scandalised.

Louisa sailed on, carried by the wind, which blew her towards Portwenn. "Bye, Danny."

With the rain carried away by the steeply sloping roof, and the stone walls easily holding off the wind that poured around their corners, and the windows shut tight to keep in the expensive heat, the doctor's surgery offered a civilised shelter from the low-pressure weather system that tried its hardest to beat against the small village on Cornwall's north shore. A calm atmosphere was promoted by the green walls, and there was an orderliness to the equipment and the way in which it was maintained. The roll of clean white paper on the examining couch seemed welcoming, as if one might be invited to sleep there.

And yet, in the privacy of this room, there were times when a human storm would blow up, and this was going to be one of those times.

"Hi, Doc," said PC Mark Mylow easily. All of life was good for him at the moment, in a way that he could not have predicted even a few months ago. He had leaped in one bound over all that he'd previously lacked — love, a sex life, a partner and children — and now all of that had been given to him by the appearance of Julie, whose encouraging smile . . . well, her smile sort of lived in him, full time, in his breast — he would have described its position there, if he'd been asked. His only anxiety now was how he was going to afford both a wedding and a baby all at the same time.

"Come in," said Martin. He went to make sure the door was firmly shut.

284

"All right, Doc? You asked me to drop by. Hope you're all right? Anything I can do to help?"

"Take a seat, please."

"Oooh, serious stuff then."

"Well, it's . . . unfortunate news, yes."

"Who is it? Who's in trouble?" A sudden panic creased his face as he suddenly thought and then said, "Not Julie, not the pregnancy, not anything to do with—"

"No, no."

"Phew, oh my God, you had me worried there." He clapped a hand to his chest and his normal benevolent expression returned.

"I just want to recap," said Martin. "You came to consult me because you were concerned that your testicles were too small and because you had had mumps as a child. You were embarking on a brand-new relationship in which you were proposing to become married and have children, and you wanted to check that the mumps hadn't affected your fertility."

"Stupid, wasn't it, thank God, there was no need to worry, after all," said Mark. "Can't tell you what a relief that is." Mark rocked back and forth in his chair, smiling. "We reckon we might have two or three children," he added. "That's how the thinking is going at the moment."

Martin handed him the single sheet of A4 paper.

"What's this?" asked Mark. He took the paper and read out loud, " 'Azoospermia', what's that then?"

"It means you're infertile."

A pained expression crossed Mark's face, but underneath he had the confidence of knowing he'd just conceived a baby, after all. "Well, it must be wrong," he said with a chuckle. "Even men with low sperm counts can do the business, you know. There's stuff about it in the pregnancy books. One persistent little blighter, that's all it takes. He swims and swims and wriggles and wriggles. Shows how lucky we were, though. Thanks for the warning, Doc, but we can be lucky again. Or maybe we might have to use a test tube. But we'll have lots of the little blighters, and you'll be a godfather to one of them, I hope."

"Mark, azoospermia means no sperm at all, persistent or otherwise."

Portwenn's policeman didn't understand. The doc must be wrong-headed, he thought. Unless he hadn't heard right. "No sperm at all?"

"Not one."

"Julie's pregnant."

"Yes."

"So, that isn't right. There's been a mix-up."

"No, I called the lab and they confirmed the result."

Mark stiffened. A flood of unhappiness, of conflict, entered the intercourse between the two men. "I don't think Julie will take very kindly to what you're insinuating, Doc."

Martin said reasonably, "I'll have to live with that." He wore an expression that came as close as might be possible, for him, to kindness.

"Yes, you will, because she is going to be my wife, and the mother of my child."

286

"Ask her who she is before you marry her, Mark."

"What's that supposed to mean?"

"Julie Mitchell's not her real name."

"I think it is." Mark was moving around on his chair as if it were on the deck of a ship in heavy seas.

"Perhaps you should ask Graham Reynolds, from the Salvation Army, who's been asked by her family to come and find her, and who has been showing photographs of her around the village. He gives a different name for her."

Mark stood up. "Well, so what if he does? She can call herself Robbie bloody Williams for all I care. It's not a problem. It's not illegal. Perhaps you didn't know that? That's my department, the law—" and here he pointed a forefinger at his own chest "—I'm the policeman, aren't I? Whereas you—" now the forefinger pointed at Martin repeatedly "—you, you, you're the . . . the member of the public."

"Her family asked the Salvation Army to trace her because her mother's dying," said Martin stonily "They didn't want to ask the police because —"

"I know what this is," said Mark, suddenly sure that he understood Martin's motives. "This is about you, isn't it? You can't bear to see me happy, can you? You haven't got anyone in your life so you don't want me to have anyone in mine. You wouldn't know a good relationship if it came up and bit you on your stuck-up —" he struggled to find the end of the insult, but couldn't so he repeated the same words twice more, emphatically, "stuck-up, stuck-up—"

"Mark," interrupted Martin.

"—-nose," finished Mark. But his voice was an awful sneer; it was a voice that didn't sound like his own but as if someone else inhabited him; meanwhile all his troubled, real thoughts were going on somewhere underneath this roiling surface.

"You're engaged to a woman who is wanted for credit card fraud and identity theft."

Mark was outraged. "I'm right and you know it. The whole of Portwenn knows it. The effort I've gone to, to welcome you to this village, trying to be your friend. And all you've ever done is snub me. You think I haven't noticed?" He was on his way to the door now. "It's the start of a new year tomorrow," he said with confidence, "and all I know is that everything's better than all the past years put together. I love Julie. And she loves me. And we're having a baby. That's all I care about."

"Her name's not Julie," said Martin quietly. "She's called Emma Lewis."

Police Constable Mark Mylow strode home and the anger burned in him so fiercely it meant his only thought was to prove Martin wrong. And yet even as he fired up his computer, entered his password and logged onto the PNC network he dreaded what he might find, and he knew that Martin would never lie. Sure enough, when he loaded the name "Emma Lewis" into the search engine it instantly showed him a picture of the woman he knew as Julie — the woman he loved, to whom he was engaged to be married, who carried his . . .

No, *not* his baby. Someone else's.

His eye caught the words "credit card fraud" and "identity theft". There were other photographs of Julie with dark hair, Julie thirty pounds heavier, Julie in scruffy jeans and a sweatshirt instead of the dresses she always wore for him. Julie without make-up, Julie as a glamour model — and for each picture there was a different name: Jane Carpenter, Louise Wood, Emma Lewis. Julie . . .

And different crimes.

He could actually hear her moving around upstairs. No wonder she hid herself away. He found that without thinking he was on his feet, and he was taking the narrow stairs two at a time, and in a few strides he was in their bedroom, where she sat at the mirror, a make-up brush in her hand.

In the mirror, she smiled at him knowingly. "Hey, you have to give a girl a little notice, you know, before you suddenly come back from work," she said.

"Why's that?" Mark felt plummeting anger.

"Well, I have to put my face on, as they say." The brush swept foundation onto her cheekbones and neck.

"Which face is that then?" asked Mark.

"You know, make-up?" She showed him the brush and smiled. "We girls don't want you to see a single blemish."

"What about the face of Jane Carpenter, or Louise Wood, or Emma Lewis?"

Julie's face straightened. She lowered the make-up brush and went completely still. After a while she said, "Oh."

"Oh," repeated Mark sarcastically. The truth of the situation was still rushing at him, and he knew he hadn't even begun to take in the disappointment, and the hurt.

"I can explain all of that."

"How?"

"Come on, Mark, you know I've had an interesting past. Part of my charm, you said so yourself. We're getting married, soon I'm going to have *your* name, and so it's like I've come home. We're in love, we're getting married, Mark, and we're having a baby together, and that's all that matters." She stood up and left the mirror behind. She moved closer to him.

"Oh yeah, about that. Our first time was only, what, a month ago?"

"Yes. And what does that tell you — only that we were meant for each other. You only had to look at me and — *bam* — I'm pregnant. You remember that look, in the Crab, and I—"

"That must have been it. A look. I only had to look at you. It wasn't going to happen any other way. Because, see, I've had a sperm test. A fertility test. And—" he shook his head "—nothing there, Julie."

Julie's expression was calm, but it was a professional kind of calm, and her turmoil was betrayed by a slight rocking on her feet, as if it had been a physical blow she'd suffered. Her profession, as a fraudster, meant she was quick to find — and pursue — a possible escape route. "Hey, Marky, we can work this out, can't we?" She took the final step that brought her close enough to touch his face, but for Mark all her charm

290

isappeared as quickly as if a light had been switched off. He grabbed her wrist and twisted it outwards. In a cold voice, and with his expression stone cold, he said, "Emma Lewis . . ."

Julie groaned and turned so her wrist became less painful in his grip. She saw, as if from a long way off, his fingers tightly pressed into her skin, in an embrace that had turned from passionate love to dispassionate, cold-hearted punishment.

Mark started again, because he couldn't believe he was going to say these words. "Emma Lewis . . . I am arresting you on suspicion of using a false identity to obtain goods by deception. You do not have to say anything but anything you do say may be taken down and used as evidence against you."

In Mrs Cronk's fish and chip shop, a stack of battered cod and plaice lay neatly on their sides, piping hot, with the batter golden and crisp. Behind the counter, Bert wielded the tongs, tugged free a bit of fish and placed it on top of the chips, deftly wrapped both into a parcel and handed it to his customer. "Right you are, Richard, enjoy." With a smile and a nod he took the money — "Oo, ta," — and tipped it into the till. "Gonna need more fish at this rate." He tapped his hand on the stainless steel service. "Next," he called cheerfully.

"Cod and chips, please."

"Coming up." Bert saw that his son, Al, loomed to one side. "Hello, boy."

"All right, Dad?"

"New Year tomorrow. Let's hope it's going to be a good one."

"Hope so, yes." Al pointed at the rack of fish. "You do this all by yourself then?"

"Can you see anyone else behind here, helping me?" He coughed against the back of his hand and wiped it on his apron.

"So, er, who taught you to cook fish overnight then?"

"Well, I taught myself, didn't I? Trial and error. The secret of a successful cod-in-batter is the lightness, isn't it? The whole thing should be light as air." He picked one out, laid it on the surface and cut a chunk off the end. "And the fish with just the right amount of muscle left in it. Pop it in your mouth and it's hot and it melts, see. Try." He handed Al the chunk. "Making a successful batter is the same as the making of a successful life. It's all in the wrist." He stirred his hand experimentally, and then wrapped up the next portion and handed it over.

The customer eyed his portion greedily. "Ta, thank you." Straightaway, behind him, was another one.

"Doreen, what'll it be?"

"Cod and chips."

Al chewed his sample of fish. "Very good, Dad." And then he spoke in a lower voice. "So where was it you were going just now, then, when you popped out and left a sign on the door that said, BACK IN FIVE MINUTES."

"Well, I popped out, as you say, for a breath of air."

"What, down to the pub? Down to the Crab?"

"Hey, you were following me? Rascally man. Nothing wrong with a refreshment break, is there? Especially not on New Year's Eve." Bert's clumsy fingers broke off a bit of fish for himself and he popped it in his mouth. "Air. Lightness, that's the key to your batter preparation."

"And what was in that box you carried back here with you?"

"Oh, sorry, didn't know it was illegal to carry a box in the streets of Portwenn."

"You're selling the fish and chips from the pub, aren't you? You're buying them off the pub, and carrying them back here, and then selling them as if you'd made them."

"So what if I bloody am? Look at all these customers." He handed thin Doreen her portion. "Thanks, Doreen, my love. Go easy on the chips or you'll be as fat as I am. Next."

"Does Mrs Cronk know you're doing this?" asked Al.

"She came in here on her way home, didn't she, and, guess what, she saw the line of customers and, suddenly, she was happy. She said, she said she wished she could have burnt her hand off long ago."

"Oh right, sure."

"Look, I'm just a Good Samaritan doing my best for a neighbour. She fell into the gutter, or into the batter or whatever, and I could have walked on by, but no, I chose to cross over the street, give her a helping hand. Put a few extra shekels in her pocket."

"You're going to cost her some shekels. The pub isn't giving you this lot for free, is it?"

"Well, it's true their charges are a bit more steep than Mrs C.'s. Quite a lot more. I was thinking, you and I should advise Mrs C. her prices are a bit out of kilter, a bit low."

"So you're paying more than what you're getting? So what are you going to tell Mrs C. when she comes back — 'Here's your bill from the Crab and Lobster'?"

"If you don't mind, Al, there's customers I have to deal with." He turned to his queue. "Hello, Richard. What'll it be?"

"Just chips."

"Coming up." Bert turned to his son. "And by the way, it's all right for you to gloat. From outside of the situation." He banged the cage of chips on its rest. "OK. So your dad's messed up. There's no need to have a go at me."

"How much is the shortfall?"

"Well. A lot. Is the figure that comes to mind."

"What are you going to do about it?"

"Well, I'm going to suffer, aren't I. Unless someone comes along to help me."

"Dad, I'm hardly going to hand you over a wad of cash so you can bail yourself out of trouble." Al took out his wallet, flipped it open and took out a good-sized wedge of twenty pound notes.

Bert fumbled with the tongs and dropped them. His attention wavered and his eye stuck to the twenties that his son Al was now fanning out in his hand like a deck of cards. "Well, that's up to you, obviously," he said. "But I would ask you one important question."

"Oh yeah?"

"What's family for?" He shook his head ruefully and tried not to look any more at the money. "Eh?"

"Ah. Well," said Al. "Thing is, when I saw you scurrying back from the pub carrying a box of fish, I had a word with Mrs Richards." He began counting the notes from one hand to the other. "And she says, she's charging you at cost, seeing as you're helping Mrs Cronk." The notes were all in his other hand, now. "So I happen to know there is no shortfall." With the dexterity of a card sharp, Al folded up his notes and put them back in his own pocket. "Nice try, Dad." He took another chunk off the battered fish and chewed on it. "Blimey. Your own son."

If there was any house, out of all the houses in England, Wales, Scotland and Ireland, that ignored utterly New Year's Eve, that allowed it to pass with no thoughts, even, of wine drinking, Scottish dancing or fireworks, it was perhaps that same small house that also doubled as a doctor's surgery, halfway up the side of a cliff in the small fishing village of Portwenn.

In fact it was worse than that, because to ignore something implied one noticed it, and worked hard to set it aside from one's thoughts, but, for Martin, New Year's Eve did not figure.

And yet, here came Louisa Glasson, who had turned down three different invitations to do instead what she actually wanted to do this New Year's Eve: once and for all *talk* to Doctor Martin Ellingham and get to the bottom of why they fell out all the time. Unlike most people, she could count on him being at home tonight.

She made the short walk down to the harbour and up the other side, clutching two bottles of wine and with her hair untied from its ponytail. She was determined to sit him down and talk to him, and she'd listen to him, get the other side of his impenetrable reserve. She imagined the bottles of wine standing between them, and the kitchen table for their elbows to rest on, and they would both talk steadily. The drug, alcohol, would help Martin to unbend, to drop his guard, and it would be like marching past the fortifications, which up to now had continually thrown her back.

And, shortly after he'd opened the door and she'd marched in, she mostly had everything she wanted. In the kitchen she plonked down the wine bottles and said, "You and I are going to have a drink, Martin, and we're finally going to sort out what we think about each other. I want to know why on earth I think about you at any moment when my mind is allowed to come to rest."

Martin frowned. "Have you been drinking?"

"Maybe. And yes I know, the liver . . . blah blah blah."

"But I don't drink," he said.

"I don't care," she said. "This evening you do drink."

"I don't drink for a particular reason," he said. "Because if I do, I fall asleep."

"Literally?"

"Is there any other way of falling asleep?"

"OK." She thought for a moment. "I'll just have to risk it." She'd pushed the first bottle forwards an inch. "So. We can talk up to the moment that you fall asleep."

She fetched two glasses, plonked them down, and poured.

So she had the wine — and him drinking it — and she also had the table to hold up their elbows. Here it was. They were face to face. There was no one else to interrupt them. It was New Year's Eve — a moment when there should be so much to talk about. They could discuss the past and make up a future; they could . . .

And yet the talking somehow didn't work. It was the thing she most wanted: his talking, their talking, together. She tried and tried again: his childhood, her childhood, what she wanted from her career, what he wanted from his career. In the end, the only subject on which she could get more than a few syllables out of him was the human body and its various malfunctions.

He was drunk; there was no doubt about that. One bottle was empty and the other was half empty. There was a different expression on his face: instead of the usual disapproval, or impatience, he wore a frightened look, and yet, she thought, there was an element of yearning there, as if he were trapped somewhere and wanted to escape.

Painfully slowly, they dribbled to the end of a topic which neither of them wanted to pursue.

"That's, er, that's actually quite common—" Martin couldn't remember even what it was they were talking about "—with a viral infection," he finished lamely, without enthusiasm. He looked at Louisa who was shaking her head as if in disagreement, but he realised she hadn't been paying attention, just as he hadn't.

"What?" he asked her; and he genuinely wanted to know the reason why she was shaking her head, with her hair falling over half her face. She looked sad, as if she'd just heard bad news. He repeated, "What is it?"

Louisa's mind was in a whirl. "I . . . I thought the wine would be . . ."

"Disinhibiting?" suggested Martin.

"Yeah. I . . . I thought we'd talk. Actually, you know. Break through."

There it was — this new expression on his face: he looked trapped. "I don't . . . really talk," he said.

"I know you don't," said Louisa, in a voice that didn't contain one jot of criticism, only understanding. And then she continued talking openly and freely as if she herself was the only person listening and yet she knew to say these words was to lay herself down in front of him, at his mercy; but there wasn't anything she wanted to do more. "I don't know," she said, "I just imagined that we'd have this great big talk, and that I'd get you drunk and seduce you. Maybe not. But I wanted to see you, you know? See the real you."

"I . . ." began Martin, and his stare was locked onto her.

"I suppose that's what I was saying before," continued Louisa. She smiled at him. "Underneath the gruff, monosyllabic, well meaning but rude surface, you're . . . gruff, monosyllabic and, well, rude."

"What happened to well meaning?"

She smiled. She got intense pleasure from thinking about and describing his character, knowing his character, and she found, oddly, that she wanted very much to say his name, she suddenly must hear herself saying it. "Martin," she said. The name floated on the very surface of her love for him. "I should be glad," she went on, "because I was right. You are exactly what it says on the tin — Doc Martin through and through." She lifted up the remaining half bottle. "I think we should just sit here and drink some more, and carry on not saying any of the stupid things that people say when they're drunk." She poured. The glug of wine leaving the bottle, and the splash of it entering her glass and his glass, filled the silence that presided over this little cottage. They were very far away from the New Year celebrations that filled so many other houses and establishments like the Crab and Lobster with revelry, with movement and dancing and the amplified human voice.

"I was—" began Martin.

"Sshh," interrupted Louisa. "No talking."

He didn't talk.

She didn't want him to talk, because she didn't want him to change one inch from the man she unaccountably found herself so attracted to.

After a while Martin said very quietly, "Well, I . . . I should remind you of the main reason that I don't drink . . . because I just fall asleep."

She looked at him, but he seemed perfectly awake; in fact he looked filled with a new energy. He looked like he was struggling.

"I don't say anything." He sounded hurt. "I'm constipated, my Auntie Joan says."

Louisa smiled and repeated, "I said no talking." Perhaps she, too, might not talk. She longed for the silence to continue so she could find out what would happen in that silence.

"And yet," Martin persisted, quietly, and slurring his words, "that's rubbish anyway. Rubbish. Things people say."

"Martin . . ."

Suddenly, he was looking at her and in his expression there was only that yearning. "You're so beautiful. You're so very beautiful, d'you know that?"

She had been greedy to hear those words for so long. "OK, I don't mind you talking, now."

He leaned forwards and said, "All I think about, every day, is just catching a glimpse of you."

She rose out of her chair an inch to reach him; their lips touched and she was startled again at how impossibly soft his lips were on hers. Their kiss had in it the memory of the first kiss in the back of the taxi, but this one worked in a new way: it wrought in Louisa a proper love that seemed knowledgeable, certain, true. A requited love.

"Louisa," he said.

"Sshh. Don't spoil it." She held his face in her hands.

"I love you," said Martin. "I love you."

"Oh . . . This bloody table's in the way." It crossed her mind to jump over, but she stepped to one side and so did he: after three strides they met and embraced, top to toe. She felt the solidity of his frame; his right arm was around her waist and his left was around her shoulder blades and the breath was squeezed out of her body by his strength and by the kiss which lasted for so long. He felt the brush of her hair over his arm and hand.

But then, after feeling light as air in his embrace, Louisa felt the terrible power of gravity begin to drag him out of her arms. Their lips, so beautifully joined and moving together, didn't so much as separate as his mouth fell from hers and his chin and nose rested heavily on her shoulder. Her stance altered to cope with the increased weight: she was trying to hold him up but couldn't. She didn't nearly have the strength. She half dropped him and half let him down onto the floor. His forehead knocked uncomfortably hard and his nose and lips were squashed in an ugly fashion against the tiles.

A single loud snore came from him.

"Martin? Martin?" She dragged at him — what should she do, get him to a sofa? She hauled with all her strength. "You're going to have to help me a little bit, Martin." She hauled again, but couldn't move him an inch. Her head swam from the drink. "Right. Um . . ." She took a moment to think: perhaps she should get help?

No . . .

She went and searched the house, bumping against the walls, staggering on her feet, and came back with a duvet and a pillow. The weight of his head, even, was a sack of potatoes when she lifted it to put the pillow underneath. She cast the duvet over him as if he were a sleeping child.

She planted a kiss on his cheek; that was perhaps the most tender moment of all.

As she walked from Martin's house the sky was filled with fireworks and the hooting of horns and the cries of the drunk and the sober as the new year came in. Spotlights were trained from fishing vessels onto the sea wall and there were lined up the bravest and boldest of Portwenn's young bachelors, their bodies shining white and naked, making comical shapes as, one by one, they jumped nude from the sea wall into the ocean and swam with all their vigour for the shore, shepherded by the fishing boats and their bright lights.

Louisa smiled; she was full of love, and pleased, right now, to be reminded of how someone had copied Martin's handwriting and put his name down for the Nuddy Jump, because, after all, he was unmarried. And, she thought, Martin had jumped that night. Naked, he had made such a terrifying leap.

The next morning, 1st January, it was Pauline who came first into the surgery. It wasn't intended that she should do so — given it was a public holiday the surgery was officially closed. But she'd left her phone charger here, so she came back to fetch it.

Meanwhile Louisa was rising groggily on the other side of the bay.

In the doctor's surgery there was no intimation that anything was wrong and Pauline thought nothing of the silence. She let herself in and went straight to her desk, ducked down to the plugs and extracted her phone charger. She would have walked straight out again had she not heard Dog's whimper just as she stepped into the hallway. "Doc?" she called out, and waited.

Again came the dog's slight whine.

Pauline's blood curdled. She'd heard those stories of dogs standing guard over their masters when something had gone wrong. She had to see.

When she reached Martin's kitchen the first thing she noticed was the two wine bottles and the two glasses standing on the table. The Doc didn't drink.

The next thing she noticed was a pair of black shoes sticking out beyond the kitchen table. A second later she had sight of him: Doc Martin, dead drunk, asleep on the kitchen floor with a duvet lying nearby; and in his arms, as he slept, was Dog, who looked up at her, confident in his new position, and wagged his tail.

Pauline's hand went to her mouth. She had her phone with a half-inch of battery left, so she thumbed the menu to "camera", and took a shot. And another. She climbed on the table and took a third one from a better angle. Within a few seconds, she'd sent copies to a select group of friends and had posted it on Facebook.

The phone rang in her hand within half a minute. It was Al. "I know," she whispered, hurrying out of the kitchen so she could talk, "it's true. He's passed out drunk on the kitchen floor and someone put down a pillow for him and a duvet." She listened for a while. "No, it is true, really really. I'm still here. Come and see for yourself if you don't believe me. I know, the dog!"

Al Large drove straight round, and brought his father Bert. Pauline waited for them in the cold sunshine out front, watching their progress down the hill and up the other side towards her.

Meanwhile, inside the house, Martin woke up and the worst thing was that he found, in his arms, in his embrace, as he lay on the kitchen floor, the wretched *dog*. He reacted as if he'd been stung by a viper, throwing the creature away from him. Groggily, he got to his feet. The wine bottles, the half-filled glasses. He must clear up. He picked up the two wine glasses. What time was it, already? He checked his watch and, with the half-full wine glass in his hand, he poured a slug of red wine down the front of his suit and shirt. He must change. He turned and walked two paces before a low beam struck his forehead. His head reeled.

And there he stood, swaying, blinded by the pain in his head, stunned, wine all down his front, when Bert and Al Large came in.

"Christ," said Al to Pauline. "See what you mean." He turned to Martin. "Happy New Year, Doc."

Bert whistled, "Pheeww, Doc, yes, Happy New Year. Looks like it, anyway. Here, you know that feeling you get when you've got a headache coming, you know, just behind the eyes and it's here too, and then it, then it spreads, you know?" He pressed a thumb into his forehead. "It throbs like a scaled-up old boiler. But it's not, it's not just there, it's also in your stomach and then in your waterworks and you've gotta run to the toilet. Oops, sorry, maybe you're not in the mood."

"That's right, I'm not in the mood. And if any of you is surprised or offended by the fact that last night I drank wine, or you've come to waste my time with infantile jokes, then you can bugger off. In fact you can bugger off anyway."

304

"Right you are, Doc. Let sleeping dogs lie, eh?"

"Not funny."

"Who was the lucky tipper, then, eh? Is it someone we know? Or, as rumoured, is it just you and your canine friend woof-woof?"

"Get out, Bert."

"How about I buy you a Bloody Mary down at the Crab? Hair of the dog, Doc?"

"Out!"

"Course, Doc. Come on, son, not much we can do to repair things here. You on Facebook, Doc? Don't suppose you are."

When all the voyeurs had left, Martin followed them outside and stayed for a while looking over the sea that was slowly building its inward tide, crawling tidily up the beach, and, when he swung his gaze to the right, he looked over the village of Portwenn, which today looked quiet and frozen in time. Some of these houses he had visited. Not many people would be working today; it was New Year's Day, a time for reflection, and for recovery. He breathed in the fresh air. His head was numb with all that had happened.

Some minutes later, he spotted Louisa walking around the edge of the harbour and up the lane towards his house. As she drew closer he saw her smile. Her gait changed: her pace slowed, and she reached him with shorter, more uncertain steps. She drew close, disturbingly close.

"I thought if you weren't used to drinking," she said, "then you wouldn't know about this brilliant hangover cure." She held up a bottle of something. "See, sometimes teach year six on a Monday morning, and this is about the only thing that makes it possible. So." She handed it to him.

"Oh. Thank you." He was aware of the terrible smell of wine, and the stain down his front.

She asked, "What happened to your head?"

"Oh. Er, nothing." He touched his forehead briefly and felt the lump growing there. "Did you want to see me for some medical advice?"

"No, no." She smiled. "Just the morning-after pill." She watched the confusion quickly cross his expression. "Joking," she said and, when he looked hurt, she insisted, "it was just a . . . a joke. It was . . . I just wondered if you wanted to see me or if . . . if there was anything else you wanted to say before you passed out last night."

"I, I embarrassed myself. I . . ."

"No, you didn't embarrass yourself. And I'm really glad that you said what you said. And I just wish that I'd had a chance to say . . . say that . . . I do, too." She looked at him seriously. "I love you, too."

He couldn't answer.

"What?" She wanted to help him. "What is it, Martin?"

"Love. It's a, it's a difficult word when you think that we don't actually know each other that well."

"Martin, we've known each other quite a while now."

"Yes, but, strictly speaking, for you to say that you, you love me, when you can't possibly know that you do, is, is, is, is . . ."

"Is what?"

"Is, is potentially delusional."

"Oh."

"And there are certain, you know, quite well-known, er, disorders where . . ."

"What disorders?" She frowned.

"Where a, a person falls, without good reason, for someone else and believes that they love them."

"I beg your pardon?"

"De Clérambault's syndrome, for instance," said Martin. "Also known as erotomania. More common in women. They fall for an older man of a higher social standing, of a higher professional standing than themselves."

"Martin, what the hell are you talking about?"

"Delusional romantic attachments, often associated with excessive, er, intrusiveness into the life of the object of the irrational affection. Stalking, if you like."

The village of Portwenn had, last night, been noisy with revelry, and now it was quiet, yes, on this New Year's Day morning, It was quiet, and pleased with itself, but, after that word "stalking" — and accompanied only by the *shussshh* of the sea on the beach — there came the faint, distant sound of a slap, as Louisa's hand stung Martin's cheek.